NINE LIVES

Dwain Gordon Fuller

ISBN 979-8-89619-879-6 Hardback
ISBN 979-8-89619-875-8 Paperback

DEDICATION

To Brexit and Milo, our family's redoubtable British Shorthair cats, who have each survived major falls and other life-threatening circumstances.

Also, to Charlie, our Bichon Frise, who sat by my desk as I wrote this novel and made occasional helpful suggestions.

ACKNOWLEDGMENTS

Nine Lives is the fourth in a series of thrillers that continues to document the dangerous lives of a young male CIA clandestine operator and a beautiful femme fatale former KGB undercover agent. This novel is the sixth one that I have written since retirement after forty years as a retinal surgeon. I remain indebted to my long-lost high school friend, Classics Professor Susan Wiltshire, who convinced me that writing could be as intellectually rewarding as repairing detached retinas.

My patient wife Patsy has continued to permit me to sit at my computer hour after hour and compose dialogue and text. It has been more years than I care to remember since I first was smitten by a beautiful nurse helping with a cardiac arrest when I was a medicine resident. However, it took me seven years to finally put a ring on the nurse's finger. Thank you, Patsy.

I also want to thank my sons, Christopher, Matthew, and Timothy, for reading my manuscripts and making helpful suggestions. Matthew, who is an English teacher, once again read this novel meticulously and found many typos, as well as grammar and syntax problems. My son Andrew, who has no taste for violence, continues to prefer Shakespeare, Tolkien, and the Bible over my efforts at authorship.

Lastly, none of these novels would have ever seen the light of day except for the work of my superb editor, Cynthia Orticio. She makes needed corrections, takes care of the artwork, obtains the copyright and ISBN numbers, and arranges for publication.

Whether I have another novel in me remains to be seen. Once a person reaches a certain age, the phrase *tempus fugit* becomes increasingly more personal.

—Dwain Fuller

"It has been the province of Nature to give this creature, the cat, nine lives instead of one."

—The Greedy and Ambitious Cat
from the Panchatantra animal fables
in Sanskrit literature, ca 500 AD

"Tybalt: What wouldst that have with me?

Mercutio: Good king of cats, nothing but one of your nine lives."

Shakespeare, *Romeo and Juliet*, III, i

TABLE OF CONTENTS

Prologue 1

Reprise 3

Chapter 1: Clean Underwear 5

Chapter 2: Timely Emesis 8

Chapter 3: New Friends 12

Chapter 4: Firepower 15

Chapter 5: Southern Vapors 19

Chapter 6: Tiny Testicles 23

Chapter 7: Free Drinks 27

Chapter 8: Hulga 30

Chapter 9: Double Green Stamps 33

Chapter 10: Room and Board 36

Chapter 11: Porch Fire 39

Chapter 12: Cavity Searches 42

Chapter 13: Bullet Proof 45

Chapter 14: Cowardly Dwarfs 48

Chapter 15: Peripatetic Male Appendage 51

Chapter 16: A Yank in Time Saves Nine 54

Chapter 17: Mission of Mercy Report 58

Chapter 18: The Dog Whisperer 62

Chapter 19: Hospital Demise 65

Chapter 20: Have Black Bag, Will Travel 68

Chapter 21: Hole Extraction 72

Chapter 22: Poking the Hornet's Nest 75

Chapter 23: A Major Bite in the Butt 78

Chapter 24: Father Jack 81

Chapter 25: Waiting for Arturo 84

Chapter 26: Paired Social Assets 87

Chapter 27: Raising the Dead 90

Chapter 28: Faux Priest 93

Chapter 29: Guerrero 96

Chapter 30: The Opera's Not Over Yet 99

Chapter 31: Mr. Crudie 103

Chapter 32: Cat Clairvoyance...106
Chapter 33: Décolletage Bad Decision.................................109
Chapter 34: Belling the Cat..112
Chapter 35: Short on Foreplay..115
Chapter 36: Waiting for the Rapture....................................118
Chapter 37: Anger Management Issues.................................122
Chapter 38: A Bad Way to Go...126
Chapter 39: A Bushel of Dynamite......................................130
Chapter 40: Wallet Conundrums...133
Chapter 41: Eye Candy...136
Chapter 42: Call to the Priesthood......................................139
Chapter 43: A Ghost...143
Chapter 44: Special Plastic Surgery.....................................146
Chapter 45: From the Texas Desert to Mexico......................150
Chapter 46: Hulga–Mia..154
Chapter 47: The Penicillin Club of Mexico..........................157
Chapter 48: A Command Performance.................................160
Chapter 49: A Hobson's Choice...163
Chapter 50: Chopin's *Nocturne Number Two*.....................166
Chapter 51: Sewer Scum..170
Chapter 52: Take It or Leave It..173
Chapter 53: A Bullet and a Shot of Whiskey.........................176
Chapter 54: Sati..180
Chapter 55: True Amazon Women..183
Chapter 56: Testosterone Crisis...186
Chapter 57: A Love Note...189
Chapter 58: Discount Breast Implants..................................192
Chapter 59: An Unusual Demise...195
Chapter 60: Secrets..198
Chapter 61: Fight or Flight...201
Chapter 62: Hell's Gate..205
Chapter 63: Paid Leave..209
Chapter 64: One Heck of a Deal...212
Chapter 65: Free Drinks–Again..215
Chapter 66: Olfactory Adventures..218
Chapter 67: Date Night..221
Chapter 68: Unhealthy Air...225
Chapter 69: Old Friends...228
Chapter 70: Mounting Body Count.......................................232

Chapter 71: Up a Brown Creek 235
Chapter 72: Catometer Readings 238
Chapter 73: Suite Rules 241
Chapter 74: Near Miss 244
Chapter 75: Almost Movie Time 247
Chapter 76: Countdown 250
Chapter 77: Lethal Camera 254
Chapter 78: Just Say "Please" 256
Chapter 79: Vampire Management 259
Chapter 80: Deep Freeze 262
Chapter 81: Money Stop 266
Chapter 82: A Partial Reveal 269
Chapter 83: Déjà Vu All Over Again 272

PROLOGUE

Nine Lives is the fourth in a series of thrillers. It can be read and enjoyed without having followed the main characters in the first three novels—*The Oven, Out of the Oven and Into the Fire,* and *Meltdown.* However, the brief synopsis that follows will provide orientation.

Newly trained CIA clandestine operator Woody Stressel is embedded as a first-year student in Grantland Medical School. He is told only that there is a strong suspicion of a mole in the CIA who has been turned by Russian agents and is fingering CIA operatives who are being kidnapped and tortured for classified information. However, no bodies are ever found. The CIA has information that suggests that someone at the medical school is involved.

Woody meets the mysterious and alluring student Alina Karnitsky across the cadaver table in gross anatomy. She speaks fluent Russian, and Woody soon learns that she is an expert in weapons and street fighting. He is concerned that Alina might be a Russian plant in the class. During a nighttime exploratory operation, Woody discovers the mutilated body of a pregnant woman in a vat of formalin in a heavily secured backroom of the gross anatomy lab. As Woody starts to uncover pieces of the missing CIA operatives puzzle, he becomes the target of assassination attempts. Woody learns that Alina is indeed a KGB agent and that her real name is Ava Volkov.

Ava tells Woody that his only chance of survival is to trust her to protect him. She and Woody become unlikely partners to solve the mystery of the CIA operatives who vanish and whose bodies are never found. The two of them barely escape being tortured and cremated and having their ashes thrown out with used kitty litter. Woody and Ava become high-value targets for both the KGB and a powerful Chicago crime syndicate. The two of them are moved to the secure CIA Camp Peary near Williamsburg, Virginia, for their safety while they decide whether to have their identities changed along with plastic surgery and relocation to a foreign country.

Woody and Ava receive death threats while at supposedly impervious Camp Peary and realize that they are not safe at the CIA facility. They make the dangerous decision to leave CIA protection, change their identities, and take a hazardous road trip to the Trans-Pecos desert in far West Texas, where Woody's mentally unbalanced and paranoid Uncle Wilbur has built an armed compound to protect himself from supposed Nazi agents. After an eventful road trip, Bob and Mary (new names) arrive to find that the only person at the compound is Leta, an inhospitable 16-year-old runaway girl who has escaped from being held captive at a desert whorehouse. Leta has a Mensa-plus IQ, a sharp tongue, and a quick trigger finger. Woody's Uncle Wilbur is mysteriously missing. The inhabitants of the compound are as likely to be blown to smithereens by Wilbur's sophisticated booby traps as to be captured and killed by KGB agents or hired criminal assassins. As bodies continue to pile up, paid killers overwhelm the compound, forcing Bob and the women to pull the "Armageddon" lever that Uncle Wilbur had designed to be used as a last resort. There is a cataclysmic explosion that reduces the compound to rubble and annihilates anyone in or near the compound. It seems impossible that Bob, Mary, and Leta could survive.

REPRISE

The heavyset man sitting at the small table in the beach restaurant motioned for the waiter to come over. The waiter, who was well tanned and had blonde hair pulled back in a long ponytail, smiled and approached the table. *"Sí, señor?"*

The customer continued, speaking in Spanish. "This red fish is really wonderful. Who is the chef?"

"You are looking at her husband," the waiter answered politely in passable Spanish. "My wife is the chef. I'm just the waiter and number one dishwasher. I'm glad that you like our food."

The man said, "There are lots of restaurants on the beach, but you people really stand out. May I ask who owns the restaurant?"

"My wife and I do. We've only been open for a few months."

"Your Spanish is pretty good, but you sound like someone from the States. Are you expats?"

The waiter nodded. "We used to live in North Dakota, but we got very tired of the terrible winters and decided to move here for a slower pace and good weather year-round."

A young woman with short auburn hair, wearing an apron, walked into the serving area from the back.

The waiter called to her. "Reba, this gentleman was complimenting your red fish."

The woman gave a big smile as she approached the table. She said in fluent Spanish, "It's my mother's old family recipe for red fish with herbs and wine dressing. I hope that you like it well enough to visit our restaurant again."

The customer nodded an enthusiastic yes. He glanced at the woman's waist and said, "Not to be rude, but you must be three months pregnant. I'm Dr Victor Hernandez, and I do most of the deliveries in town. I can spot an early pregnancy a block away."

Reba gently put her hand on her abdomen and answered, "I'm certainly not offended. You do indeed have a well-trained eye. Perhaps you will be kind enough to leave a business card for me."

"Of course," the doctor replied. "Tell you what—I'll trade you my card for one of the restaurant cards. He looked at the card that the waiter gave him and said, "Ellie's. That's an elegant name for your establishment."

The man stood up and placed some money on the table. "I need to get back to the office." He winked and said, "But you can be sure that I will return and bring either my wife or my girlfriend—depending on which one has been the nicest to me lately."

Just after the doctor left, a young woman entered the restaurant with a large basket. "Back from the grocery store," she said in good Spanish. "This should take care of everything Reba needs to prepare for tomorrow. It's a Friday, so we should be busy."

"How's school going, Maria?" Reba asked.

"It's painful. In all modesty, I'm much smarter than my classmates. Once my Spanish gets better, I need to get into the university here in town."

The three people walked back into the kitchen.

Maria said, "I'm certainly not going to complain, but waking up to a perfect morning every day could get old after a while. How long are we going to stay dead?"

The man looked at Maria and replied very seriously, "For a long, long time."

CHAPTER 1

CLEAN UNDERWEAR

It was 10 PM and the last customers had just left Ellie's Restaurant on the beach.

Maria locked the front door and headed back to the kitchen where Jack was drying a large stack of dishes. Reba sat at a small desk in the corner, counting a stack of Mexican paper pesos and coins.

Maria said, "Man, we were super busy tonight. Jack and I could hardly take orders and get food to the tables fast enough. If our volume continues to grow, we really are going to need help. There is no way Reba can continue to crank out so many orders."

"Amen," replied Reba. "Standing over a hot stove was not exactly what I agreed to when I married Jack."

Jack smiled and said, "Remember, my beautiful princess, you wrote the vows for the wedding and could easily have deleted the 'for better or worse' part. The really worst part would have been being blown into bloody little pieces when Uncle Wilbur's compound exploded. Our escape was nothing short of a miracle. We can all thank my crazy uncle for the brilliance of his survival plans."

Reba stood up, walked over to Jack, and gave him a kiss on the lips. "I am indeed a lucky woman. No complaints here."

Jack smiled and rubbed Reba's stomach, then asked, "And how is little Rufus doing in there?"

Reba shook her head, "You have no clue whether this child will be a boy or a girl. And you can bet the farm that no son of ours would ever be named Rufus."

Maria said, "I am also grateful to Wilbur that we are all alive, but it's hard for me to forget that I was sleeping with a cannibal who may have had me in his future dinner plans."

Before Reba or Jack could respond, there was a sudden loud crash, and glass shards sprayed the back part of the kitchen.

Jack ran for the back door, flung it open, and looked out into the dark alley. There was a screech of spinning tires as a small sedan with no lights raced away.

Jack closed the door and bolted it. He walked back into the kitchen with a troubled look on his face. "I wonder if that was just an adolescent prank or if it was a serious message. My bet is that some slimy character will arrive tomorrow and tell us that we need to pay for protection."

Reba frowned and replied, "Trouble in Paradise—and we have no weapons. I was really enjoying not having to spend my life on full alert. Maybe it will turn out to be a one-time thing from someone who hates gringos."

Maria chimed in, "Or it could be someone sent by one of the other restaurants on the beach that doesn't like competition. Too bad that Ellie's man-eating Belgian Malinois guard dogs are not still with us."

Jack said, "It works out well that we are living above the restaurant and can keep constant surveillance."

Maria hesitated as if debating whether to speak or not. After a moment she said, "Guess I better fess up. When I was walking home from the market today there was a little incident. Some creep came up behind me and tried to pull my skirt down."

"What happened?" Reba asked with concern.

"I was really pissed off, so I dislocated one of his arms and gave him a drop kick in the crotch. He was moaning and writhing on the ground when I walked away."

Jack shook his head. "Maria, our CIA tutor, Becky Reagor, taught Reba and me the absolute importance of never standing out if a person wants to disappear into a new community. I bet your disabling this pervert was the talk of the town in all the bars tonight."

"Just a minute, Mr. Holier than Thou!" Maria responded heatedly. "You've never been forced to work in a whorehouse where each horrible night was spent dealing with heavy-breathing old men who were trying to rip your clothes off. What would you have done if some weird man on the street tried to yank your pants down?"

Jack smiled slightly, then said, "I'd just want to be sure that I had clean underwear on."

Maria scowled and turned to Reba, asking, "Now aren't you sorry that you married this a-hole? Tell this idiot what you would have done in my place."

Reba did not hesitate. "I would have broken both arms and sent him to the hospital missing most of his teeth. No problem here with what you did. If there are any consequences, we will deal with them."

Jack looked at Maria and said apologetically, "My bad, Maria. You did not deserve a lecture. One thing's for sure—Reba has turned you into a very proficient street fighter. All those hours she spent drilling you at the compound have really paid off."

Reba said, "I really feel naked without my Makarov pistol. We need to figure out a way to get our hands on some weapons without arousing suspicion. Hopefully, Maria's encounter on the street and the broken window will both just blow over. The last thing I need to complicate my pregnancy is sleeping with one eye open and a weapon under my pillow."

Jack nodded in agreement. "I really hope that I am wrong, but I am willing to bet all the money on the table over there that we will have an unpleasant visitor tomorrow. Which reminds me—we need to stash all those pesos in the wall safe before we go to bed tonight. I'll make a deposit at the bank tomorrow morning."

CHAPTER 2

TIMELY EMESIS

Reba and Maria were up early the next morning working in the kitchen preparing for the opening of Ellie's Restaurant at 11 AM for lunch. Maria was making large bowls of salad, while Reba was kneading masa harina corn flour to turn small dough balls into tortillas with a wooden corn press. Jack had taken a quick shower after his run on the beach before sunrise and then left to deposit the previous day's earnings into an outdoor bank deposit box.

There was an insistent knocking on the back door. "That has to be our seafood delivery for the day," Maria said as she walked to the back door and unbolted it.

A muscular man with a bushy beard pushed his way through the doorway.

"A pleasant good morning, ladies," he said in perfect English. "I am Rodolfo, and I am here to present a business proposal. I will cut quickly to the chase. Life in this beautiful beach town is more dangerous than you might think. There are several criminal gangs here that specialize in robbing businesses such as yours. Their modus operandi is to burst into a store or restaurant, rob the patrons, and empty the cash registers. They are well armed and are in and out of the business in two minutes or less. The local police have proved powerless to stop them. Here is where I and my partners can be of help by offering protection."

Reba looked directly at the man and said, "Bad news for you and your partners, Rodolfo. We are not going to get forced into the protection racket that you and your friends are running. Now, kindly back your large butt out of the door and don't come back unless you want more trouble than you can handle."

The man's face hardened. "Little mother, you obviously don't understand what a bargain our protection plan would be for you. Two weeks ago, the El Caballo Restaurant near here mysteriously burned to the ground. Strangely enough, the owner had recently refused our kind offer to keep his place safe. His stupidity turned out to be very costly."

Reba said coldly, "We'll just take our chances. Now get the hell out of our business."

Rodolfo shook his head. "You may wonder why I speak such good English. I spent four years in the States and graduated cum laude with a combined degree in history and psychology from Columbia University. My final paper was entitled 'The Balance of Power in Small Societies.' Implicit in my paper was the concept that might usually makes right." The man pulled a snub-nosed revolver out of his pocket and pointed it at Reba.

"This, Sweetie, is what power looks like. You have no bargaining position at all. Tell you what. I'll give you and your husband some time to think rationally before you make a terrible choice. Plan on my coming back just before the restaurant closes tonight with some papers for you to sign."

Maria suddenly gave a shriek and started vomiting. Rodolfo turned to look at her. Quick as a cat, Reba lunged forward, slapped the gun out of his hand, and grabbed it in mid-air. She pointed the gun at Rodolfo's head.

"Surely a scholar such as yourself knows that the balance of power can change abruptly in small societies. Last chance for you to make a good decision before I blow you away and tell the police that you tried to rape me. If you aren't out the back door by the time I count to three, you're going to need good funeral insurance."

The man snarled, "I bet a fancy woman like you doesn't have any idea how to use that gun. Better give it back to me before you get hurt." Rodolfo extended his hand and stepped toward Reba. "Give it to me, you bitch."

There was a single blast from the pistol. The bullet disintegrated Rodolfo's left earlobe. He screamed as blood started trickling down his neck.

"The next shot will be right between your eyes," Reba said with no emotion.

Rodolfo headed for the back door, but stopped to scream, "You are a dead person walking, you whore! I'll be back!"

Just as Rodolfo exited out the back door, Jack rushed into the kitchen. "I just heard a gunshot! What happened?"

Reba said calmly, "You were so right about a heavy coming by today to give us an offer that we could not refuse about protection for the restaurant. I politely declined, then the man got ugly and pulled a gun. With some timely vomiting help from Maria, I took the gun away from him and had to shoot off one of his earlobes to get him to leave. But he promised to come back. At least we have one gun now with several shells remaining."

Jack shook his head. "First, Maria roughs up some street pervert, then you have to shoot a protection goon. Not exactly the way to stay off the radar in a small town. No question that we need to get our hands on some substantial firepower if we plan to stay alive. Trouble just seems to follow us wherever we go."

Jack paused, then turned to Maria. "What's with the vomiting, Maria? Are you sick?"

Maria shook her head. "Jack, you have forgotten that I have the unique ability to upchuck whenever I want to. I felt certain that barfing loudly and spewing vomit would distract the protection man long enough for Reba to disarm him."

Reba quickly said, "Brilliant work, Maria! The only thing more effective than a speeding bullet is projectile vomiting. Well done, young lady." She hesitated, then added, "Jack, the protection thug spoke perfect English and claimed to have spent four years in the States getting a degree in history and psychology at Columbia University. He was not the usual dirt bag criminal who gets into the protection racket."

Jack responded, "We need to give serious thought to how to stay alive if he comes back tonight with friends. Blowing off someone's earlobe is not exactly the way to win a friend for life."

Maria said, "Getting back to running a restaurant, we have lunch to serve in less than four hours. Time for all of us to pitch in and get the food ready. I think our growing notoriety in the community may turn out to be a big draw."

Jack responded, "Agreed. I'll start peeling the shrimp while I think about how to get some weapons for us. And I may have a possible source."

CHAPTER 3

NEW FRIENDS

Lunchtime was very busy at the restaurant. Reba was a whirling dervish in the kitchen grilling fish, frying shrimp, and warming the corn tortillas in the large oven. Maria prepared salad plates, delivered food to the tables, and was the cashier. Jack acted as combination waiter and bartender. Finally, just after 1 PM, things slowed down enough for Reba to sit down in the kitchen.

Jack came into the kitchen and put a hand on Reba's shoulder. "Honey, why don't you put your feet up and let me get you some food? You haven't stopped working since early morning."

Reba smiled and replied, "I'm really fine. If you will get me a Coke out of the fridge and give me a salad and a corn tortilla, I will recharge my batteries in a hurry."

Maria joined Reba and Jack in the kitchen and grabbed a dish cloth to wipe the beads of perspiration off her face. "Whew!" she exclaimed. "We've all been busier than the proverbial one-legged man in a butt-kicking contest. Thank goodness there are only a few people still out there. The dining room is becoming more and more like a sauna. We need to invest in some better air conditioning—and also get the lazy workers to move faster on finishing the patio dining area with the huge overhead fans."

Jack said, "Two more weeks on the patio. And we absolutely have to find some restaurant help quickly. Three people just can't run this place. It would be ideal if we could hire a good cook to work under Reba's direction. We also need a waiter. It is tough trying to take orders and also mix drinks when we get really busy. Which reminds me, we need to order some more liquor before the busy weekend arrives."

A deep man's voice came into the kitchen. "Hola, Jack. I brought my wife to try your restaurant's great redfish. Sorry to come so late, but I had a difficult delivery that took a long time."

Jack went into the dining room and shook hands with the portly gentleman. "Doc, for you, it's never too late." He turned to the buxom woman standing by the doctor. "My Spanish is not great, but I'm Jack Roberts. My wife and I own the restaurant."

The woman smiled and answered, "I'm Sofia, Victor Hernandez's wife. It is a pleasure to meet you. Victor came home raving about your wife's redfish. I am really looking forward to trying it."

Reba and Maria came out of the kitchen. Jack turned to them. "You two come on over and meet Dr. Hernandez's wife, Sofia."

Reba walked up to Sofia, shook her hand, and said, "I am Reba Roberts." She hesitated, then added, "Your husband is fortunate to have such a beautiful wife."

Sofia smiled. "I used to be his nurse, but now I get to manage him and his money."

Jack laughed. He turned to Maria and said, "And this is Maria Williams. She is my older sister's daughter who has been visiting us for several months to learn Spanish. She has become almost completely fluent."

Maria smiled at the doctor and his wife and said in good Spanish, "Don't believe everything Jack tells you. I have a way to go before I approach fluency."

Reba motioned toward a table. "Please have a seat, and Jack will bring you menus and whatever you wish to drink. If redfish is to be your choice, I'll head back to the kitchen and start grilling."

* * * * *

The doctor and his wife declined dessert, but both accepted Jack's offer to bring them café espresso and asked for Reba, Jack, and Maria to join them at the table.

Reba smiled, looked at Sofia, and said in excellent Spanish, "I hope that you liked my redfish as much as your husband has."

Sofia gave a small frown and answered, "To be perfectly truthful, the salad with mango dressing was the best part of the meal. Sometimes redfish just doesn't turn out very well."

Victor looked at his wife disapprovingly and said, "I thought the redfish was excellent. Sofia always complains about the food even in fancy restaurants in Mexico City. She is very spoiled."

Reba smiled again and said, "I am glad that Sofia liked the salad. Maria gets all of the credit for that."

Victor Hernandez looked at Maria and asked with a smile, "Young lady, do you realize that you are the talk of the town? People's tongues are wagging about how you laid out the police chief's son Eduardo yesterday morning after he tried to pull down your skirt in public. He has been a bully ever since he was in the first grade. Eduardo was in a lot of fights in school, and apparently never lost a single one. How you handled him so easily shocked people since the young man always brags about his training in judo. I bet you have a lot of curiosity seekers tonight at dinner who just want to lay eyes on you."

Maria answered modestly, "Eduardo's not so tough. Taking care of him was really nothing special."

There was a brief lull in the conversation. Jack started to speak, then stopped. He looked at Reba who nodded slightly.

Jack turned to the doctor and said, "We don't know you very well at all, but we have some real problems. Can I ask you to go into the kitchen with me and get some advice from a man who clearly knows this town?"

Victor nodded and answered, "Of course. And if it's about the man with part of his ear missing, there is a great deal to talk about."

CHAPTER 4

FIREPOWER

Jack and Victor Hernandez sat down at a small work table in the kitchen with their coffee cups. "How can I be of help, Jack?" the doctor asked.

Jack hesitated, then said, "Doctor Hernandez"—and paused, as if undecided whether to continue or not.

"Jack," the doctor interrupted, "Please call me Victor. I only go by doctor when I have my magic white coat on."

Jack smiled and continued. "I have no idea whether I can trust you or not, Victor, but there is no one else in town I can turn to. Reba and I have two current big problems. The easier one is our immediate need for help at the restaurant. We had no idea that we would get busy so quickly. Any suggestions that you might have for a cook and a waiter would be greatly appreciated. Reba is already working way too hard, and as her pregnancy progresses, she won't be able to stay on her feet all day long."

Victor responded, "I can help with that. What is the second problem?"

Jack continued. "Someone came down the alley last night and shot out one of our back windows. By the time I could rush to the alley door, a car with no headlights sped off. I predicted that sometime today we would be presented with a 'take it or else' ultimatum about paying for protection. While I was at the bank early this morning, a heavy named Rodolfo showed up and pulled a pistol on Reba when she told him in no uncertain terms that we would never agree to extortion. My wife disarmed him and ended up having to shoot him to get him to leave. Rodolfo promised to return tonight to settle the score."

Victor thought a moment, then began to speak. "Rodolfo Mendez and his friends can be a really big problem for you. Mendez grew up several towns down the beach and was an exceptional student in school. A wealthy New York attorney on vacation met Rodolfo at a hotel bar where the young man worked and was so impressed that he used his money and influence to get Rodolfo admitted to Columbia University. The idea was that Rodolfo would graduate, then return to his town in Mexico to teach underprivileged students. However, early in the first year after Rodolfo returned to teach, he was charged with having a sexual relationship with a 16-year-old girl in one of his classes and was fired."

"Sounds like a great guy already," Jack interjected.

"Since age 16 is over the age of consent in Mexico, Mendez was never charged with a crime. But the girl's father was threatening to kill him, so he moved to our town and fell in with some of the local petty criminals who were involved in prostitution and marijuana. Recently, Rodolfo convinced his partners that offering protection for businesses could be very profitable. A number of stores and restaurants in town now pay a monthly extortion fee out of fear for the safety of their businesses and their families."

"Why not go to the police?" Jack asked.

"Miguel Cardenas is our very weak police chief. Most people are convinced that he is on the take from the local criminals. A few threatened business owners filed complaints early on, but no action was ever taken by the city attorney or police. And, as you might imagine, bad things started happening to the complainants' businesses. The owners quickly saw the handwriting on the wall and started paying for protection. But there was one business owner who flat out refused to pay up and threatened to kill Rodolfo if he came back on his property."

Jack said, "That must have been the owner of the El Caballo Restaurant that burned down recently. Rodolfo used that incident as a threat when he was talking with Reba."

The doctor nodded and responded, "The fire occurred in the wee hours of the morning. The owner, Juan Lopez, was asleep above the restaurant and sustained major third-degree burns. He was flown to a burn unit in Mexico City, but lived only a few hours. Strange as it may seem, the fire and Juan's death could help deal with both of your problems."

"How so?" Jack asked with a puzzled look.

"Juan Lopez has a niece named Hulga who is on the SWAT team for the police in Detroit, Michigan. Her mother was a beauty from the Sonora region and was unusually tall. As a college student she worked one summer at an archeological site in the Sonora Desert where she met a Norwegian archeologist named Geir Larsen who was also very tall. They ultimately married and produced a huge daughter whom they named 'Hulga,' which is Norwegian for 'danger' or 'threat.' Hulga studied police work in college and ended up in Detroit and became a member of the police SWAT team there."

Victor paused to take a sip of his coffee, giving Jack a chance to say, "That's an interesting story, but how does it help Reba, Maria, and me stay alive?"

"Simple," Victor responded. "Hulga loved her uncle and visited him at least once a year. The word is that she is terribly upset about how her uncle died. Hulga is arriving some time tomorrow, apparently with vengeance on her mind. I'm betting that you can talk her into helping you part-time at the restaurant in exchange for room and board. She is a very intimidating person who is well over six feet tall and weighs in at least 220 pounds. If she stays with you, she should be a strong deterrent to any funny business from Rodolfo and his arsonist cronies."

Jack said, "That sounds very promising. But tonight may be dicey if Rodolfo and his thug buddies show up. You don't know much about Reba and me, but let me just say that we are very experienced with firearms and martial arts. We can take care of ourselves. Our immediate problem is no firepower. Do you know how we can purchase at least three good pistols and some ammunition without arousing suspicion from the law? We can afford any price that would be charged."

Victor sat silently for a minute with a wrinkled brow. Then he said cautiously, "I can get my hands on three unregistered Walther PPKs that would be perfect for concealed carry since they can fit in a pocket or be tucked in at the waist. And I can provide ammunition. But it is important that these guns can never be traced to me. The best way to make the transfer is for you to call me in my office late afternoon and tell me that Maria has fainted in the kitchen. I will rush over in my white coat to tend to her and will have the guns and ammunition in my doctor's bag."

"How much will we owe you? We are not poor."

Victor answered, "We can decide that later." Then he added cryptically, "I may need some important help from you and Reba in the near future."

CHAPTER 5

SOUTHERN VAPORS

Shortly after Victor and his wife left, the dining room cleared out completely. Maria locked the front door and changed the red neon sign in the window from "OPENED" to "CLOSED UNTIL 5 PM." Reba, Jack, and Maria began hasty preparations for the dinner crowd, which seldom started showing up before early evening. Jack related to Reba and Maria his conversation with Victor and the planned faux emergency visit to deliver the revolvers.

Maria took a small curtsy. "I am really good at faking Southern vapors. This will give me a chance to display my thespian skills."

Jack smiled and said mischievously, "Don't be too realistic, or Dr. Hernandez may be forced to resort to the age-old treatment of an impromptu nicotine enema to rouse you."

Reba shook her head and said, "That treatment is total BS and never really happened."

"Au contraire, my fair lady," Jack replied. "In the late 1700s, smoke enemas were considered the treatment of choice for drowning victims and for people near death."

"Please spare us the scatological details," Reba interrupted. She looked at Maria and muttered "just hopeless" under her breath.

Jack waited a moment and then asked innocently, "What did you two ladies think of Victor's beautiful wife?"

Maria frowned and answered, "Kind of pretty in a buxom sort of way. But that dress Sofia was wearing made me think that she was an entrant in the annual All-Mexico Mega Cleavage contest."

"Agreed," Reba said emphatically. "Maria and I have both been blessed by nature, but that woman looks like she has a serious glandular disorder. And I bet her brain is the size of an English green pea."

Jack shook his head and said, "Jealousy is such an ugly emotion. Victor told me that Sofia has an advanced degree in aeronautical engineering and also reads to the blind children at the local orphanage every weekend."

Reba turned to Maria and said, "Just ignore him. When Jack's BS machine goes into overdrive, there is just no stopping it until it blows a fuse. Five o'clock will be here before we know it. We need to get hopping in the kitchen."

* * * * *

By 5 PM the restaurant was ready for the expected later influx of dinner guests. Jack picked up the phone to call Dr. Hernandez's office and report that Maria had collapsed in the kitchen. But before he could complete dialing, there was the distinctive roar of a Harley in the parking lot. A slender man with beady black eyes and a large scar on one cheek stomped into the restaurant and seated himself at the bar. He was wearing a motorcycle jacket that had "Road King" lettered on the back in gold.

The man pounded on the bar until Maria came into the dining room from the kitchen. He pointed at Maria and ordered, "*Cerveza*, you *puta*, before I slap your ugly face."

Maria's head was flooded with a rush of terrible memories from the time she was forced to work in the desert whorehouse in Texas. But she calmly took a cold stein out of the refrigerator, filled it with beer, and walked up to the man.

She held the beer in the air and said, "Now's your chance to apologize for your rudeness, Road King, if you really want this beer."

The man snarled, "Not on your life, bitch" as he grabbed Maria's free hand. Maria smashed the stein down on his head and sent him sprawling to the floor. The man began to curse and reached into his jacket, pulling out a pistol. Maria kicked the pistol out of his hand and snatched it off the floor. She pointed the gun at him and said, "Time for you to leave unless you want to get hurt really bad."

Jack heard the noise and rushed into the dining room. He quickly assessed the situation. "Do you need any help, Maria?"

"No. Everything is fine. This gentleman is just leaving. Turns out he's not old enough to drink alcohol or to own a firearm."

Maria looked down at the man who was still cursing and said, "Such terrible language. I know that your mother would be ashamed of you. OK, dirtbag, I'm going to give you ten seconds to be back on your motorcycle and haul ass before I have to shoot you in self-defense."

Jack looked at the man with disgust. "Better get moving. The lady can shoot, and you wouldn't be the first sleazebag she has taken out."

Still snarling, the man stood up and stuck his hand out. "Give me my gun back, you bitch."

Maria shook her head and replied, "You may be Mr. Road King in your dreams, but you clearly are not responsible enough to own a weapon. It's mine now. If you don't head for the door immediately, I'll show you what a good shot I am. I think that I'll shoot you between the legs first—then go for the kill shot."

Still cursing, the man headed for the door. He screamed over his shoulder, "This place is gonna burn!"

Reba had come into the dining room and heard the last part of the conversation. She said, "I am willing to bet that motorcycle man had something to do with the El Caballo Restaurant burning down. We are going to need weapons more than ever now. Jack, time for Maria to faint dead away in the kitchen and for you to place an emergency call to Victor."

It took less than five minutes for Victor to arrive wearing his white coat and carrying a large doctor bag. Inside were three Walther PPK pistols in pristine condition, as well as extra ammunition.

Reba took one of the guns and sighted down the barrel. "Pretty sweet. Not as easy to handle as my Makarov, but plenty of stopping power. Doc, you are a real life saver. If Rodolfo and his buddies come back tonight looking for trouble, we will be more than happy to accommodate them. We need to pay you for the weapons—anything you ask."

Victor shook his head. "Just doing my part to reduce the rat population in town. As I told Jack earlier, there is something you people can do for me, but it won't be easy or safe. And it may be above your pay grade. We can talk about it tomorrow after Hulga arrives. Now, I need to head for the hospital. I've got two women there pretty far along in labor. Lunch was so good today that my wife and I may come back for dinner tonight if neither baby gets stuck in the chute."

CHAPTER 6

TINY TESTICLES

By 8 PM there was a good dinner crowd at Ellie's Restaurant, and Reba, Maria, and Jack were a constant blur of activity. Shortly after 9:30 PM when there were several open tables, Dr. Hernandez and his wife came into the restaurant. Jack greeted them and directed them to a quiet place in the back.

"Any problems?" Victor asked.

"No so far," Jack responded. "But we feel a lot more secure after your visit to treat Maria." Then Jack sat down at the table and quietly told the couple about the visit from Road King and his threat to burn down the restaurant.

Victor listened intently before speaking. "The man with the scar who rode up on the Harley is a flunky for Rodolfo Mendez. His name is Diego Moreno, and he is mean as a snake. Moreno was in prison for two years for assault and robbery. I wouldn't be surprised if arson is one of his skills. My guess is that Rodolfo sent his gofer to case out your restaurant."

Jack asked, "What's your guess about Rodolfo's next move? Do you think he will show up here tonight with some of his heavies?"

Victor shook his head. "Probably not. It would be bad PR for him to start a fight with so many people around. Keep in mind what initially was a pure business proposition from him has changed to a crushing desire for revenge. For the rest of his life, every time Rodolfo looks in the mirror, he is going to see part of one ear missing and remember the woman who humiliated him. I don't mean to frighten you, but to Rodolfo's warped mind the only way to settle the score will be to orchestrate a terrible death for your wife."

Jack replied grimly, "We don't frighten. I am not at liberty to fill you in on our past, but suffice it to say that Rodolfo and his goons are not the biggest threat we have ever faced. We moved to Mexico to find a simple life, free from sleeping with one eye open and being armed day and night. Things are sure not working out that way."

Victor looked quizzically at Jack and asked, "Are you and Reba ex-military? Are you running from the law?"

"Neither," Jack answered. "That's all that I am going to say. Now, how about some chicken instead of fish for tonight? Reba has made an incredible dish of barbecued chicken breasts with arugula and red grape salad with lemon vinaigrette."

"Sounds fantastic," Sofia said quickly. "And it will be good for my husband's expanding waist line."

Just as the doctor and his wife were finishing their meal, there was a loud bang as the front door was shoved open forcefully. The police chief's son, Eduardo Cardenas, stomped in with a very large man in a police uniform trailing behind him. "We're here to arrest the bitch who attacked me in town this morning. Sergeant Ortiz has the court order. Send her out, now!" The sergeant gave a mean laugh and took a pair of handcuffs off his belt and waved them menacingly.

Victor quickly stood up and pointed a finger at the man in the sergeant's uniform.

"That man is not a policeman. He's a former professional boxer who runs a sleazy gym down by the railroad tracks."

The large man moved toward Victor with one fist raised above his head. "You talk too much, you *hijo de puta*. Time for me to shut your mouth."

Jack quickly stepped between the angry man and Victor. He looked directly at the approaching man and said quietly, "Friend, let me help you make a better decision. I suggest that you and your little friend march back out the door before I have to send you to the hospital."

The large man sneered and said loudly, "You don't know who you're talking to, punk. I'm a Golden Gloves champion and can kick your ass with one hand tied behind my back."

The man moved surprisingly quickly toward Jack and launched a lightning fist toward his face. Jack ducked, but took a blow to the side of his head that stunned him for a moment. As the boxer moved in for a knockout blow, Jack quickly recovered and butted the man in his stomach. Jack parried the next wild swing, grabbed the man's long hair, and drove his face into the wall so hard that the plaster shattered. At that moment the police chief's son rushed toward Jack with a pistol in his hand and screamed, "Back off, asshole! Put your hands up in the air! Now!" He pointed the gun at Jack and said, "You have two seconds to call on the Virgin Mary before I blow you away!

"One…"

Hearing the commotion, Reba came into the dining room holding a large steak knife. She hurled the knife at Eduardo and stuck it deeply into his shoulder. He screamed and fired the gun wildly into the wall before dropping it. Maria appeared from the kitchen with one of the recently delivered revolvers in her hand.

"The party's over, children. You two rats are way out of your league. Which one of you should I exterminate first?"

Maria paused, then said, "I have a better idea. Jack, keep these losers covered." She flipped the revolver to Jack who caught it. The big man was standing in the corner with blood pouring from his broken nose and a deep laceration just above one eye. He looked dazed and not eager to go another round with Jack.

Maria walked over to Eduardo who was still on the floor cursing, with blood drenching his shirt from the knife that was still buried in his shoulder. She reached down and jerked the knife out. Eduardo gave a shriek.

"Now, Mr. Macho, stand up slowly and unbuckle your belt." Eduardo stood up slowly and hissed, "You are dead, bitch."

"My, my, such terrible language. Drop your pants, cry baby, or I'll bury this knife in one of your eyes."

Eduardo looked hopefully at the big man who still seemed shell shocked. Then Eduardo slowly dropped his pants.

Maria said, "Just to show you what a nice person I am, I'm going to let you keep your shorts on and not let the world see your tiny testicles. But your pants stay here."

Jack pointed the pistol at Eduardo and his bodyguard. "It's getting late. You two children should be in bed. Head out before something much worse happens to you. And don't forget to say your prayers tonight and thank the good Lord that you both are still alive."

There was a moment of indecision, then the two men headed for the door. Eduardo turned around and said coldly, "This deal's not over. Not by a long shot."

CHAPTER 7

FREE DRINKS

A number of the remaining diners had hurriedly exited as soon as Eduardo and his friend had entered the restaurant. People at the back of the restaurant with no safe exit had hit the floor when Eduardo pulled a gun. Now they were back at their tables, buzzing about how the owners of Ellie's had called Eduardo's bluff and humiliated him and his bodyguard.

Jack walked to the middle of the restaurant and announced to the remaining patrons, "We are very sorry for this unfortunate interruption of your meals. Our pledge to you is to keep Ellie's a safe place for you and your friends. Drinks are on the house until closing!"

By closing time at 11 PM only the doctor and his wife remained. Some of the guests had left the restaurant a bit wobbly after enthusiastically accepting the free drinks offer. Jack and Reba joined Victor and Sofia at their table for a late cup of coffee.

Victor smiled and said, "I usually don't use caffeine this late, but after all of the excitement tonight, I won't be sleeping much anyway. You two, as well as Maria, are just amazing. I don't know what your background is, but you three make a lethal team."

Reba answered modestly, "We can take care of ourselves. I hope what happened tonight won't make people afraid to come to our restaurant."

Sofia shook her head. "You three are quickly becoming local celebrities. Nobody in town likes that bully Eduardo, and they will be happy to learn that Maria humiliated him twice in one day. I was hoping that she would jerk his shorts down and send him out naked. I bet that he has a tiny penis."

Victor looked at his wife and said, "No need to discuss the poor man's anatomy. Not every woman is as lucky as you, my dear."

Sofia laughed and replied, "Smart women learn pretty quickly that money trumps male anatomy any day of the week."

Victor was suddenly serious. "You people have created enough enemies in two days to last a lifetime. Rodolfo is sure to seek revenge for his missing earlobe, and he has to make it plain that no business can refuse his protection services without paying a huge price. And you can be certain that Eduardo will not let his humiliation by a woman go unanswered. It is fortunate that Hulga arrives in town tomorrow. I will bring her for lunch unless half the mothers in town go into labor in the morning. She is a very intimidating woman."

Jack replied, "Great timing for us. Hopefully, we can convince her to stay with us and help with the restaurant. And, although I haven't seen Hulga, just for the record, I can promise you that if she and Reba went into a dark alley, only Reba would come out."

The doctor shook his head. "I wouldn't be too sure of that, my friend. Hulga is very large, but she moves like a ballerina. She also is a weapons expert. And she definitely has a mean streak."

Jack started to respond, but Reba interrupted him. "That's enough singing my praises, Jack. But there's no question that if you and I went into a dark alley which one of us would need an ambulance."

Reba turned to Victor and said, "We have a large extra bedroom upstairs that would work well for Hulga if she decides to stay with us and help in the restaurant. If she is as formidable as you say, having her around might be a good deterrent to keep local rats away."

Jack asked Victor, "What is your best guess about the next move by Rodolfo or Eduardo? Any chance that they might team up together?"

"Very likely," Victor answered. "I have no doubt that Eduardo's father is getting paid well for turning a blind eye to the prostitution and drug sales that Rodolfo is running. After Eduardo goes whining to him about his two unfortunate encounters with the new gringo woman in town, my guess is that Miguel will call Rodolfo for some retaliation help. There is nothing worse for a Mexican male than having his machismo publicly challenged."

Reba asked, "Victor, do you think what happened tonight will make Rodolfo more cautious now that he knows that we can defend ourselves?"

Victor nodded in agreement. "Probably so. But it won't deter Rodolfo and Eduardo and his father for long. They will just plot more carefully before they strike. I think burning your restaurant to the ground will be high on their list. But Rodolfo for sure will want to eliminate Reba in some horrible way. Eduardo will have his sights on Maria with a similar intent."

There was a pause in the conversation. After a moment Sofia stood up and put her hand on her husband's shoulder. "Time for bed, Victor. I need my beauty sleep. And if you snore again, you'll be having your sweet dreams on the couch."

As Victor rose to join his wife, he looked at Jack and Reba and said, "I have a friend who raises German Shepherd guard dogs in Mexico City. These animals are in great demand for rich families there. The trainer owes me a big favor. I might be able to get you bumped to the front of the line. But these dogs are not cheap."

Reba spoke and said, "We are experienced with Belgian Malinois guard dogs. In fact, one saved my life. Having a trained guard dog at the restaurant would really bump up our protection. If you can get the dog, we can produce the money."

"I will see what I can do. And don't forget that there is a very important personal matter that I need to discuss with the two of you. But it can wait until Hulga is here and we know what she is going to do. I'll bring Hulga for lunch tomorrow, and we can see if Reba would really be willing to go into a dark alley with her."

CHAPTER 8

HULGA

Jack and Maria left the restaurant at 6 AM to run on the beach. Reba was up starting food preparations with her new compact Walther revolver in a lightweight concealed waist holster. Ellie's Restaurant had survived the night unscathed, although Jack had been up in the middle of the night to check on some strange noises behind the restaurant that proved to be a pack of scavenger dogs looking for food.

The living area above the restaurant was large and contained several bedrooms. Jack had converted one spare room into a small gym with weights and a treadmill where he, Reba, and Maria worked out at least five days a week. Reba planned to keep exercising as long into her pregnancy as possible and was frequently on the treadmill running at a fast speed with sweat soaking her shorts and top. She continued to work with Maria on hand-to-hand combat skills.

Jack and Maria came back into the kitchen breathing hard from a race back to the restaurant from the beach. Maria said to Reba with some annoyance, "Jack would never have beaten me if I hadn't stumbled in a sinkhole in the sand."

Jack shook his head. "Maria, I was so far ahead of you by that time that all you could see was my taillights. Once I kicked on the afterburners, you were eating sand."

Maria turned to Reba and said sarcastically, "If your husband were Pinocchio, you could get him to tell whoppers at night just like now and find a new means of conjugal entertainment."

Reba shook her head. "Maria, you are a striking young woman, but one who needs a bit of work on social refinement."

Maria replied, "Being a conscripted worker in a whorehouse does not give much time for work on social graces. I'll start polishing my social graces when your husband starts working on telling the truth."

Reba smiled and said, "Maria, we love you and still would even if you were a mass murderess. But that's enough quibbling for now. We are certain to have a large lunch crowd after the fireworks at the restaurant last night. And don't forget that Victor will be bringing Hulga. We all need to be welcoming and pleasant if we want to convince her to move in upstairs and help protect this place. And maybe we can give her a hand in finding the thugs who burned her uncle's restaurant down. Now we need to hit the kitchen like three whirling dervishes."

* * * * *

The lunch crowd started arriving early. It was predominantly locals with a sprinkling of tourists. Just before 2 PM, Victor arrived with Hulga. She was a striking woman who was well over six feet tall and had a large, muscular frame. Hulga's face was surprisingly pretty despite a very noticeable scar at the top of her forehead. Her hair was jet black and cut short with a prominent gray streak running from front to back. Hulga was wearing khaki slacks and a muscle shirt that accentuated her biceps.

Victor headed for an empty table before Jack could intercept them. Hulga stayed in the doorway and surveyed the patrons carefully before walking over to Victor and motioning to another table in the back of the restaurant against the wall. Victor nodded, and the two of them relocated, with Hulga facing the front of the restaurant.

Jack brought a menu over to Victor and Hulga. He smiled and said, "Victor, please introduce me to your attractive lunch companion."

Victor stood to shake Jack's hand and turned to the seated woman. "Jack Roberts, this is Juan Lopez's niece, Hulga Larsen, who will be visiting in town for an indeterminate period of time. Hulga, Jack and his wife Reba own this restaurant."

Hulga stayed seated but extended her hand to give Jack a bone-crushing handshake. "Nice to meet you, Jack. You look like you have hoisted a few weights in your day. Is there a gym in town where I can work out?"

Jack replied, "Let's get you two fed first, then we can talk about a gym and other things that may interest you."

Victor said apologetically, "Sorry to show up just as Reba and you are closing down the lunch period. But I had a little fellow who was bound and determined not to leave his cozy little uterus home. I finally had to use high forceps and try not to smush his brain or one of his eyeballs with the blades while I was coaxing him out. I swear, nobody should ever use high forceps unless they are religious and on very good terms with the Mother Mary."

Just at that moment, Reba came out of the kitchen wearing an apron with her hair pulled up and walked over to the table where her husband was standing. She turned to the woman and said pleasantly, "You must be Hulga. I'm Jack's wife Reba, as well as the chef, cook, and business manager of Ellie's Restaurant. I would be honored to serve both of you with anything on the menu."

Hulga did not speak for a minute as she looked Reba up and down carefully. Then she said, "Victor told me about all the excitement that has been going on in your restaurant recently and how you took care of a thug who was threatening you. I was expecting you to be much larger and meaner looking."

Hulga kept staring at Reba as if deciding if she could take her in a fight. There was an awkward moment, then Reba said quietly, "Miss Larsen, the answer to your obvious unspoken question is that you wouldn't stand a chance. Now, let's talk about lunch for you two hungry people."

CHAPTER 9

DOUBLE GREEN STAMPS

Hulga used two steins of beer to wash down a huge platter of ground beef tacos and a mound of fried rice and beans. For dessert she had a large plate of fried plantains. However, Hulga kept a close watch on the other guests in the restaurant as well as the front door. Victor settled for a salad and a glass of wine since he said his wife was putting him on a diet.

By closing time at 2 PM the restaurant was empty except for Hulga and the doctor, who were having coffee. Jack and Reba came to the table and sat down. Victor stood up and said, "It's back to the office for me. We are offering double green stamps on all Pap smears this afternoon, so things will be busy. I know that you two and Hulga have some things to discuss."

Hulga gave Victor an indulgent smile and said, "Victor, don't give up your day job for standup comedy just yet. You need to work on some better lines. I'll come by your office later this afternoon when the line of patients dies down. But don't plan on my taking you up on your double green stamps offer."

Victor smiled and replied, "It would be my honor to provide medical services for you at a steeply discounted rate."

As Victor was leaving through the front door, Hulga called out, "Don't hold your breath on that one."

Maria cleared the coffee cups, then came back and sat down at the table. Hulga gave her a close up and down inspection, then spoke. "Maria, I understand that you are famous for disabling the sheriff's son who tried to disrobe you in public.

"For an encore, you disarmed a nasty man who came into the restaurant and pulled a gun on you after you decked him with a pitcher of beer. You and Reba are both very pretty and hardly seem the type to be proficient at generating violence. And Victor tells me that Jack is a super stud."

There was a moment of silence, then Reba said, "Hulga, we are not at liberty to tell you much about the past of any of us. Let me just say that we are very experienced with weapons and street fighting and have a number of notches on our belts. Victor told us that you are on a SWAT team in Detroit and came here to take care of the people who burned your uncle's restaurant to the ground and sent him to the hospital with fatal burns. You are going to need some help."

Hulga shook her head. "I can take care of this problem all by myself. Frankly, I think that the tales of you ladies' heroism are likely greatly exaggerated. Not to be rude, but you people impress me as candy-asses."

Jack looked at Hulga and asked, "Do you have a weapon? You are sure going to need one. The people who burned your uncle out are hardened criminals, and they play for keeps. We have been told that if we don't pay a large monthly fee for protection, our restaurant will also go up in smoke some night. Seems to me that we may have some mutual interests here."

Reba turned to Hulga and said, "Not to brag, but if you went into a dark alley with any one of the three of us, you would never come out. Being as large as you are is a real handicap against a trained fighter. Once you start nosing around town trying to find out who killed your uncle, you sure won't be safe in a hotel room at night. A few thousand pesos to the night clerk will buy a duplicate key to your room. Morning would find you stiff and cold in your bed with an expertly placed gunshot wound to your head."

Hulga snapped, "You are wasting your time. I don't scare easy."

Jack added, "Not to be unkind, but being a hotshot police officer in Detroit won't buy you much here in Mexico. You are going to need help to stay alive once you start searching for your uncle's killers. And we are the people who have the best chance to keep you out of a large pine box."

There was a sudden gunshot with the almost simultaneous sound of shattering glass from the kitchen.

Hulga screamed "incoming!" and dived under the table, sending two chairs across the room. Jack, Reba, and Maria did not move. Hulga sheepishly stood up. "Aren't you going to go see who's shooting at you?"

"No point," Jack replied. "That was a rifle shot, so whoever fired the shot is not close by. This is the second time we have had a window in the kitchen shot out. This time I think the shot was a welcome-to-town greeting for you. Victor said that your coming here to find the people who burned your uncle out was not a secret. Obviously, you are already on the radar of the killers."

Maria could not resist saying slyly to Hulga, "Not to be rude, but we candy-asses didn't flinch while you were diving under the table."

Hulga bristled and started to give a heated reply, but thought better of it and simply clenched and unclenched her fists. After a moment she said almost calmly, "OK, how would you suggest that we work together to stay alive and also take care of my uncle's killers?"

Reba asked, "Are you planning to stay in a hotel in town?"

Hulga replied, "Victor asked me to bunk in with Sofia and him. But that would not be my first choice. Not to be crude, but Sofia has her poor husband's balls in an iron grip. Theirs is not a peaceful household. Also, I now understand that staying there would put the doctor and his wife in danger. Do you have a better suggestion?"

"Much better," Jack replied. "Let's get another cup of coffee and have a serious conversation."

CHAPTER 10

ROOM AND BOARD

Hulga was a bit subdued as well as embarrassed after the gunshot caused her to dive under the table while her hosts stayed sitting with seemingly little concern. She rather begrudgingly turned to Jack and said, "You are probably right that trying to find out who killed my uncle and burned his restaurant down will make me a target and having help makes sense. What ideas do the three of you have?"

Reba, not Jack, replied. "Hulga, the first thing you need to decide is where you are going to stay to reduce your risk of waking up in a bloody bed with rigor mortis. We have an offer to make. If you will agree to help out in our restaurant, we will provide room and board and protection. There is a large upstairs where we all live, and there is an empty bedroom with its own bath and a view of the street. You will be much safer there than in a hotel or at your uncle's house. And I should mention that Victor is negotiating to get us a German Shepherd guard dog from an expert trainer in Mexico City."

Hulga hesitated for a minute, then asked, "Exactly what would I be expected to do in the restaurant?"

Maria interjected very seriously, "You would have to take over my job of keeping the bathrooms clean. Most of our male customers seem to delight in trying to pee on the ceiling."

Before Hulga could object, Reba laughed and said, "Maria is just teasing you. We can use help in almost all areas—serving, cooking, cleaning, shopping, etc."

Hulga asked, "How does this help me find my uncle's killers, which is the only reason I am here?"

Jack responded, "We have also been threatened with being burned out if we don't agree to pay a monthly protection fee to some local thugs. The town's police chief apparently is on the take from the bad guys and is of no help. The gunshot a few minutes ago was just another warning that these guys mean business. You can be sure that we are never going to submit to extortion. There is little doubt that the protection racket men are the ones who killed your uncle. We are just as interested as you are in eliminating these scumbags."

Hulga made up her mind quickly. "No choice but to accept your offer. I travel light, but my suitcase is at Victor's house. At some point I will need to go get it."

Maria mischievously said, "Hulga, be sure not to forget your double green stamps when you see your uncle."

Hulga's face reddened and she replied sharply, "Maria, you are something of a wiseass. Surely your mother told you that children should be seen and not heard."

Maria replied very seriously, "Tell you what, Sweetie. Let's you and me step outside and see who comes back inside. The only way you could ever hurt me would be if you sat on me."

Hulga began to breathe rapidly, stood up, and clenched her fists. Reba quickly intervened. "Enough! You two. I have no idea why Maria is being so rude. But maybe being called a candy-ass offended her. If we are going to survive, we all will have to work together as a unit with no little interpersonal squabbles."

"Sorry, Hulga," Maria said. "You are right—I am something of a wiseass. Working in a whorehouse does that to a person."

Hulga looked shocked and started to speak, but Jack cut her off. "No need for any of us to share personal secrets right now. There will be plenty of time for that later. The main thing we need to take care of immediately is to identify for Hulga the bad guys we know about to date. Reba and Maria met the first lowlife. One of them can tell you about it."

Maria nodded at Reba, who paused then began speaking. "Two days ago, a man named Rodolfo Mendez forced his way into the restaurant's back door early in the morning and advised Maria and me that unless we started paying him and his men for protection, really bad things could happen to us. He mentioned that your uncle refused to pay for protection shortly before his restaurant burned down. When

I told him that we would never submit to distortion, he got angry and pulled a gun. I had to disarm him and shoot one of his earlobes off before he would leave. He told me that I was a dead person walking."

Jack added, "Rodolfo was educated in the United States at Columbia and clearly is no dummy. Your uncle warned us that he and his men are very dangerous and will have no hesitation to kill. I feel almost certain that they are the ones who killed your uncle."

Maria said, "My turn for a lowlife story—short and sweet. When I was walking home from the market earlier in the week, the police chief's son, Eduardo Cardenas, came up behind me and tried to yank my skirt down. I had to jerk his shoulder out of joint and rearrange his testicles. A day later he and some big goon bodyguard dressed up as policemen came to the restaurant on the pretense of having a warrant for my arrest. Jack took care of the goon, and Reba and I disarmed Eduardo and sent him packing without his pants."

Hulga absorbed all of the information, then said calmly, "I need a weapon. I can shoot with the best of them."

Jack replied, "Victor somehow managed to get three Walther PPKs for us. He may be able to get one for you. In the meantime, we have the two pistols we took away from the police chief's son and Rodolfo."

Hulga said, "Strange that Victor has access to guns. To my knowledge, he has never had any interest in weapons." She paused for a moment before speaking, then said, "There's something strange about Victor. He seems happy and jovial on the surface, but he gets occasional looks of stark terror on his face that he tries to hide. Something is really scaring him."

CHAPTER 11

PORCH FIRE

At 6 AM the next morning, Jack was working out in the gym upstairs that he had outfitted with a treadmill, weights, and several large mats. Hulga came into the room wearing workout clothes. She saw Jack and said with surprise, "I thought this early you people would still be in bed."

Jack smiled. "No lazy butts in this family. All three of us adhere to Benjamin Franklin's admonition, 'Early to bed and early to rise keeps a person healthy, wealthy—and alive.'"

Hulga shook her head. "Old Ben Franklin is probably turning over in his grave the way you have messed up his 'Poor Richard's Almanac' maxim."

Jack replied, "Seriously, if a person is the target of really bad guys, spending a lot of time in bed is a sure way to end up dead. Reba was here ahead of me and has already run on the treadmill, lifted some weights, and worked on her combat skills on the mat. Maria went running on the beach, but at my insistence, she went well armed. She should be back at any time. By the way—how were your new quarters last night?"

Hulga answered, "Not bad at all. But I did wake up with a bruised back. It must have been the English green pea that someone put under my mattress."

Jack laughed and said, "You obviously read a lot of Hans Christian Andersen's fairy tales when you were a kid. I'm curious. What was your major in college?"

"Strangely enough, my undergraduate degree was in English, but I later got a master's degree in criminology."

There was a pause in the conversation, then Hulga asked, "How much are you trying to bench press there?"

Jack answered, "Not trying—doing, Hulga. I just put up 275 pounds."

Hula asked, "How much do you weigh, Jack?"

Jack shook his head. "Hulga, didn't your mother tell you that it is rude to ask a man his weight?"

Hulga smiled and replied, "That only applies to asking a woman, dummy. Seriously, how much do you weigh? I'm betting 225 pounds."

Jack answered, "You hit it right on the head. Why do you ask?"

"Not to impugn your masculinity, but a real he-man should be able to press at least 100 pounds more than his weight. So, 275 is not very impressive. Put 325 on the bar and stand back."

Jack stood up, added weights, then pointed to the bench and said, "When pigs fly, Hulga. Be my guest. I will spot for you."

Hulga said firmly, "No thanks. You weren't using one. Spotters are for sissies."

Hulga lay down on the bench, grabbed the bar, and hoisted the weight rapidly five times with little effort. "Piece of cake," she said as she stood up.

Jack shook his head and said, "I am impressed. As easily as you did that, I bet that you could bench a lot more."

Before Hulga could answer, Maria came into the room with sweat dripping from her face. "Three miles on the beach in 17 minutes! Not bad for running on sand."

Hulga gave Maria a small smile and said, "I hope nobody tried to yank your shorts down. Maybe wearing suspenders would give you an extra margin of safety."

Maria started to give a sharp retort, but hesitated before she spoke. "You know, Hulga, we all are going to have to get along and work together to stay alive and eliminate the men who burned your uncle to death. So, I'm going to pretend that I didn't hear your smartass remark and just start doing my pushups."

There was a tense moment of silence before Reba hurried into the room with a look of concern on her face. "I smelled smoke a few minutes ago while I was working on the lunch menu. On the back porch I found a blazing burlap bag. I put the fire out with the kitchen fire extinguisher. Inside the bag was a large dog's head with both eyes gouged out."

"That's a cheery good morning," Jack said. "I take it as a warning that when the bad guys choose to strike, we will be blind like the dog and not know it before it happens."

Hulga nodded in agreement. "Not to confuse the issue, but when I saw Victor yesterday afternoon to pick up my suitcase, he seemed really shaken. As I was leaving, he said something cryptic—'Things are really closing in on me. Tell Jack that I have to see him tomorrow before it's too late.'"

CHAPTER 12

CAVITY SEARCHES

Shortly after 7 AM there was an insistent knock on the front door of the restaurant. When Maria went to the door and looked out through the small peephole, she saw a very anxious Victor Hernandez. There were beads of sweat on his face that had dripped down to streak the green scrub top he was wearing. Victor headed rapidly to the kitchen as soon as Maria let him in. Reba turned from the stove and was surprised to see Victor.

She smiled and said, "We don't do breakfast, Victor, but I can whip you up some scrambled eggs and sausage if you like."

Victor shook his head and replied, "If I ate now, I would throw up immediately. My stomach has been churning all night, and I didn't sleep a wink. Where's Jack?"

Maria volunteered, "He's showering after working out. But we have good water pressure at the kitchen sink, which means he is out of the shower."

"I really need to talk with Jack—with all of you," Victor blurted out. "This may be my last day on earth."

Jack came into the kitchen with his hair slicked back, wearing a white t-shirt and beach shorts. "Thank God," Victor exclaimed. "I've got lots to tell everyone. Can we all sit down?"

Once everyone sat down at the large kitchen table, Victor began to speak rapidly. "Rodolfo Mendez is threatening to kill me. He has recruited some really bad actors from Mexico City who are part of a narcotics group that smuggles heroin into the United States. Either I agree to help them, or they will ruin my practice and likely kill me."

Reba had a puzzled look. "Victor, please slow down. You are talking so fast that it is hard to follow you. Just how are you supposed to help them?"

Victor took a deep breath, then started talking rapidly again. "These people are getting heroin into the U.S. by using human mules. Cavity searches for women are not uncommon at the border. What they want me to do is insert a double condom stuffed with heroin as deeply as possible into the vaginal canal of a woman. Then, they want me to draw off two pints of the woman's blood, soak a lot of cotton pads with blood, and stuff them tightly up the birth canal. Next, I am to smear blood on the outside of the pelvis and down the woman's legs and also bloody up a pair of panties for her to wear."

Reba said, "This would give the appearance of a life-threatening vaginal hemorrhage. No agent at the border would want to do a cavity search of a woman who might be at risk of bleeding out and dying."

Victor nodded. "It's even more clever than that. I'm supposed to put a very tight tourniquet on each arm long enough to make little blood spots on the skin. Then I am to write a note on a prescription pad stating that the woman has hemophilia and had a miscarriage with vaginal bleeding that cannot be stopped, and that she needs to get to a hospital in the U.S. that has large quantities of fresh frozen plasma to save her life."

Jack said, "This plan is too sophisticated for Rodolfo to conjure up by himself. There had to be some input from a doctor."

Reba added, "Clever indeed. Drawing off two pints of blood would also give the woman a fast heart rate that would be expected with heavy bleeding."

Victor replied, "Exactly. Rodolfo has a local ambulance driver who is on the payroll who will drive the woman through border customs, then drop her off at a motel where the heroin will be recovered."

Maria asked, "Why would a woman agree to take this risk?"

Victor replied, "Money. Big money for a poor woman who is living hand-to-mouth. And it beats selling their bodies on the street."

Jack said, "What happens if you refuse to cooperate with these dirtbags?"

Victor made an ominous slicing sign across his neck. "Rodolfo told me that first he and his partners will ruin my practice, then kill Sofia and me if I still refuse to help them. Either way, I am ruined. Rodolfo sent an underling to visit me just as the office was closing yesterday. The man told me that if I didn't cooperate there would soon be blood a foot deep in my waiting room. After a slaughter in the office, you can bet no patient will dare to come back."

Victor continued gloomily, "The man last night gave me a phone number. He said that if I didn't call before midnight to agree to help them, today would be a very bad one in the office. There's just no way out for me. I spent all last night thinking of putting a bullet into my brain."

Hulga was listening intently and breathing harder and harder. The veins on her neck were standing out. Then she spoke angrily. "Victor, I will sit in your waiting room starting this morning. I swear that none of your patients will ever be hurt. Describe for me what the man from last night looked like."

Victor looked uncertain and hesitated before speaking. "The person was short and skinny and had a pock-marked face. He had short greasy hair with really large ears and walked with a limp. My guess is that he is an expendable hired gun and not part of Rodolfo's professional criminals."

Hulga turned to Jack and said, "How about a loan of one of the Walther pistols that Victor supplied? Believe me, I can shoot the testicles off a mosquito at fifty yards."

Victor had stopped sweating profusely, but he looked unconvinced that the chances of his long-term survival had greatly improved. He turned to Hulga and said, "I have another Walther PPK at the office that you can use. But if you have to shoot someone, please do it in the parking lot and not in the office."

Jack asked Hulga, "Don't you think one of us should go with you in case more than one thug shows up?"

Hulga feigned a look of great disappointment and said, "Jack, you really know how to hurt a girl's feelings. Surely you know the motto of the Texas Rangers—'One riot, one Ranger.' In this situation it is 'One riot, one Hulga.' I can take care of myself, big boy."

CHAPTER 13

BULLET PROOF

Hulga joined the small group of patients queued up outside Victor's office waiting for it to open at 9 AM. Among them was a nun in a black habit with a wimple and coif. She appeared nervous and kept looking around at the other people. Hulga moved close to the nun and encountered a strong tobacco smell.

Hulga addressed the nun, "Good morning, sister. I hope that you have nothing serious that brings you to see Dr. Hernandez. You know, he's particularly good at treating gonorrhea among women from your cloister."

The nun began to edge away from Hulga, then broke into a dash for the street. Hulga sprinted after the nun, quickly caught her, and ripped her wimple and coif off. The nun had been transformed from a holy sister to a man with a pocked face and large ears. Hulga had a firm grip on one arm of the struggling man, but the other arm was free and suddenly produced a snub-nosed revolver that the man fired point blank into Hulga's chest.

Hulga rocked back, then picked the man up and walked to the street. She stood there holding the thrashing man over her head. "Surprise, scumbag. I'm bullet proof. Let's see if you are truck proof!" Hulga threw the man in front of a large truck that came speeding down the street. There was a loud thump and a screech of brakes as the man was hurled up into the air and came crashing down onto the pavement.

As a crowd gathered, Hulga shouted, "Get the police! That man dressed like a nun tried to kill me!" Then Hulga walked calmly around the medical building into the alley and disappeared.

Ten minutes later Hulga was in the kitchen of Ellie's Restaurant having a cup of coffee and French toast that Reba had made. Maria,

Jack, and Reba sat at the table waiting to hear from Hulga. "So, what happened?" Maria asked impatiently.

"Problem solved, at least for now. The man with the pocked face and large ears was waiting with other patients in front of Victor's office dressed as a nun. There was something odd looking about the sister. When she scratched her crotch with the habit on, I knew that there had to be a man inside the nun's garb. I moved closer to her and smelled tobacco smoke. The fake nun got nervous and bolted, but I ran her down and jerked off her wimple and coif. Bingo. Sudden sex change. The pious sister was now a rat-faced killer with big ears. He pulled a pistol and shot me in the chest."

"Shot you in the chest?" Reba said with great concern. "You should be dead by now!"

Hulga shook her head. "Don't underestimate me. I was wearing a small boron carbide breast plate that stopped the bullet."

"What happened to the man?" Jack asked.

"Kind of a sad story. He was so remorseful after trying to kill me that he stepped in front of a speeding truck. If the loser survived, he won't be back in action for a long time."

Maria looked at Hulga and asked, "Are we all correct in assuming that the man had an assist in getting in front of the truck?"

Hulga smiled slightly as she answered, "I'm taking the Fifth on that one."

Jack said, "Great work, Hulga. This may temporarily take the pressure off Victor, but losing one lower echelon worker won't stop Rodolfo and his imported professionals for long. Extortion money is just peanuts compared to a heroin mega payday. I think that we are all sitting on a time bomb that is just waiting to explode. Any suggestions from our august war council?"

Maria immediately replied, "I think that we have to strike first and make those people afraid to mess with us."

Reba countered, "The problem with that approach is that Rodolfo has a lot more resources at his disposal than we do. In a war of attrition, we lose for sure. No way we will ever get any help from the local police department with Miguel Cardenas in charge. He's sitting fat and happy with crime money flowing into his bank account."

Jack mused, "Too bad we are not in the U.S. where we could call in the feds since narcotics are involved."

Hulga said, "Staying armed and alert may be all we can do right now. I think I need to sleep at Victor's office for a while in case there is trouble at night. My guess is that the bad guys will want to make a statement by trying to burn down Victor's clinic or this restaurant. Having the guard dog Victor has promised you would be a huge help as an early alarm system. Any idea when the dog might arrive?"

Jack shook his head. "Victor was not sure if he could get us put at the front of the line with his friend the trainer in Mexico City. Good guard dogs are in great demand by wealthy families in Mexico."

Suddenly there was a loud thump from the front of the restaurant. Jack drew his pistol and moved cautiously to the door. The carcass of a headless dog crawling with maggots lay on the porch. There was a crudely lettered note in blood stuck to the dog's body with a large nail which said in Spanish—

Are you sure that you assholes are maggot proof?

CHAPTER 14

COWARDLY DWARFS

Lunch time at the restaurant was busy but uneventful. Hulga turned out to be a welcome help in the kitchen and quickly took over some of Reba's chef duties. Periodically, however, Hulga would walk out front and scan the dining room, looking for any suspicious patrons. Jack was busy taking orders, managing the bar, and working the cash register. Maria served most of the food and kept the tables clean. The three women, as well as Jack, worked with concealed weapons in waist holders.

Shortly after 2 PM the restaurant was empty, and Reba and Hulga were working on food for dinner. Maria and Jack quickly cleared the tables and loaded the large commercial dishwasher, which was a rarity in Mexican restaurants in the early 1960s. Hulga walked over to the dishwasher and said, "This machine must have cost a fortune. Which one of you people is a trust baby?"

"No such luck," Jack replied. Then he added slyly, "But my wife was a very successful stripper in Vegas before we had to get married, and she invested her money wisely." A coffee cup whizzed by Jack's head and shattered against the wall.

Reba gave Jack a death stare and said, "You're living dangerously, Jack. I missed your head on purpose, but one more offensive whopper about me, and the next launch will be a perfect strike much lower down. You will wish that you had invested in a reinforced protective cup."

Jack turned to Hulga and said, "I married a very violent woman who has a perverse desire to emasculate all the men in her life."

Reba looked up from the potatoes that she was peeling and shook a warning finger at her husband. Jack made a dramatic gesture of crossing his hands over his crotch in mock fear.

Maria laughed. "Hulga, these two children specialize in getting into petty fights. Most of the time the only adult in this family is me."

There was an urgent knock on the back door which Maria carefully answered before letting Victor inside. He seemed less agitated than he had been earlier in the day. Victor sat down at the work table and asked hopefully, "Any leftovers from lunch? My appetite has suddenly returned."

Reba nodded yes and said, "How about some beef tacos with a salad?"

"Perfect. I may actually be able to keep the food down now that I know that the man with the pock-marked face is in the hospital with multiple broken bones and a concussion. My patients told me that he showed up at the office this morning dressed like a nun and packing heat. Some good Samaritan disarmed him before he could get into the office and start slaughtering any of my patients. Then the man wandered into traffic and got hit by a big truck." Victor paused, then asked, "Is that about right?"

"Close enough," Hulga answered with a perfectly straight face.

Just as Reba was serving Victor his late lunch, there was a loud banging on the front door, and a harsh voice shouted, "Police! Let us in before we knock the door down!"

Jack went to the door with one hand near his concealed waist holster. He opened the door. Several men in police uniforms with guns drawn stormed into the restaurant led by a short, squat man with a police chief badge.

"I'm Chief Cardenas, and we are here to arrest Hulga Larsen for assaulting a patient of Dr. Hernandez this morning while the poor man was waiting for the office to open."

Hulga came into the room and towered over the chief and his deputies, all of whom backed up a couple of steps. She walked up to the chief, looked down at him, and asked politely, "Can I see the warrant for my arrest?"

The chief stuttered a moment, then said, "It's being processed right now."

Hulga frowned and said, "I'm a policewoman back in the States. No warrant, no arrest. OK, Short Shit, it's time for you and all of your cowardly dwarfs to move your asses quickly out of here before you all get hurt. Everybody knows that you are on the take from the heroin mob. I would consider shooting you to be a community service. If you are even halfway smart, you won't give me the chance."

Jack, Reba, and Maria came into the dining area quietly and stood staring silently at the chief and his men.

Then Jack said, "Cardenas, you have no idea how far out of your league you are. Unless you and your men want a quick ticket to the funeral home, I would suggest an expeditious retreat."

Several of the policemen had already holstered their weapons and started backing toward the door. Then, they suddenly broke ranks and exited en masse, leaving the chief alone.

Hulga moved closer to the chief and said, "If you are still here in five more seconds, I'm going to squash you like a cockroach." She took another step toward the chief, who bolted and ran out of the door screaming, "I'm the law! I'll be back!"

There was a moment of silence after the police left, then Maria gave a thumbs-up to Hulga. "I just love your alliteration—'Short Shit.' Absolutely perfect for that little creep."

CHAPTER 15

PERIPATETIC MALE APPENDAGE

Victor came into the front of the restaurant once the police had made a hasty exit. "I thought it best if I tried to stay out of this. Hulga and Jack certainly put Miguel Cardenas in his place. The problem is that making this little man lose face in front of his officers and demeaning his manhood will make him homicidal. We all need to watch our backs. I still am expecting an attempt to burn us both out."

Hulga asked, "Victor, any idea when the guard dog might come?"

Victor said, "Good news on that front. The dog will arrive tomorrow in a special truck."

Reba asked, "How in the world did you convince your friend to bump us to the front of the line? That dog must have cost a fortune. We need to pay you back."

Victor responded, "The man owes me a really big favor. Not to break a medical confidence, but let me just say that two years ago when my friend's wife was out of town for two weeks on a trip with girlfriends, he showed a lack of discretion and ended up with a drippy problem with his member. I managed to load him up with penicillin and get him totally cleaned up before his wife returned. To say that he is eternally grateful is an understatement."

Maria asked, "Does the dog have a name?"

Victor nodded yes. "The dog's name is 'Chingón.'"

Reba had a puzzled look as she took a few seconds to flip through her mental Rolodex of Spanish words. Then she smiled. "I think 'Chingón' is slang for 'bad ass' in Spanish."

Victor nodded. "Exacto. My trainer friend told me that the previous owner's family are all fluent in English and called the dog 'B.A.'—short for 'Bad Ass.'"

Jack smiled and made an exaggerated sign of the cross. "The dog may eat us all up before he attacks his first bad guy."

Victor replied seriously, "Could well be. My friend was adamant that the new owners know that he is not responsible for anything that this dog does. In fact, a release is coming with the dog that one of you has to sign. Apparently, B.A. had a short stay with a prominent attorney's family in Mexico City where he bit the man's wife and daughter for no apparent reason. The lawyer wanted to put the dog down, but my friend insisted on refunding his money and saving the dog. The good news for you people is that B.A. is up to date on his rabies shots."

"Well, that's a great relief," Jack said sarcastically. "Usually, guard dogs are not placed until the new owner spends several days with the dog and the trainer. If only Ellie were still with us."

"Ellie?" Hulga asked. "That's the name of your restaurant."

Reba replied, "Ellie was a close friend who had two Belgian Malinois guard dogs that were spectacular. Both she and the dogs died in the line of duty."

Hulga said, "I have some good news for you people. In my early police career, I spent three years in the Canine Division with some pretty ferocious German Shepherds. There is no dog that I can't handle. I'll have Mr. Bad Ass eating out of my hand the first day and sleeping in my bed that night."

"Well, that's a relief," Reba said. "Since you are going to be sleeping in at Victor's office for a while, the dog can warn you if Rodolfo and his thugs decide to make a midnight arson visit."

Jack turned to Victor and asked, "Will you and Sofia feel safe in your home at night? Rodolfo is not going to be happy that Hulga put his hired gun in the hospital and out of action indefinitely."

Victor replied, "My office is a much more valuable target than the house in terms of forcing me to cooperate. Also, I sleep with one eye open and keep a shotgun by the bed. I think killing me will be

Rodolfo's last resort since I am the only doctor in town who still has a valid medical license."

Reba said, "Too bad that we didn't have a chance to squeeze the pock-faced man and find out what he knows about Rodolfo's new heavies and how the heroin gets into town." There was a moment of silence, then Reba's face brightened. "I think that it would be a fine Christian gesture for someone from the convent to visit the poor fellow in the hospital tomorrow and wish him Godspeed with his recovery."

Jack smiled and exclaimed, "Capital idea! Now all we need is a habit and headgear."

Victor's face brightened. "As luck would have it, one of my patient's daughters was a nun who got pregnant in some supernatural way and had to leave the convent and marry her old high school boyfriend. Her mother was very disappointed and mentioned that she has kept all of her daughter's convent clothes. I've been treating the mother's diabetes for years without charging her."

Reba asked, "Do you think that she would let you borrow some nun garb?"

Victor shook his head. "Not a chance in Hades. But I'm seeing the woman at 9 AM tomorrow. She lives alone, and I know that she does not have a dog. I can detain her in the office for a while."

Reba smiled and said, "Say no more. Just give me the address. And, Victor, I'm sure with your hospital connections that you can find what room Mr. Pock Face is in."

Maria stood up and gave a short burst of applause. "Hot dog! Tomorrow promises to be an exciting day. First, grand larceny, then a hospital visit, and last but not least, B.A. arrives and promptly takes a big chomp out of our dog whisperer's generous butt. I'm going to have trouble sleeping tonight."

Hulga gave Maria a death stare.

"Just yanking your chain, Hulga. No insult intended."

Hulga kept staring at Maria and said, "Keep on yanking my chain, little wiseass, and one day the chain is going to fly right back and knock the crap out of you."

CHAPTER 16

A YANK IN TIME SAVES NINE

At mid-morning the next day a nun entered the hospital with her head bowed reverently and a silver cross around her neck. Her habit was a bit short, but not enough to cause any suspicious looks. An orderly made the sign of the cross as the nun walked slowly down the hall toward the main hospital elevator. She responded to the orderly with a soft "bless you, my son." Once the creaky elevator reached the third floor, the nun exited and walked past the nurses' station where a nurse was busily writing in a chart.

Suddenly a naked old man tottered into the hall from his room across from the nursing station and started screaming, "Help! Help! They're trying to kill me!" The man lost his balance and fell very hard to the floor, striking his head with a loud thump. An orderly appeared and reached the patient just as the nurse did. The man began to have seizure movements and started vomiting.

"He's going to aspirate!" the nurse shouted as she knelt down and turned the man's head to the side.

The nun continued down the hall with a slight smile on her face. Once she reached the room at the very end of the hall, she stopped to read the patient sign that read "Reynaldo Huertas—No Visitors." Then she opened the door silently and disappeared inside. A man with a bruised, pock-marked face lay in the bed, seemingly asleep, with one leg up in traction and a weight attached. Both arms were in casts above the elbow. The nun carefully moved the call button away from the bed. Then she quietly tore a wide piece of adhesive tape from a roll on the side table. With a lightning quick move, she slapped the tape over the man's mouth. His eyes popped open and he began to struggle and tried to scream.

The nun reached into a slit in the side of the habit and produced a pistol that she pointed at the man's head. "One more sound out of you, Reynaldo, and you are heading straight for hell without stopping at purgatory to collect two hundred dollars. You and I are going to have a friendly little chat, or I am going to have to hurt you really bad. *Lo entiendes?*" Reynaldo had a malignant look of hatred on his face and shook his head 'no' as he extended the middle finger of each hand that protruded from the casts.

"Not a very nice gesture to make to a holy woman of the church, Reynaldo. You should recognize this gun with a silencer. It's the one that you intended to use to kill patients in Dr. Hernandez' office. But you are so incompetent that you dropped the gun on the street when you stupidly walked in front of a truck." Reynaldo began to struggle and try to scream.

The nun shook her head. "Reynaldo, you are such a slow learner. What part of 'Don't make any sounds' is so hard to understand? Let me make myself plain. If I have to correct you again, as God is my witness, I will put a bullet right in your brain and consider it a community service. Please nod if you understand things better now." Reynaldo did not respond.

"Tell you what, hot shot. While you think about making a smart decision, I'm going to take a chance and untape your mouth. If you yell for help, it will be the very last thing you ever do." The nun kept the gun pointed at Reynaldo's head with one hand while she ripped the tape off his mouth. He gasped but did not cry out. Then the man suddenly spit at the nun who ducked to the side.

The nun said quietly, "I really underestimated just how stupid you are. Let me help you stay alive a little longer." She turned and grabbed the catheter that was attached to a bag of yellow urine hooked to the side of the bed. She gave it a yank. The man in bed groaned and had a new look of fear in his eyes.

"Let me explain some basic physiology to you, my friend. This catheter is in your bladder. It has a balloon that is blown up to keep it from coming out. If you are not more cooperative, I will have to jerk the catheter so hard that the balloon will be forced down your urethra and out the tip of your male part. It will hurt so bad that you will wish you were dead. And you will be a dribbler for life with absolutely no ability to satisfy a woman ever again. Now, for the last time, please nod if you understand the rules of the game."

Reynaldo remained immobile, but when the nun reached for the catheter, he nodded a slight yes.

"Now that we have a clear understanding, it's time for us to play the questions and answers game. Question number one: Rodolfo has two new men in town to help manage his heroin trade. Who are they, and where did they come from?"

Reynaldo hesitated long enough for the nun to give his catheter a forceful yank.

The man groaned and gagged like he was about to throw up. His eyes were dilated, and his face had beads of sweat. The heart monitor showed a heart rate of 100 and gave out one warning beep before the woman snatched the plug out of the wall. A red tinge appeared in the catheter bag.

"I need names, Reynaldo, and you better not bullshit me unless you want to see me again very soon."

The man in the bed was a professional killer, but he had never considered that he might be the victim instead of the assassin. It was clear to him that the person in the nun garb would not hesitate to put a bullet in his head. Reluctantly, Reynaldo began to talk. Whenever he hesitated too long, the nun would give the catheter another quick pull that magically loosened the man's tongue.

The nun had learned a great deal before voices appeared outside the door. She quickly put her gun away and whispered to the man, "Say one thing wrong, and I swear that I will come back tonight and finish you off."

The door opened and the nurse who had been attending the old man who had fallen came in with a pain pill for the patient. She seemed surprised to see the nun and said, "Sister, I hope that I am not interrupting anything. I'll poke this pill in Mr. Huertas' mouth and give him some water to swallow it. Then I'll leave you two alone. I sense that this gentleman can use more religious guidance."

"No problem, nurse. Mr. Huertas and I have had a serious talk about the condition of his soul. I am confident that Mr. Huertas will be a changed man when he is finally able to leave the hospital. I need to get back to the convent for morning prayers, so I'll leave you to tend to the patient's physical needs."

The nun walked to the door, but stopped to give a warning stare to the patient before she left and disappeared down the staircase outside the room. A minute later she was in the alley behind the hospital and looked very much like a tourist, wearing sandals, shorts, and a halter. The habit and other parts of the nun garb had been folded and placed into a beach basket that she was carrying. Mission accomplished. The nun had much to tell her sisters back in the convent.

CHAPTER 17

MISSION OF MERCY REPORT

Reba used her key to come into the kitchen of Ellie's from the back of the restaurant. She found Maria busy making a huge bowl of green salad with mango slices, pecans, and small peppers. Hulga was hard at work turning out corn tortillas. Jack came into the kitchen from the dining area pushing a vacuum cleaner. He saw Reba and announced with a smile, "The holy sister has returned from her hospital mission of mercy. So, did she save another soul from perdition, or did she have to administer last rites to the patient?"

Reba shook her head as she looked at her husband. "Your Catholic theology is a bit weak. Surely you know that only priests can perform last rites for a dying person. However, the patient today tried to spit on the visiting nun and did come very close to needing terminal rites."

Maria asked, "So what did you learn, Reba? Did you convince Pock Face to sing?"

Reba answered, "Mr. Huertas was not very cooperative until I started yanking his catheter and describing just how uncomfortable pulling the catheter out of his male appendage would be, and how he would never, ever again have a good erection for life. This terrified him more than the threat of putting a bullet into his small brain."

"Typical male," Hulga sniffed. "They worry more about their dicks than about being killed."

"As a woman of vast experience, I can echo that remark," Maria quickly agreed.

Jack parked the vacuum cleaner in the corner and sat down at the table. "Time for a five-minute work break so Sister Reba can give us all the details of her hospital visit." Everyone joined Jack at the table in the kitchen.

Reba began, "Getting into the house of Victor's patient was a piece of cake. I walked around to the back door and opened the simple lock with a bump key. The woman obviously has left her daughter's room as a memorial of sorts. There was a Catholic Bible on the nightstand and a closet with several habits and other pieces of nun garb. I put what I needed into a beach bag and changed in an empty stall at one of the public bathrooms. People at the hospital obviously are accustomed to having nuns visit patients and simply smiled or nodded at me.

"I will spare unnecessary details except to say that I found Mr. Huertas asleep with one leg up in traction and both arms in long casts. By sticking my newly acquired Walther in the man's face and giving the man's catheter some serious yanks, I was able to learn a few interesting things. First, Reynaldo was hired by Rodolfo to create chaos in Victor's office by shooting the place up. Of course, he swore that he did not plan to hurt anyone there. My guess is that Pock Face is a professional killer with a 'Have Gun, Will Travel' business card."

Hulga asked, "Do you think that this dirtbag also has a subspecialty in arson?"

"I asked Reynaldo pointedly if he knew anything about plans to burn down our restaurant or Victor's office or house. He stuck to his story even when I pulled his catheter hard enough to make blood come into his catheter bag. I tend to believe his story that he was in town for a quick specific job followed by a hasty exit out of town."

Jack asked, "Did you learn anything about the two new heavies in town who apparently are here to set up a narcotic pipeline across the border?"

"Not much," Reba answered. "Reynaldo said that they are from Mexico City and would just as soon kill you as look at you."

Maria frowned and said, "That's quite a compliment from one professional assassin to another."

Hulga paused a moment, then said angrily, "Rodolfo Mendez and his people burned my uncle's restaurant down and also burned him to death. I'm here for revenge. Since the police in town are crooked, I'll begin by taking Rodolfo out myself."

Jack shook his head. "This is not the Wild West where you send a challenge to Rodolfo and meet him on the street and face off at twenty paces to determine who can draw faster. You won't see Rodolfo until he wants you to see him, and only when the odds are heavily in his favor. The man is mean as a snake, but he is no dummy."

Reba said, "Victor missed the deadline he was given to agree to help with prepping women with vaginal heroin to get past border inspectors. Plan A was to send a shooter to Victor's office to create chaos as an inducement to reconsider. But now that Hulga has put Reynaldo on the injured reserve list for several months, Rodolfo will have to find a replacement. After the word gets out about what happened to Reynaldo, I don't think many professional hit men will be lining up for the job."

Jack nodded in agreement. "No way Rodolfo or any one of his professional thugs will take the risk of being a public shooter in Victor's office. They may just move ahead to Plan B and burn down Victor's office."

"Doesn't Chingón the German Shepherd guard dog, aka B.A., arrive sometime today?" Hulga asked. "After he and I become best friends, I plan to sleep in Victor's office at night all snuggled up with the dog."

Maria got a wicked smile on her face and asked innocently, "Isn't bestiality still a crime even in Mexico?"

Hulga's face became red. She stood up quickly, grabbed Maria's chair, and lifted the chair and Maria high in the air. She said angrily, "One more smartass remark out of this little girl, and I will have no choice but to hurt her."

Maria reached down and grabbed a fistfull of Hulga's hair and dived off the chair, pulling Hulga to the floor. Hulga gave a bull roar and stood up with mayhem in her eyes. Reba darted between the two of them.

"That's enough, you two idiots! We've got plenty of problems without my having to referee hen fights.... Maria, your remark was crude and totally uncalled for. I want you to apologize to Hulga now, or you will have to deal with me."

There was a tense pause—then Maria mumbled, "I apologize."

Before Hulga could respond, there was an insistent loud banging on the front door of the restaurant.

CHAPTER 18

THE DOG WHISPERER

Jack went to the door, pistol in hand, and slowly opened it. There was a man in a delivery uniform standing there. Before Jack could speak, the man said, "I'm here with the dog from Mexico. I'll unload the cage from the truck, but you folks will have to let him out. This is one mean son-of-a-bitch dog who has a record of biting people without any reason. I plan to be back in the truck when you new owners get acquainted with this killer dog. And you can keep the cage."

Saying this, the man opened the back of the panel truck and set up a small ramp that let him roll the cage down to the ground. Inside was a large black and tan German Shepherd that was looking intently through the steel bars. By this time, Reba, Maria, and Hulga had joined Jack outside.

Hulga walked up toward the cage. As she drew close, the dog began to snarl and show its sharp teeth. She gave a short whistle and said, "Chingón is an absolutely gorgeous Shepherd. That black muzzle is really striking. And he must weigh at least ninety pounds."

By this time the driver was back in the panel truck. He gunned the engine and spewed gravel as he sped away.

Maria suggested, "Why don't we let the dog whisperer make friends with that beast first, and the rest of us can applaud while looking through the front window? I have read that German Shepherds have an even stronger bite force than Ellie's Belgian Malinois, which we saw easily remove body parts from bad guys."

Hulga looked at Jack and said, "So the restaurant is named after this Ellie person who had the guard dogs. I understand that the dogs died, but what happened to the woman?"

Jack gave a disapproving look at Maria and answered, "A long story from a different life that we are not at liberty to discuss. What say we let B.A., the killer, out and see what happens? We all need more excitement and danger in our lives. Anyone who hides inside is a giant candy-ass."

Hulga walked up to the cage and unlatched the door and opened it. For a moment the dog sat motionless. "Come on out, Big Boy," Hulga said firmly.

Chingón sprang from the cage and leaped right at Hulga. She caught him in mid-air and clamped his jaws shut with one strong hand. Surprisingly enough, the dog did not snarl or struggle. Hulga set the dog down in front of her, then released his jaw and whispered into his ear. Chingón gave a low growl, and Hulga gave him a soft slap on his nose. Nothing happened for a tense moment, then the Shepherd began to lick Hulga's hand.

"Well, I'll be double damned," Jack said softly. "The lady is a real genuine dog whisperer. Maybe she can teach me to be a wife whisperer."

Reba smiled and looked at Jack. "In your dreams, Tarzan. Maybe you can learn to be a chimpanzee whisperer."

Hulga took the leash that had been wired to the top of the cage and hooked it to Chingón's collar. The dog did not object. "The dog and I have bonded. Now that we are friends, he has given me permission to call him by his nickname, B.A. Let's go inside, and I will introduce each of you to him. Once he knows and trusts you, he will give up his life for any of us. I bet the big fellow could use some water and food. After the lunch crowd is gone, I'll take Bad Ass down to the end of the beach and work with him."

Jack quickly cautioned, "Hulga, be sure to take a weapon when you go. There is no doubt that you are now on Rodolfo's hit list just like us."

Chingón followed Hulga to the kitchen and devoured a meal of beef strips before walking to the back door and waiting for Hulga to take him out behind the restaurant to do his business. The German Shepherd then lay down in a back corner of the kitchen, staying on full alert, but never growling.

After the lunch crowd thinned out, Hulga helped with the cleanup, then put a leash on the big German Shepherd and headed down the beach. Once she reached an isolated area, she began to try different commands in Spanish to see which ones B.A. would recognize. It did not take her long to learn that the Shepherd had been trained in English, which surprised her.

Hulga found an old baseball on the beach and hurled it as far as she could after she had given the dog a "Stay" command. She then ordered, "Go Get!" B.A. took off like a cannon shot and raced down the beach in a blur before grabbing the ball and racing back. After thirty minutes Hulga had discovered most of the commands that the trainer had used with the dog. She had not been able to try "Take Down" or "Kill" and was not sure whether the guard dog would recognize these commands or how he might respond.

Suddenly, there was a pistol shot that hit the sand right in front of Hulga. A second shot followed with a bullet zinging right by Hulga's head. She dropped to a kneeling position and fired a shot toward an old deserted beach house 30 yards farther down the beach. Her bullet shattered the glass window in the sagging front door. A person darted from the house and jumped on a motorbike that roared and blasted a cloud of sand into the air before getting enough traction to take off.

Hulga shouted, "Take down!" The German Shepherd responded instantly and raced after the motorbike, quickly catching it and leaping on the back of the driver, who screamed and lost control of the bike which spun out in the sand.

Chingón pinned the person to the ground with his jaws clamped on one leg. Hulga had sprinted after the dog and covered the distance to the struggling person in huge strides. Just as she got close, the person on the ground produced a pistol and pointed it at the Shepherd's head.

"No!" screamed Hulga. She dove on top of the person, knocking the pistol out of his hand. Hulga grabbed the hair of the gunman and turned his face toward her. She found herself looking into the frightened face of a teenage boy with a wimpy mustache and bad acne.

CHAPTER 19

HOSPITAL DEMISE

Hulga came into the kitchen with B.A. and sat down at the table where Maria was working on a huge bowl of salad. Reba was at the sink shucking oysters. Jack was busy stacking plates that he was taking out of the commercial dishwasher.

"Well," Jack said, "what did you learn about Super Dog?"

Hulga replied, "First, this animal is really special. I estimate that he can run almost 35 miles an hour, which is really fast for a German Shepherd—or any dog. I quickly learned that B.A. has been taught with English commands, not Spanish. But I wasn't sure if he knew a takedown or kill command. However, I can now confirm that this animal knows exactly how to respond to an order to take someone down.

"A person started taking pot shots at me with a pistol from an old deserted beach shack while I was working with B.A. I sent a friendly bullet back his way, and the shooter leaped onto a motorbike and tried to flee. B.A. ran him down in a flash, knocked him off the bike, and held him down until I arrived. It turns out that the shooter is a thirteen-year-old kid. We had a little Come to Jesus talk right on the beach. When I suggested that I might have to send him to glory right there on the beach, he almost wet his pants and started shaking and crying."

Reba interrupted, "Did you learn if Rodolfo sent him?"

Hulga nodded yes. "The boy said that some man with part of an ear missing came up to him downtown and offered him a fistful of pesos to watch the restaurant and trail me if I left. His orders were to scare me by firing some shots at me if I went into an area without many people. The man gave the boy a gun and told him how to use it.

Rodolfo also told the boy that if he did not return the gun, he would send someone to kill his mother who is a maid at the main hotel."

"What a great father figure," Jack said sarcastically. "Where are the boy and the gun now?"

"I'm a pretty tough woman," Hulga responded. "But I couldn't keep from feeling sorry for the boy. I learned that his father is in prison. His mother is trying to feed herself, the boy, and his young sister by working at a menial job. I ended up giving the gun back to the boy after I took all of the remaining shells out." Hulga hesitated as if trying to decide if there was something else she should share.

Maria said, "Fess up, Hulga. There is something else we should know. I can read it in your eyes."

Hulga stared at Maria and then said quietly, "I gave the boy fifty American dollars before I let him go."

"Oh, my gosh!" exclaimed Maria. "That really shoots your tough woman image to hell."

Before Hulga could respond, there was a knock on the back door. Jack put his hand on the pistol at his waist and slowly opened the door. Victor came quickly in and was obviously disturbed. He quickly asked, "Reba, did you go see Reynaldo Huertes today at the hospital?"

Reba answered, "Yes. I went as a nun after I borrowed clothes from your patient. We had a friendly little chat, then I left when the nurse came in to give him a pain pill. The man has multiple fractures and won't be back in action anytime soon."

Victor shook his head and said, "Reynaldo won't be back in action ever again unless the devil has a squad of shooters in hell. Early this afternoon he was found dead in his bed with no obvious evidence of foul play."

Jack responded, "As a wannabe doctor, I wonder if he threw a pulmonary embolus. Lying in bed all the time would be a perfect set up."

Victor replied, "That's a good layman's guess, but that's not the answer. I got called to pronounce the patient and sign the death certificate. Acting on a hunch, I had the lab draw a stat potassium blood level. The report just came back at 20 milli-equivalents per liter, which is way above the level that causes cardiac arrest. The good Señor Huertes was murdered."

Reba said, "Good thing I got to him before whoever did the injection since I learned some interesting things. I guess loose lips not only sink ships—they can also get you killed."

Jack asked, "Victor, any trouble at your office or home since we last talked?"

"All quiet for now. It's like the calm before a hurricane strikes. Hulga, are you still willing to sleep at my office with the guard dog? I know that it's just a matter of time until Rodolfo and his men make a move."

"Of course, Victor. It turns out that this Shepherd is a super dog and very well trained. Please tell your friend just how grateful we all are. Now changing the subject, do you know a woman who works at the big hotel as a maid and has at least one young son?"

Victor nodded. "That's easy. Carmen Gutierrez. Her husband went to prison three years ago after he got into a poker fight and stuck a stiletto through a man's heart. Poor Carmen has really been struggling to support her family since she lost her husband's income. She is a very religious woman who happens to be beautiful as well. She is a maid at the hotel, but the rumor is that for the right amount of money, she will occasionally provide services beyond room cleaning. Of course, her children don't know. It's really a sad story."

Hulga asked, "Does she have a son who is about thirteen years old with a wimpy mustache?"

Victor answered, "That's Luis. He is super bright and often plays chess in the square and makes money by beating more experienced players. I have been helping him with his acne. In fact, I see the whole family and never charge them. I hope the Good Lord is taking note of this and will shorten my stay in purgatory."

Reba smiled and said, "Victor, you are such a good man that I bet the angels put you on a golden skateboard and let you zip through the Pearly Gates."

Victor shook his head and replied, "I'll be lucky to get out of purgatory in a hundred years. As a young man, I was a real hellraiser and woman chaser."

CHAPTER 20

HAVE BLACK BAG, WILL TRAVEL

Victor's incriminating self-assessment was interrupted by a furious banging on the back door. Jack opened the door carefully to see a young boy crying. He blurted out, "He's going to kill my mother! Please help us!"

Victor had a look of surprise on his face. "It's Luis. You can let him in."

Hulga said, "That's the kid who shot at me."

Victor went to the door, led the trembling boy in, and sat him down at the table. "Stop crying and tell us what's going on. Who said that they were going to kill your mother?"

Luis was breathing hard and had trouble talking. Hulga walked over to him and put a hand on his shoulder. She said kindly, "Luis, it's going to be all right, I promise you. Tell us—Did you take the gun back to the man with part of his ear missing?"

Luis nodded yes. He gasped a couple of times, then managed to say, "When I told him that I only shot twice and then got taken down by a dog and a woman, he became very angry and slapped my face. Then he reloaded the gun and tried to give it back to me. He said the woman was a murderer who had escaped from prison and needed to be killed before she could hurt more people."

Victor said, "Luis, the very bad person is the man who gave you the gun in the first place. Why did he give the gun back to you?"

Luis choked up again before he could manage to say, "The man told me that the woman was hiding out at this restaurant, and that I was to go there and kill her with the gun. He said that I would be a hero. When I refused, the man began screaming and said if I did not do what he told me to do, he would kill my mother. And then he said…" At this point Luis burst into tears.

Victor asked kindly, "Luis, tell us what the man said."

Luis struggled to compose himself. "The man said… He said that my mother is a dirty whore at the hotel and not a maid." Luis started breathing hard and began shaking.

"Then what happened?" Victor encouraged.

The boy finally was able to say, "I threw the gun down and ran."

Hulga took the boy's hand and said, "No one will hurt your mother. I promise. Is your mother still at the hotel now?"

Luis nodded yes.

Hulga asked, "Is your sister in school?"

Luis shook his head no, then answered, "Nina is only four years old. She is at a neighbor's house."

Hulga said, "Luis, I need you to be a very brave boy. You and I and my dog are going to get your sister and bring her back here. My friends here will take care of your mother."

Luis seemed uncertain, then stood up and walked out of the back door with Hulga and B.A.

Reba turned to Jack. "We've got to get Luis's mother away from the hotel. The question is whether we can find her there, and if we can convince her to come with us."

Maria said, "As a person who, unfortunately, is very experienced in the world's oldest female profession, perhaps I should go along to help encourage Luis's mother that she can trust a bunch of gringos. Also, having one more gun along can't hurt."

Jack replied, "Someone has to stay at the restaurant in case Rodolfo sends a hired man with a can of gasoline and a match. And there's still a lot to do in the kitchen before we can serve dinner. Reba and I will try to make this a quick trip."

Jack turned to Victor. "What can you tell us about the layout of the hotel? Do you think Carmen is actually a prostitute working for Rodolfo?"

Victor shook his head. "I'm certain she works at the hotel as a maid, but it would not surprise me if she occasionally freelances on the side if the opportunity arises during her day shift. Carmen is almost a saint, but she gets paid so little cleaning rooms that I can understand her being willing to do almost anything to feed her children."

Victor continued, "I have been called on a number of occasions to see sick people in the hotel, so I know the layout pretty well. I will make a sketch here on this napkin."

As Victor began drawing, Reba walked over to Jack and took his hand and asked wistfully, "Why couldn't we have just stayed quietly dead like we planned? Trouble just seems to follow us everywhere. Victor gave me one of the brochures from the office that he provides for his pregnant patients. It has a list of Do's and Don'ts for the mothers in waiting. And one of the absolute No's is getting into an unnecessary gun fight."

Jack squeezed Reba's hand and gave her a kiss on the cheek. "We still have an extra bedroom upstairs. I think that we should hire Carmen to work in the restaurant and provide room and board for the children and her. She'll be a whole lot safer here than at the hotel."

Victor said, "I have a good idea how to get Carmen out of the hotel without you two storming the hotel with guns a-blazing."

Reba smiled at Jack and said, "The good Dr. Hernandez clearly underestimates us." She turned to Victor. "We have no intention of having to use guns. Jack will wait outside while I go into the hotel and cruise the halls until I find a pretty maid and convince her to leave with me."

Victor asked with concern, "But what if you run into Rodolfo or one of his thug friends and they start to get ugly?"

Reba replied simply, "I will be armed. These guys are amateurs. Jack and I are professionals."

Victor responded, "That may indeed be true, but a safer plan would be for me to take my black bag, go to the hotel on a medical call, find Carmen, and bring her out to you and Jack."

"There's one big flaw in your brilliant plan, kind sir," Reba responded. "You are pretty high up on Rodolfo's hit list now that you have refused to help him smuggle heroin across the border. If you run into him, he may just shoot you on sight."

Victor replied, "I'm still his best hope for doctoring up women's vaginas with blood to conceal hidden drugs. He's not going to kill me until he is absolutely certain that I won't play along. And I'm certain that he thinks with enough pressure I'll still crumble."

Reba spoke up. "Let me improve on your plan, Victor. I think that you should make an urgent visit to see a person in the hotel who may be dying. That being the case, it would be appropriate for a nun to join you. And I still have the nun outfit I borrowed from your patient's house."

Victor stood up. "Have black bag, will travel. I'll head to the office, wait ten minutes, then start walking to the hotel. You can change in one of the public dressing rooms and join me in the lobby."

CHAPTER 21

HOLE EXTRACTION

Victor was at the desk having a whispered conversation with the desk clerk when a nun came through the front door. The doctor turned toward the nun and said, "Sister Teresa, I'm so glad you got my message. I'm afraid the woman I am going to see is very sick. She may need a priest later."

Victor said "gracias" to the clerk and discreetly left some pesos on the desk. He and Sister Teresa walked to the elevator and disappeared as the door closed behind them.

"What did you learn from the man at the desk?" Reba asked.

"I told him that I had received a call from Carmen and that she is having severe belly pains and has fainted once. A few pesos served to persuade him to tell me that she likely was working on the third floor at this time of day. Hopefully, we can see her in the hall or find her cleaning cart outside of a room."

There were two halls on the third floor that met at right angles near the elevators.

Victor and Reba picked one and walked toward it. They looked down the hall and found it deserted. People who were leaving had already checked out, and it was still too early for check-in.

"No Carmen there," Victor said. "Let's check the other hall." At the very end of the second hall, they saw a cleaning cart parked in front of a room. They walked carefully down the hall and found that the door to the room was closed.

"That's odd," Reba whispered. "Cleaning people always leave the door open while they work."

Victor whispered back, "Unless Carmen is in there making an impromptu customer very happy." He knelt down and took a small flashlight out of his bag and shined it at the door jamb. "It looks like the dead bolt is in place, so whoever is in the room is planning on privacy."

Suddenly, the sound of a slap could be heard through the door, followed by a woman crying. There was another slap, then an angry voice said, "Stop crying, you bitch, or I'll give you something to really cry about. I asked your worthless son to perform a small errand for me. He smarted off, then ran away. If you don't get him to come back to see me at the hotel before the day is over, something very bad is going to happen to you and him. Do you understand, you dirty slut?"

The nun motioned for Victor to wait down the hall. She slipped a small blade into the door lock and kicked the door open. Rodolfo whirled around and grabbed a small pistol from his pocket. He was shocked to find that he was pointing his weapon at a nun. There was a moment of indecision, but he kept the pistol elevated.

The nun pointed an index finger at Rodolfo and said gravely, "Rodolfo Mendez, the Lord has sent me to warn you that you have been consigned to hell's fire for eternity. You will be meeting the Lord much sooner than you had planned. I have also been sent to take Señora Gutierrez from this den of iniquity." The nun beckoned to the woman and said, "Come with me, my daughter."

Carmen started to stand, but Rodolfo shoved her back down on the bed. "Not so fast, you whore. I've got more business with you." He turned to the nun and snarled, "Religion is all bullshit. I've never shot a nun before, but today might be a good day to start. If you don't get your ass in gear and clear out of here in the next five seconds, I'll have to shoot you in self-defense."

Rodolfo moved closer to the nun and waved the gun in her face. He started counting—"five, four, three, two…" By the count of one, the nun had slipped her hand inside the slit of her dress and fired through the garment. The bullet struck Rodolfo in the leg. He screamed and fired a wild shot that passed through the door. The nun was lightning quick as she slapped the gun from his hand.

She drew her gun from her skirt and pointed it at Rodolfo, who was clutching his bleeding leg and moaning. "Listen, asshole. You and your thug friends are trying to play way above your level. If you cause any more trouble for Dr. Hernandez or the people who own Ellie's Restaurant, I personally will expedite your trip to hell.

"I doubt you are smart enough to make the right decision here, so I would suggest that you start thinking about cremation versus an underground burial. Once I get back to the convent, I'll say a special prayer for you and light a candle."

Rodolfo had a look of total hatred on his face as he hissed, "Once you light that candle, Sister, go right ahead and shove it up your ass! We'll soon find out who is playing above their level."

The nun clucked her tongue. "Such filthy language. I'll need to shower right after I report to the Mother Superior." She then beckoned to the woman on the bed who sat there with a look of utter disbelief on her face. "Carmen, come with me. Your son and daughter are safe. My friends and I will take care of you and your family."

Carmen looked uncertain about what to do, but once she glanced at Rodolfo who had slumped down on the floor and was cursing, she stood up and walked toward the nun.

Sister Teresa took a hard look at Rodolfo and said, "Be sure to get a tetanus shot, dirtbag. It would be a pity if you were to die from lockjaw."

Reba took Carmen's hand and led her out into the hall. Victor was nowhere to be seen. Just as the two approached the elevator, the door opened, and the police chief and two of his deputies rushed out, barely glancing at the nun and her companion as they ran down the hall.

CHAPTER 22

POKING THE HORNET'S NEST

Reba hustled Carmen down the stairwell to a rear exit that Victor had sketched on a napkin back at the restaurant. As they walked, Reba reassured Carmen that her children were safe and waiting for her. When the two women reached one of the public changing stations, Reba urged Carmen inside with her. There was a rapid transformation as the nun reached behind a large trash barrel and retrieved a beach bag that contained her clothes. Carmen watched in amazement as the sister underwent a rapid metamorphosis and became a typical tourist in less than thirty seconds.

Ten minutes later, Reba and Carmen entered the kitchen of Ellie's Restaurant. Luis and Nina were sitting at the table with a bottle of Coke and a sandwich. When they saw their mother, the two children burst into tears and ran to her. Carmen was overcome with emotion and began to sob as she wrapped Luis and Nina in her arms.

Jack was at one of the work counters expertly slicing fish flanks while Maria was busy washing vegetables. Hulga was feeding the big German Shepherd, who was no longer suspicious of the children. But when Carmen entered the dog looked away from his food and gave a low growl. "It's all right, B.A.," Hulga said. "Carmen is a friend." The dog was satisfied and resumed eating.

Maria stopped washing vegetables and looked at Reba. "We are all on tenterhooks. Tell us what happened at the hotel. I detected a faint whiff of gunpowder when you walked in. There must have been some shots fired."

Reba answered, "All in good time, my impatient young friend. First things first. Jack, use your best junior high Spanish and explain to Carmen why she and the children are here."

Before Jack could speak, Carmen said in almost perfect English, "You don't have to use Spanish. I have watched American TV for years and have been able to practice my English with tourists."

Jack looked at Reba with an exaggerated frown and said, "Junior high Spanish, my hiney. That's a very demeaning remark. I'm at least at the high school level. But English is easier."

There was a pause, then Jack continued. "Carmen, there are some very important things we need to share with you." He stopped speaking and looked at Luis and Nina. Carmen nodded in understanding and said in Spanish, "Children, please take your drinks and sandwiches and go finish them in the dining room while we talk. I'll come get you in a few minutes."

After the children left, Jack continued and explained in detail what had happened with Luis and Hulga on the beach. Carmen gave a short gasp, and her eyes filled with tears. When she heard how Luis had come to the restaurant crying and afraid for his mother's life, she bowed her head and crossed herself.

Maria interrupted impatiently, "Reba, please tell us what happened at the hotel and why you have a smell of gunpowder."

Reba answered, "To give you the Cliff's Notes version, Victor greased the desk clerk's palm and learned that Carmen was cleaning on the third floor. We found the room where her cleaning cart was parked, but the door was closed and locked. Then we heard sounds of slaps and a very angry man shouting inside. I sent Victor home, picked the door lock, and surprised our old slimeball friend Rodolfo abusing Carmen. He was not intimidated by a nun and pulled a gun, threatening to kill me. It was time for a major attitude adjustment, so I had to shoot him in the leg and disarm him."

"Touché!" Maria exclaimed. "But you should have wiped this rodent off the face of the earth."

"I did tell him that he and his thugs were trying to play way above their level, and if they made any more trouble for Victor or the people who own Ellie's Restaurant Super Nun would come back to eliminate him."

Jack said, "I know that you had no choice, Reba, but if we keep poking a hornet's nest, eventually we are going to get stung. Did Rodolfo seem frightened?"

"Not much. When I stated that as soon as I got back to the convent, I would light a votive candle for him, the rude man suggested what I could do with the candle."

Maria laughed and advised, "Reba, just be sure to blow the candle out before you insert it!"

Reba shook her head. "Maria, once again, your social deportment could stand some polishing."

Maria quickly retorted, "Please keep in mind that you are dealing with a girl whose resume includes being forced to work in a whorehouse. Social refinement of the women there was not a prime goal of management. A good body and flexible hip joints were much more important assets."

Carmen looked at Maria with shock on her face.

Jack looked at Maria and said sternly, "No more personal biographical details, please. You need to grab a dictionary and look up the meaning of 'incognito.'"

Reba turned to Carmen and asked, "Where do you and your children live?"

Carmen replied, "We live in a small apartment away from the beach. Rent is due next week, but I am going to have trouble paying it if we plan to keep on eating."

"Perfect," Reba replied. "You won't be safe there anyway. We have lots of space above the restaurant with a large bedroom that is vacant. If you and your children move in with us, we will hire you for more than you were making at the hotel to help with the restaurant. We are getting busier and busier and can really use another person."

Suddenly there was the loud sound of a single gunshot with the zing of a bullet that embedded itself in the thick wall separating the kitchen from the dining area, causing a shower of plaster.

Jack said, "This is really getting old. That sounded like a small caliber pistol not too far away." The German Shepherd raced to the door with a loud bark. Hulga was right behind him and announced as she quickly opened the door, "B.A. and I will take care of this little problem. Fear not."

CHAPTER 23

A MAJOR BITE IN THE BUTT

Nina ran back into the kitchen after the gunshot, jumped into her mother's lap, and began crying. In contrast, Luis calmly walked into the kitchen and went to inspect the site in the plaster wall where the bullet had struck. Then, without a word, he found the vacuum cleaner and began to clean up the plaster shards and dust on the floor.

Carmen had a concerned look on her face as she looked at Jack and asked, "Are you sure that we are safer here than in our apartment? This place is looking like a war zone."

Reba replied before Jack could speak. "Carmen, you have seen Rodolfo at his best when he was slapping you around in the hotel. He and the thugs that he imported from Mexico City are cold-blooded killers. Anyone who challenges them is quickly slated for elimination. Rodolfo sent your son out to take shots at our friend Hulga in an attempt to persuade her not to investigate the death of her uncle. When Luis reported to Rodolfo that he had been taken down by a dog and Hulga, the man became furious and ordered Luis to come to the restaurant and find and kill our friend Hulga. Rodolfo told your son that if he did not follow this order, he would have you killed."

Carmen had placed her hands over Nina's ears as Reba spoke. Reba continued, "Carmen, you need to trust us. I cannot tell you everything, but Jack and I are extremely well trained in weapons and self-defense. Hulga is a SWAT police officer in Detroit, and Maria is no slouch at taking care of herself. Rodolfo is already into extortion and prostitution and is now trying to establish a narcotics business smuggling heroin across the border into the U.S. He and his associates will not hesitate to kill anyone in their way."

Maria walked over to Carmen and took Nina from her mother's lap. "Nina, would you like to learn to play jacks? I bought some in the market yesterday. Let's go back to the front of the restaurant and use one of the large tables. I bet you can beat Luis after I get finished teaching you."

Nina was uncertain whether to go with Maria or not. She looked at her mother, who smiled and nodded. After the girl and Maria had left, Jack turned to Luis and said, "We need a surveillance man while we talk with your mother. People have threatened to burn our restaurant down. If you can sit by the front window and keep a watch on the street for any suspicious people, that would be a big help. And if your mother agrees to move in with us, I'll teach you how to use a pistol safely." Luis nodded enthusiastically and headed out of the kitchen.

Reba sat down by Carmen and said, "Your son Luis seems very bright. Victor told us that he is excellent at chess."

Carmen nodded and answered, "Luis has a very high IQ. And I have spent a great deal of time teaching him at home."

Reba had a puzzled look on her face. "Not to be rude, but you are very well spoken. It seems strange that you are working as a maid in a hotel."

Carmen teared up and had to wipe her eyes before she answered hesitatingly, as if speaking was very painful. "I lacked only one year of finishing university in Guadalajara when I met my husband, Arturo. He had come back to school after being in the military for several years. Arturo was charming and handsome. I fell hopelessly in love with him. After a few weeks we decided to get married and obtained the necessary blood tests and chest x-rays. We were married by a Civil Registry official with four friends in attendance as witnesses.

"I quickly became pregnant, and we both dropped out of school. Arturo's father had a plumbing business in Tapalpa, high up in the Sierra Madre. We moved there, and my husband started working for his father. His family was not very accepting of me since we never had a Catholic ceremony. Arturo hated plumbing, but was forced to take over the business when his father had a sudden heart attack. His mother lived only a few months after she lost her husband."

Carmen's story was interrupted by a knock on the back door. Jack cautiously opened the door with one hand on his waist holster. Hulga and B.A. came in.

Hulga was holding a bloody piece of cloth that appeared to have shreds of flesh attached to it. "I don't think that slimeball will be back anytime soon," she said triumphantly. "This Shepherd is in a class all by himself."

Reba asked, "Can we assume that you are holding a piece of clothing that the gunman was wearing?"

Hulga nodded and said, "Right on target. When B.A. and I hit the alley, there was a man running away about twenty-five yards in front of us. I ordered 'Take down.' B.A. flew after the man and caught him just as he was jumping into a waiting car. Super Dog took a huge chomp out of the guy's rear end and brought a piece of his pants with hunks of flesh on it back to me. The car sped away."

Reba walked over to Hulga, took the bloody specimen from her, and went to the work sink to wash the blood away. She held up a piece of the flesh and said, "Really bad news for the shooter. This looks like part of his anal sphincter. Nobody will ever accuse him of being a tight ass in the future. I hope the loser can afford colostomy bags."

CHAPTER 24

FATHER JACK

Reba was up early the next morning to work out in the upstairs gym and put some miles on the treadmill before Jack came back from a run on the beach with Maria. The previous evening had been busy in the restaurant, but was totally uneventful except for an American tourist who drank too much and had to be escorted out.

Reba came into the kitchen after showering and was surprised to see Carmen already at work preparing tortillas.

Carmen smiled at Reba and said, "I hope that you are not offended, but I modified your corn tortilla recipe a bit. My mother was an expert cook and taught me a few things."

Reba replied, "Not offended at all. How did you change things?"

Carmen took a spatula and lifted a steaming tortilla off the large cast-iron comal on the stove and expertly flipped it high into the air, landing it in the center of a plate in her other hand. "Give this a try and see what you think, Reba. But be careful; it's really hot."

Reba let the tortilla cool briefly and then picked it up and took a bite. She nodded and said, "No question—much better texture and flavor. Whatever you did is a definite improvement."

"I tasted one of the tortillas last night and thought it was missing something. Do you just use masa harina corn flour, salt, and water with no oil?"

Reba nodded yes. "You must have added something."

Carmen replied, "I added just a small amount of lard and also did all of the mixing by hand. This gives a better taste to the tortillas and makes them fluffier. Luis and Nina are both very good with the tortilla press. We can put them to work in the kitchen. I can also make sopapillas that will melt in your mouth."

Reba said, "Carmen, now that you and the children have moved in, why don't we make you in charge of tortillas and sopapillas?"

"That's fine with me. But I can handle both of those jobs with one hand behind my back. I will have lots of extra time to help with cooking and cleaning as well."

Reba asked, "Carmen, did Jack and Hulga bring everything you need when they borrowed Victor's pickup truck late last night and went to your apartment?"

"Yes. They got everything in one trip. It's a furnished apartment, so there was no heavy furniture to deal with. I'm just thankful that they didn't run into any trouble with Rodolfo's people."

Jack and Maria came into the kitchen hot and sweaty after their run on the beach. They both grabbed a bottle of water out of the large refrigerator and sat down at the table to drink.

"Any trouble?" Reba asked.

"None," Jack replied. "But there was an old man fishing down the beach who would take a quick glance at us, then look away. I feel certain that he was watching us to report to Rodolfo and his people."

There was a sudden large thump from upstairs. Carmen looked nervously at the ceiling.

"Nothing to worry about, Carmen," Maria said. The Hulk's sister is in the gym up there hoisting weights. It sounds like Hulga just tried to clean and jerk more than she could handle."

There was a rap at the back door. Jack peered through the peephole and opened the door for Victor, who came in sniffing the air.

"The smell of tortillas cooking. Ambrosia for the gods," he exclaimed.

Reba asked, "How about a cup of coffee and a couple of fried eggs wrapped up in one of Carmen's new and improved tortillas?"

"You twisted my arm," Victor answered with a smile. "I'm starving. My wife, Sofia, has me on a low-calorie diet that wouldn't keep a mouse alive. In exchange for breakfast, I'll share some interesting news with you. A cab driver dropped a man off at the hospital ER yesterday with a gunshot wound of his right leg. The man had lost a fair amount of blood and received two units of blood on the way to the OR. The surgeon on call graduated near the bottom of his medical school class. The nurses call him '007—licensed to kill.' I wouldn't let him operate on my dog."

Jack said, "Don't keep us in suspense, Victor. Is Rodolfo the rat going to make it, or does my beautiful wife get another notch on her gun?"

"The surgeon was able to locate the bullet and remove it. Kind of like the blind hog finding an acorn. Fortunately for Rodolfo, the shot missed his femoral artery. He'll be in the hospital for at least a week, but he will likely make a complete recovery."

Jack had a slight smile as he asked, "Any chance that the patient has a Foley catheter in?"

Victor nodded and said, "Yes. Why do you ask?"

Jack replied, "Just wondering if one of the saintly nuns from the convent should visit the patient and give the catheter tube a few hard yanks to continue Rodolfo's attitude adjustment."

Reba shook her head. "That holy sister has been kicked out of the convent and has gone to Las Vegas to be a stripper. If anyone saintly visits Rodolfo, it needs to be a priest like Father Jack."

CHAPTER 25

WAITING FOR ARTURO

The morning went by quickly with a good lunch crowd. By 2 PM the restaurant was empty and the kitchen was clean with the large dishwasher chugging away.

Carmen went upstairs to put Nina down for a nap. Luis objected strenuously, but his mother convinced him to start some summer reading upstairs for an hour.

Reba, Maria, Hulga, and Jack sat at the kitchen work table to finish their late lunches. Maria looked at Jack and asked, "So, do we just sit here and wait for all hell to break loose, or do we try to deliver a knockout blow? The only way I see that we can win this fight is to convince Rodolfo and his goons that most of them won't survive a battle."

Hulga spoke up. "My sole purpose for being back in Mexico is to deliver justice to whomever burned my uncle to death and destroyed his restaurant. There is little doubt that Rodolfo gave the order even if he didn't spray the accelerant and light the match. I have a good mind to go to the hospital and put a bullet through his head."

Reba said quickly, "Don't be a fool, Hulga. Do this and you'll end up in a Mexican prison for life. The police chief has sold his soul to Rodolfo and would call for federal help in a heartbeat if someone assassinated Rodolfo in his hospital bed. There is no way that you would ever get back across the border to the United States."

Jack said, "I agree completely. Stupid move. I think that the pressure is off Victor for a while. My guess is that the heroin smuggling gambit will be in a hold pattern until Rodolfo gets back on his feet. Burning his office down at this stage would make little sense as long as there is any hope of scaring Victor into helping set up vagina mules for drug smuggling."

Reba chimed in, "One thing to remember is that Rodolfo seems to be trying to start a mom-and-pop narcotic smuggling organization to supplement his extortion and prostitution business. He did bring in a couple of killers from Mexico City who likely were small-time players in the narcotics trade there. Maybe Rodolfo's goal is to get a successful local pipeline established and hope to be invited to join one of the large drug cartels."

Hulga frowned and said, "I have to admit that you people are right that my sending Rodolfo to his permanent reward by shooting him in his hospital bed would not be very smart. We need to eliminate him and his heavies in what appears to be self-defense or a seeming accident."

Carmen came back into the room and sat down at the table. "I had to lie down with Nina until she fell asleep. Once Luis starts reading, he may disappear for several hours. I'm ready to start on dinner whenever Reba gives me the word."

Maria gave a thumbs-up sign to Carmen. "You have cute kids. We are all going to work to keep you and them safe." She paused and then said, "Carmen, how about the rest of your story after you and Arturo moved to Tapalpa. You must have been pregnant with Luis then."

Carmen nodded. "I told you how much Arturo hated taking over his father's plumbing business. However, he ran the business well, and we were financially secure. But after a few years he became very depressed and paranoid. He started hearing voices. At times he would come out of his depression and suddenly become almost manic. During these times he would make bad business decisions. Then he began drinking and gambling. Arturo ran through our savings and ignored the plumbing business until it went bankrupt."

"How awful," Reba said.

Carmen teared up before saying, "And then it got worse. Arturo started telling me that God was talking to him and telling him to be his avenger of evil people. One night Arturo got into an argument during a poker game when he accused another man of cheating. The player pulled a gun and shot at Arturo. Fortunately, the shot only grazed one arm. The man tried to fire again but the gun jammed. According to witnesses, Arturo pulled a knife out and stabbed the man in the heart, and then screamed, "The Lord's will be done!"

Reba shook her head. "Heavenly God! The story did get a lot worse. From what you say, surely Arturo has to have had some type of psychosis. I'm surprised that he went to prison for what sounds like self-defense as well as a psychotic episode."

Carmen wiped her eyes and replied softly, "Arturo never had a chance. We could not afford a good attorney, and the man who died was the nephew of a state politician. We lost our house since I could not make the mortgage payments. Cruel children at school started taunting Luis about being a murderer's child. There was no choice but to move some place different and make a new start."

Maria said, "Not to be a pretend psychiatrist, Carmen, but when I was in school, I always read way above grade level. I became fascinated by mental illness. My lay diagnosis of your husband is schizoaffective disorder. These people have a mixture of schizophrenia and bipolar with voices, paranoia, as well as deep depressions alternating with manic periods during which time they can make very bad decisions."

Carmen nodded her head. "Once Arturo was in prison, he finally got to see a psychiatrist who started him on a new drug called lithium as well as Thorazine. When he writes me once a month, his letters seem much better organized."

Hulga shook her head. "Not to be cruel, Carmen, but I would have dumped that man the day he hit prison. You are a beautiful woman and could find another husband by just batting your eyes."

Carmen lost control and began to sob. She finally managed to say, "I am a very bad woman. God is punishing me for things that I am too ashamed to tell. I could never love another man like I love Arturo. He is eligible for parole in five years. As God is my witness, I will be waiting for him."

CHAPTER 26

PAIRED SOCIAL ASSETS

Victor and his wife Sofia came to Ellie's for a late dinner. Sofia's two proudest possessions were on display, with a plunging neckline and a diamond pendant nestled between the paired assets. When the couple came in, Reba sidled up behind Jack who was manning the bar and whispered, "If you stare too long, you might go blind, Casanova."

Jack laughed and replied, "Not a problem, Sweetie. I'm only going to risk one eye. Besides, I've never had much interest in animal husbandry."

Victor and Sofia stayed late for after-dinner coffee. Jack and Reba joined them at their table since the dining area was almost empty. Reba turned to Sofia and said pleasantly, "I hope that you found the food to your satisfaction tonight."

Sofia replied, "Everything was good—except the ceviche could have used more cilantro. But I must compliment you on the tortillas tonight. The previous ones we've had here were, if you will excuse the expression, gringo tortillas."

Victor started to apologize for his wife, but Reba interrupted quickly. "Thank you for your critique, Sofia. We'll have to work on the ceviche. However, now that Carmen is working at the restaurant, we will definitely be serving more authentic Mexican food in the future. The woman certainly knows her way around the kitchen."

Sofia paused, then said with a condescending expression on her face, "I understand that Carmen also knows her way around the back halls in the hotel."

Victor shook his head. "Sorry, folks. Sofia promised to be on her best behavior tonight."

Sofia gave her husband a withering look, then said pointedly, "Sometimes at night it can get very cold at our house."

Maria, who had just cleared the cash register, brought a carafe of hot coffee out from the kitchen to refill Victor's cup and heard the last part of the table conversation. Just as she was about to disappear back into the kitchen, she turned around and waited for Reba to look at her. Then Maria made the letter "P" in American Sign Language followed by a "W." Reba had to cough several times to keep from laughing out loud.

As Maria disappeared into the kitchen, Carmen came into the dining area to clean the table that the last customers had just vacated. Victor stood up and said, "Carmen, I am so glad that you and the children have found a safe place to stay." Sofia totally ignored Carmen.

Carmen smiled at Victor and replied, "Dr. Hernandez, we feel blessed to be here. I cannot tell you how grateful we are for your medical care. Now that I have this better position at the restaurant and no apartment rent to pay, we plan to be able to take care of our medical bills in the future."

Victor said, "It is always my pleasure to see you and your family." Sofia gave her husband a look of strong disapproval.

As soon as Carmen had gone back to the kitchen with a stack of dirty dishes, Jack stood up and motioned for Victor to follow him outside. "Sofia, I need to borrow your husband for a moment to get some more business advice. You and Reba can compare notes about your respective husbands' bedroom skills while we are gone."

Sofia gave a slight smile and replied, "I have just ordered some instruction books with pictures to help Victor, who is such a slow learner."

When Jack and Victor reached the porch in front of the restaurant, Jack stood close to the doctor and asked, "Victor, my friend, is there any way that you could get your hands on a priest's cassock and clerical collar? I have been told that Rodolfo has requested a visit from a priest to work on the state of his wretched soul."

Victor replied quietly, "It just so happens that my thrift store has those precise items. Can I come by tomorrow early and trade you those things for breakfast?"

"Of course," Jack replied.

"Besides the clothes, I'll also give you an exact location in the hospital for the penitent. But be aware that the police chief has set up a rotation of eight-hour guards outside the hospital room door. His worthless son Eduardo has been deputized and is taking one of the shifts. So, you may need to take something more powerful than a Douay Bible with you."

Jack nodded. "Understood."

When the men came back inside to join the ladies at the table, Jack asked, "Which one of us won the 'Lover of the Year' award?"

Sofia quickly answered, "It was a tie. On a scale of one to ten, each of you got a three."

Reba put her chin into her hands, then surreptitiously flashed a quick ten fingers for Jack to see. He smiled.

Victor took Sofia's hand and helped her stand up. "My lovely wife and I have to be heading a la casa. One of the instruction books that she ordered for me came in the mail today, and I need her to explain some of the pictures to me before bedtime."

After the doctor and his wife left, Reba said to Jack, "Sofia is one of the least likable people I have ever met. I'm sure all she does at home is lie in bed, eat bonbons, and order Victor around. If I were him, I'd be scared to death that one night she might turn over in bed and suffocate me."

Jack laughed. "Was I hearing things, Reba? I could swear that after Sofia treated Carmen as if she were total trash, Carmen made a slight 'moo' sound as she turned to leave the room."

Reba nodded and replied, "I heard that, too. But I thought I was imagining things. Carmen is obviously more spunky than we thought. In a cat fight to the death between Carmen and Sofia, I'd have to put my money on Carmen."

"Me, too," Jack replied. "Now I need some sleep since I have to be well rested for my ecclesiastical mission of mercy to the hospital tomorrow."

CHAPTER 27

RAISING THE DEAD

Victor arrived early the next morning with a small duffle bag. Inside was a black cassock and a clerical collar. While Jack went upstairs to try the cassock on for fit, Reba and Carmen made Victor a hearty plate of Mexican chocolate waffles and bacon. Victor sat down at the table with a large smile and put a bite of waffle into his mouth. "Good thing that Sofia doesn't see me loading in this many morning calories. She would put me on bread and water if she could."

Reba asked Victor, "How on earth did you acquire the priest clothes for Jack? I hope that you didn't resort to breaking and entering like I did for the nun's outfit."

Victor only smiled and said, "I have my ways that must remain secret."

Reba said, "Speaking of Catholic garb reminds me that I need to return the nun's clothes that I borrowed from your patient. Any idea, Victor, how I can do this discreetly without risking getting caught while jimmying the back door lock?"

Victor replied, "I'm guessing that my patient's daughter had several habits in her closet. Her mother is unlikely to miss one. Why don't you hang onto the clothes in case the need for another mission of mercy arises?"

Before Reba could respond, Jack came back into the kitchen wearing the cassock and clerical collar that Victor had brought.

Maria turned from the sink where she was washing vegetables and exclaimed, "That is one hot priest! Keeping his vows of abstinence won't be easy with all the young female parishioners hitting on him."

Reba shook her head and said, "That priest is already spoken for, and I'm carrying his baby."

Hulga came into the kitchen after exercising B.A. in time to hear Reba's remark and immediately wagged her finger at Jack, saying, "Huge scandal! I'm calling the pope immediately. That man needs to be emasculated on the spot!"

Jack laughed and replied, "So, Hulga, what do you think? Do I look authentic?"

Hulga replied, "Two obvious problems, Faux Father. Your wedding band is silver, not gold, and it has a small stone in it. Much too flashy for a real priest. And, the other problem is that you have a long ponytail which your diocesan bishop definitely would not allow."

Reba said, "Good points. Leaving the ring behind is easy. And as much as I would hate to do it, I need to snip off the ponytail. Pull up a seat, Big Boy, and I'll be your tonsorial artist."

Jack frowned as he sat down and said, "Ugh. I am not eager for this masculinity-robbing procedure."

Maria said slyly, "This is just like Samson and Delilah—except not only will Jack be weak, but also impotent for life."

Reba smiled and responded, "Don't worry, Sweetie. I have magic ways to raise the dead."

After a few snips, the blond ponytail was on the floor. Reba smoothed the back of Jack's hair to make it more priest-like. She left the room and came back with a hand mirror. Jack surveyed himself and said, "A number 10 priest if I have ever seen one." He lifted the front of the cassock and said, "Check out my authentic black slacks and black dress shoes."

"Yikes!" screeched Maria in mock alarm. "A flasher priest! Lock up the women and children before it's too late!"

Jack replied, "Comedy hour is over. I need to wolf down a chocolate waffle and have a cup of coffee before I leave for my priestly duties at the hospital. I'll take a small Bible as well as my pistol."

Victor stood up from the table and said, "I need to get rolling to start seeing patients at the office. Reba and Carmen, thank you for a great breakfast. Jack, Rodolfo is in the trauma ward in Room 222. There definitely will be an armed guard in front of the room. I told you previously that the worthless police chief has deputized his equally worthless son Eduardo to help with guard duty. Eduardo is a hothead, so I would hope that it's someone less likely to shoot a man of the cloth. But I know that you can take care of yourself."

Five minutes later, Jack ducked into the customers' bathroom. When he came out to leave, Hulga asked, "Commando Priest, before you leave on your mission of mercy, tell us if there's any chance that you'll need to perform last rites on the piece of human garbage in the hospital bed."

Jack shook his head. "My goal today is to scare Rodolfo so badly that he will soil his drawers and think carefully before he or his men mess with us anymore. The problem is that Rodolfo and his thugs likely can recruit some more drug trade heavies if need be. We won't win a war of attrition."

There was a loud rapping on the back door. Jack opened the door carefully to find Victor standing there short of breath. "I have some news that you need to know before you go to the hospital," he gasped. Victor sat down in a chair, working to catch his breath. Jack said, "Take it easy, Victor, and let me grab you a glass of water while your blood pressure and heart rate go down."

After a couple of minutes and several gulps of water, Victor began to talk. "I haven't run that fast since I was in grade school and weighed fifty kilos." He took another mouthful of water before speaking again. "I had barely walked three blocks from here and was almost to the market when a black sedan came slowly down the street. There was a burst of machine gun fire from one of the car's windows, and a man sitting by himself at an outdoor restaurant was riddled with bullets. His head exploded as he fell to the floor gushing blood."

Reba immediately asked, "Who was the victim, Victor?"

Victor took another drink of water and shook his head. "I have no idea. The man was a stranger."

Hulga smiled and said, "You folks aren't very good at deductive criminal reasoning. I would bet my whole retirement that I know who this man is and why he was blown to smithereens in broad daylight."

CHAPTER 28

FAUX PRIEST

Jack turned to Hulga and said, "Not to doubt your prodigious police skills, but I see no way that you could have any information about the stranger who just got hyperventilated by a machine gun near the marketplace."

Hulga replied, "I don't know much about your and Reba's background, and I don't doubt that the two of you make a lethal team, but neither of you has police skills like I do. Detroit is a tough town, and my eight years on the force has taught me a great deal."

Reba said, "We are all eager to hear what you have to say, Hulga."

Hulga paused, then began. "As I understand things, Rodolfo is a small-time crook specializing in extortion and prostitution. Suddenly, he gets the brilliant idea to start smuggling heroin across the border in women's bloody vaginas as alleged life-and-death emergencies that need a U.S. border hospital. Rodolfo then hires a couple of heavies who apparently have experience in the drug trade. My guess is that these two men were previously bit players in a much larger crime group.

"Getting a finger into the Mexican drug trade is not like opening a flower shop on the square. The men who run the big narcotic groups in Mexico don't look kindly on interlopers. I believe that the dead man was one of the two people Rodolfo recently hired. The deceased's previous boss likely sent a hit team out as a lethal warning to Rodolfo and anyone else who might be foolish enough to try to start a mom-and-pop drug operation."

"Very interesting," Jack said. "Maybe Rodolfo will get taken out, too, and save us the trouble."

Hulga answered, "It's not that simple. The boss who sent the machine gun assassin might decide to make Rodolfo an offer that he can't afford to turn down—namely, to share profits from the local extortion and prostitution rackets with the crime boss's group or to end up very dead. In return, Rodolfo might be given a small piece of the narcotics action. If that happens, Rodolfo will have lots of potential new firepower backing him up."

Reba said, "That would likely mean goodbye to Shangri-La for us and Ellie's Restaurant. I want to live to have this baby and see him or her grow up. Maybe we should consider letting our old CIA mentor, Becky Reagor, know that rumors of our death were greatly exaggerated and that we want to reconsider relocation to a secret third-world country."

"I'm not going to agree to that!" Maria said emphatically. "I vote to shoot as many of these bastards as we can and hold out as long as possible. A good start would be for Father Jack to visit Rodolfo in the hospital this morning and put a bullet through his head."

Jack was silent for a moment, then said mysteriously, "There's more than one way to skin a cat. I need to call Victor and see if he can provide some more priestly accoutrements for me before I head to the hospital." Jack walked to the phone at the checkout desk in the dining area, dialed a number, and spoke briefly. When he came back, he said, "Wish me luck. I'm off on an important ecclesiastical mission."

* * * * *

Thirty minutes later a young priest walked into the hospital and quietly took the stairs to the second floor. Room 222 was halfway down the north hall, heading away from the central nursing station. There were two young nurses charting who glanced up at the priest and quickly returned to their work. Jack could see that there was a man sitting in front of Room 222. As Jack drew closer, he recognized Eduardo Cardenas, the son of the police chief, Miguel Cardenas. Eduardo had his feet propped up on a second chair and was reading a magazine with a grin on his face. The new deputy was so absorbed in the magazine that he did not look up until Jack was very close.

"Peace to you, my son," Jack said as he made the sign of the cross. Eduardo hastily closed the *Playboy* magazine he had been leering at. Jack paused a moment then said, "Lust is one of the cardinal sins that will get you into purgatory. I think that I need to pray for your blackened soul before the devil calls you home early."

Eduardo's face darkened. "Spare me your holier-than-thou BS lecture," he snarled. "Everybody knows that most of you priests are pedophiles who can only get it up with children." Eduardo reached into his pocket and pulled out a pistol that he pointed at the priest. "Haul ass, you pedo, before I give you something to really pray about."

The priest shook his head and said sadly, "Blasphemy, my child. Let me take the flesh magazine away that Satan is using to tempt you." Jack reached for the *Playboy*. Eduardo tried to slap his hand away, but Jack grabbed Eduardo's arm, jerked him out of the chair, and smashed a knee into his face. Before the startled man could respond, Jack had his powerful arm around Eduardo's neck with enough pressure that the man could only gasp. Jack lifted the man off his feet and took a few steps down the hall to the laundry chute, shoving Eduardo in head first. There was a gratifying bumping sound as Eduardo headed down to the basement.

The priest straightened his cassock, then collected the pistol that Eduardo had dropped on the floor. He paused before the door of Room 222 and listened intently. There was no sound. Just before Jack started to ease the door open, his sixth sense made him stop. He hit the floor just before a bullet from inside the room crashed through the wooden door at waist level and buried itself in the opposite wall.

Jack crawled a few feet to the next hospital room, jerked the door open, and moved quickly inside. There was a woman sitting on a bedpan who gave a shriek. Jack said, "The Lord be with you," as he dashed to the window and opened it and stepped out onto the small balcony.

CHAPTER 29

GUERRERO

Jack eyed the balcony of Rodolfo's room before he climbed up onto the four-foot railing and balanced there for a moment to look at the hard concrete fifteen feet below. Then he squatted and exploded into the air. His leap was just long enough to allow him to grasp the bottom of the railing of Rodolfo's balcony. The priest in his cowl made a strange sight as he hung there a moment listening for any activity inside the room. All was quiet. Jack used his arm strength and hands to silently pull himself up and over the railing onto the balcony.

The room curtains were closed, but the window was open. Jack parted the curtains slightly and was able to see Rodolfo standing by the door on high alert with a small revolver in his hand. His injured leg was wrapped in bandages with a small area of fresh blood in the calf area. Jack knew that he had little time to act following the obvious sound of gunfire in the hospital. There was also the certainty that the woman on the bedpan would have immediately called hospital security about a priest barging into her room with the likely embellishment that the not-so-holy man had attempted to molest her.

Jack reached into the slit in the cowl and produced a small wire-pull smoke grenade from his pocket. He breathed a 'thank you, Victor' as he pulled the wire and tossed the grenade at Rodolfo's feet. The room was almost immediately filled with billows of gray smoke. Rodolfo got off one desperate shot before Jack tackled him and smashed his head into the floor. By this time there was no visibility at all, but Jack was able to pull Rodolfo to his feet and force the arm with the gun behind the struggling man's back.

Jack ordered harshly, "Drop the gun or I'll rip your shoulder out of the socket."

Rodolfo struggled and cursed, but did not release the gun until there was a loud popping sound from his shoulder joint. He screamed as the gun fell to the floor.

There was a sudden urgent knocking at the locked door. "Police! Let us in!"

Jack pulled the Walther pistol from his pocket and fired a shot through the very top of the door. The knocking immediately stopped followed by loud voices in Spanish and retreating footsteps.

Jack kept the pressure on Rodolfo's arm and whispered into his ear, "Pay close attention, you miserable little piece of garbage, unless you want to cash in your chips way early. You and your little friends are trying to play way above your league. So far you have lost part of one ear and been shot in the leg. One of the two new thugs that you recruited to help you start up your own little drug trade was gunned down near the marketplace this morning with a burst of machine-gun fire. The big boys don't take kindly to competition. You may be the next one they take out.

"If you like living, don't mess with Dr. Hernandez or anyone at Ellie's Restaurant again. This is the last warning that you are going to get. Now, here's one nice little reminder to help you make good decisions in the future." Saying this, Jack grabbed Rodolfo's thumb on the hand behind his back and broke it with a loud crack. He shoved Rodolfo to the floor and moved quickly to the window through the clearing smoke, hanging on the lower part of the balcony railing before dropping to the street below and landing with a parachute roll. Jack stood up, pulled the cowl over his head, and left it and the clerical collar in the alley, heading for the street in a leisurely walk.

Close to the end of an alley, a large gray cat was sitting on a short post. As Jack approached, he noticed that the cat looked underfed and had blood on one side of its face. There was a garbage can near the cat. Jack opened the lid and found the remnants of a fish meal. He walked up close to the cat and extended the food. The cat stood up and hissed, then took the food and devoured it.

Jack spoke to the cat. "You are a very handsome fellow who must like to fight. Since you have no collar, I'm assuming that you are a stray. You may not know it, but I am a professional cat whisperer." Jack slowly extended an index finger and touched the cat's nose. The cat did not move. "OK, Buddy, you are going home with me." Jack picked up the cat and walked into the street and headed for Ellie's, avoiding the front of the hospital where two police cars with flashing lights were parked.

* * * * *

Jack unlocked the back door of the restaurant and walked in holding the cat. Reba looked up and said with a smile, "It looks like the priest has been defrocked." She paused with a perplexed look on her face and then asked, "Was the hospital giving away free cats today?"

Jack replied, "No such luck. I had to pay a man a thousand American dollars for this exotic attack cat. This beast is trained to claw the eyes out of bad guys."

Maria, who was preparing a huge bowl of guacamole, quickly chimed in, "The famous Jack Roberts' BS machine is going into overdrive. His proud possession is a rather handsome British Shorthair which is half starved. Does the cat have a name?"

Jack thought for a moment, then said, "Since this beast is an attack specialist, I'm going to call him 'Guerrero,' which is Spanish for 'warrior.' Once I get Guerrero fixed up with a bowl of milk, I will tell you all about my rather eventful trip to the hospital. And, by the way, Rodolfo sends his warmest regards to all of you."

CHAPTER 30

THE OPERA'S NOT OVER YET

Lunchtime at the restaurant was fast approaching, and preparations in the kitchen continued at a rapid pace as Jack began to tell of his ecclesiastical trip to the hospital. When he got to the part about the smoke grenade, Reba said, "Halt. Where did you get the grenade? The last time I checked the fruit market was fresh out of them."

Jack said, "You will recall that just before I left this morning, I spoke to Victor on the phone and told you that I needed to stop off at his office for some more priestly accessories. Victor is really amazing. He seems to have an endless supply of specialty items at his disposal. He was able to go to the back of his office and return with the smoke grenade in a paper bag."

Reba shook her head. "Something seems a bit out of whack here. Victor appears to be a very friendly man who runs a medical practice in a small Mexican beach town and has a domineering wife who keeps his testicles in her Gucci purse. Yet, on a moment's notice, the good Doctor Hernandez was able to come up with three fancy Walther PPK pistols, as well as a full priest outfit. Then, today, out of nowhere, he produces a smoke grenade. It doesn't add up."

Jack nodded and replied, "I agree that it seems strange. But I trust Victor, even though we know almost nothing about his background. I see no other choice for us."

Maria asked, "Is there any chance that Victor is shrewdly playing the middle and will sell us out when the time is right?"

Carmen, who had been working on making several gallons of iced tea, suddenly spoke up. "Victor Hernandez is a good man—a very good man." Then she bowed her head as if apologizing for speaking out of turn and returned to her work.

Just at that moment, Hulga came in through the back door with B.A., whom she had taken out for a walk. The dog saw Guerrero drinking milk from a bowl on the floor and growled, walking toward the cat. To everyone's surprise, Guerrero held his ground and hissed. When B.A. came close, the cat slashed out with a quick paw and gave B.A. a bloody gash on his nose. The surprised animal gave a little whimper and backed off.

Maria moved toward Guerrero to grab the animal and take him out of danger. "Don't touch the cat," Hulga ordered. "Let those two work it out. Either B.A. will have the cat as a quick hors d'oeuvre, or they will become friends."

There was a standoff for a minute, then Guerrero resumed drinking milk. B.A. seemed uncertain what to do. Hulga walked over to him and put her hand on his head. "Good boy, B.A. You and the cat need to be friends." The dog looked up at Hulga, then went to the back of the kitchen and lay down.

Lunch was busy, and the dining area was almost full until shortly before closing time at 2 PM. Victor arrived just as the last couple was paying their bill. He apologized to Jack, who was manning the cash register. "Sorry, I never seem to be able to get here on time for lunch. I was busy trying to deliver a woman who would easily tip the scales at 150 kilos. I felt like I was working as a spelunker. The man who impregnated her could probably get a job in a carnival side show."

Jack smiled and said, "That's exactly how I put myself through college!"

Reba shook her head. "Careful, Jack, you're about to short out your BS machine."

Victor laughed, then asked, "Any chance that you folks can find some food scraps for me?"

"Of course," Reba replied. "We'll all take a break before we finish cleaning up and sit down with you. How about beef tamales and a salad?"

"Sounds perfect."

As Victor ate, Jack recounted his morning adventures to Victor and Hulga, who had missed the first telling. Victor listened attentively, then said, "The word on the street is that the second drug person Rodolfo hired left town in a hurry this morning after his colleague was blown to bits downtown. That leaves Rodolfo with just his regular low-level criminal support staff, who won't be much help setting up a drug business."

Hulga joined the conversation, "If those losers are even halfway smart, they would haul ass on the next bus out of town. My concern is that the head of the narcotics cartel who ordered the execution this morning may still try to work out a deal with Rodolfo. That would be very bad news for us."

Jack replied, "Well, one good thing is Rodolfo will be benched for a while with the gunshot wound to his leg, as well as the shoulder I wrenched out of joint this morning. The broken thumb may also help slow him down. I think I made it very clear to him today that there will be a heavy price to pay if he messes with any of us again."

Hulga asked Victor, "Do you think Rodolfo's plans to burn your office down are still on hold for a while? This might be a perfect time for Rodolfo to strike since he has a perfect alibi while he is confined to the hospital."

Victor answered, "I still would like for you and your dog to sleep at my office for a while longer. There is no way to know whether Rodolfo might be able to enlist some new resources."

Carmen's son Luis came into the kitchen with an envelope in his hand. He handed the envelope to Jack and said, "I was playing chess in the park after lunch today when a Cadillac limousine pulled up. A man who was very well dressed and wearing dark sunglasses got out of the back of the limo and walked directly over to me. He smiled, sat down, and lit up a fancy cigarillo. Then he said, 'I understand that you are very good at chess. Have you won any money yet today?'

"I reached into my pocket and pulled out an American five-dollar bill. The man then said, 'Tell you what, young man. Let's you and I play. If I beat you, I get your money, but if you win...'" He paused to pull a hundred-dollar bill out of the inside pocket of his suit coat. "'This Benjamin is yours.'

"There was no way I could turn that deal down. We started playing, and the man checkmated me in only sixteen moves. I've never played anybody as good as he was. Then he said, 'You need some more work on your game, muchacho. But you can keep your money— and if you do a small favor for me, you can have the hundred-dollar bill also.' He asked me to deliver this envelope to the man at this restaurant."

Jack took the envelope and held it up to the light. Then he opened it and unfolded a white sheet of paper that was inside. His eyes widened, then he placed the paper on the table for everyone to read the words that were written in a very neat hand:

La gorda aún no ha cantado.

CHAPTER 31

MR. CRUDIE

Reba picked up the piece of paper and said, "Easy Spanish to translate—'The fat lady has not yet sung.' But, Victor, what do you think this note means in terms of our survival?"

Victor replied, "It's clearly a warning, like the dog's head with the eyes gouged out. To me, it means that Rodolfo has struck a deal with some heavies out of Mexico City who are interested in developing new territory. He now has a formidable support group."

Hulga said, "The fancy man in the Caddy limo was likely a member of the governing body of the crime cartel who was sent here to scout things out and decide whether Rodolfo would be incorporated or liquidated. It looks like Rodolfo may have made the cut. I wouldn't be surprised if arson is back on the agenda.

"The cartel has a number of low-level workers, any one of whom is bright enough to pour some gasoline and throw a lighted match. Having Hulga and her German Shepherd sleep at my office is suddenly much more urgent."

Maria asked, "Since the crooked police chief is in bed with Rodolfo and turns a blind eye to his extortion and prostitution business, I wonder if the chief is now part of the new local crime syndicate? He and his son both still have to be super pissed after getting humiliated publicly. Seeing us all dead would really make their day."

"Don't you mean make their decade?" Jack asked.

Victor stood up. "It's back to the hospital. I have three ladies in labor. Each night I say a prayer of gratitude to the Catholic Church for making birth control a mortal sin. It's surprising that some of the local families aren't living in a shoe like the little old lady in the nursery rhyme."

Maria said with a sly smile, "Victor, you are a busy OB doctor, but I bet you don't know what woman holds the record for most live births."

Victor puzzled for a moment, then replied, "No idea, I'm afraid."

Maria said, "I have always been able to recall a great deal of minutia. The record was set in the sixteenth century by a Russian woman, Valentina Vassilyeva, who birthed sixty-nine children. As I recall, she had sixteen pairs of twins, seven sets of triplets, and four sets of quadruplets."

Reba said, "That poor lady!"

"Poor lady?" Jack asked. "How about poor man? The fellow must have had calluses on his male member."

Reba shook her head and gave Jack a death stare.

Maria smiled and said, "And Reba has accused me of lacking in social deportment. How about Mr. Crudie here? At least I have the excuse of being trapped in a desert whorehouse for several months among people whose forte was not refined speech."

Reba looked at Maria disapprovingly, then quickly turned to Victor and said, "Maria sometimes confabulates. I would simply ignore that remark."

Victor had a puzzled look on his face, then commented, "I'm not sure if I am more amazed at the number of births or the fact that Maria remembered all of the details. She must have a photographic memory."

Reba said, "Our little Miss Maria has an IQ off the chart, and her brain has a built-in high-resolution camera."

Victor started walking toward the door, but paused to say with a smile, "Great lunch. Just put it on my tab."

Once the kitchen was clean, it was all-hands-on-deck to prepare for the dinner crowd. By 7 PM the dining area and bar seats were full with a number of people waiting to be seated. The patio area was close to being finished and would be pressed into immediate use. One of the diners complimented Reba on the food and laughingly called it "Comida Gringo Mexicana."

The evening passed uneventfully with nothing to suggest an impending retaliation from Rodolfo or any of his new friends. However, just as the front door was being shut to be locked at 10 PM, a tall, well-dressed man slipped into the restaurant trailed by a short but very muscular companion.

Jack said politely, "Sorry, Sir, but the kitchen is shut down and we are closing." The man gave Jack an ice-cold look and replied, "This place is about to be closed permanently unless you start ponying up the weekly protection fee. Rodolfo has really let things slide. But this town is now under new management. Let me explain things very clearly. If you don't come up with two hundred American dollars every Friday night, this restaurant will be burned to the ground by a mysterious fire. Do I make myself perfectly clear?"

Jack stared at the man and said, "We will never, ever agree to this extortion. Now get your fat ass out of our restaurant and never come back unless you want to get hurt very badly."

The man's face reddened as he turned to his companion. "Angel, this *estúpido cabrón* needs a little persuasion."

Angel pulled out a pistol with a silencer on the end and pointed it at Jack. The well-dressed man said, "We need to hear you say, right now, that you agree to our very fair deal. Angel has a little tremor and sometimes pulls the trigger when he doesn't mean to. Would a quick ten-to-one countdown help you make the right decision?"

There was a sudden loud bang followed by a scream from Angel as he dropped the pistol and looked with disbelief at blood oozing from his upper arm.

Reba stood in the doorway to the kitchen with a revolver in her hand that was still smoking. "Looks like the fat lady actually has sung. Perhaps you two pieces of human garbage have hearing problems. My husband asked you politely to leave before you got hurt. If you don't start moving your asses *muy rápidamente*, I plan to rid the world of you two vermin. Now move!"

Reba fired a shot right at the feet of the tall man who abruptly turned and moved quickly to the door. He hesitated to shout angrily, "You two idiots have just signed your death warrants!"

CHAPTER 32

CAT CLAIRVOYANCE

By 11:30 PM the kitchen was clean, and the small puddle of blood in the dining area had been removed. Preliminary work for lunch the next day had been completed. There were a large number of avocados in a basket, ready to make fresh guacamole. Maria had finished making the dough for corn tortillas, and Carmen had prepared two large Tres Leches cakes. Jack had contributed by peeling a mound of shrimp and placing it in the refrigerator. Hulga had left with B.A. to sleep at Victor's office shortly after the shooting.

Reba was sitting at a table in the kitchen going over the market list for the next day. She looked up and yawned. "I'm heading to bed. It's been a long day."

Jack replied, "Me, I'm wide awake and feeling frisky."

Reba looked at Jack and shook her head. "This definitely won't be a lucky night for you. I am exhausted. Shooting a scumbag always seems to make me very sleepy."

Jack suddenly had a small grin as he said, "Allow me to quote St. Paul in the book of Corinthians. I learned this scripture in high school Bible class and just knew that at some point it would come in handy. Now for the edification of all you Bible illiterates, I quote: 'The husband should fulfill his marital duty to his wife, and likewise the wife to her husband.... Do not deprive each other except by mutual consent for a time, so that you may devote yourselves to prayer.'"

Maria interjected, "You two newlyweds spend way too much time having public discussions about sex. Believe it or not, the rest of us have zero interest in how you resolve this seemingly vital question of connubial privilege. And, speaking of scriptures, I had a scary customer when I was a prisoner in the whorehouse who showed up with a Bible and a large cross around his neck. He insisted on a lengthy prayer before assaulting me."

Reba shook her head and said, "TMI, Maria. TMI. And regarding Jack's scripture, I plan to be an atheist as soon as my head hits the pillow."

* * * * *

The entire house was soon quiet. But just before 2 AM, Guerrero, who was sleeping in the kitchen, began to caterwaul. Jack awakened and lay in bed for a minute thinking, "That damn cat must smell a female in heat. He won't shut up until I let him out the back door."

Jack walked down the stairs thinking, "I never should have picked that stray up."

He turned the light on in the kitchen and walked toward the back door to let Guerrero out for a feline tryst. But just before he turned the lock, a voice said urgently, "Don't open the door. Someone's out there."

Jack turned to see Maria holding a pistol. She said, "That's not a mating call from the cat—it's a warning cry. And I am starting to smell smoke."

Maria brushed by Jack and opened the door with the pistol at the ready. A pile of rags on the back porch was blazing and licking at the wall of the house. A heavy odor of gasoline was present. Jack grabbed a fire extinguisher from its holder on the wall and began to extinguish the blaze.

Maria ran to the sink and doused herself with water from the spray hose, then dashed through the flames out into the alley. She could just make out a figure at the end of the alley jumping into a waiting vehicle that sped off. By the time Maria turned around, the fire on the porch had been extinguished before it spread to the house.

Jack had soot on his face and one eyebrow was singed. He threw the empty fire extinguisher into the large trash can by the back door. He took a deep breath and said, "Another few minutes and this house would have been a blazing inferno. Thank goodness for Guerrero. He saved the restaurant and likely our lives. And, as for you, Super Girl—dashing through the flames to be a heroine was flat-out stupid. There could have been a gunman out there just waiting to shoot anyone dumb enough to rush into the alley."

"Good point, Jack. But I hoped to be able to capture someone we could grill for information. Besides, I was armed and likely a whole lot smarter than someone who majored in arson in high school."

Jack shook his head. "Last time I checked, a plethora of IQ points usually won't stop a speeding bullet."

Maria said, "The car at the end of the alley that sped off had taillights that looked like a Cadillac. I'm guessing the mob man who came to the restaurant tonight was super pissed and decided to strike back quickly. He's bound to be staying at the main hotel, which means that his Caddy will be in the locked parking lot."

"So?" Jack asked.

"So, we need to give him something to worry about. The night is young. I think that we should sneak into the parking lot and disable his car. Also, if the engine is still warm, we will know that it is likely that he was the chauffeur for the arsonist."

Jack thought for a moment, then replied, "If I do a risk/benefit analysis, my brain tells me the risk far outweighs any possible benefit."

Just as he finished speaking, Guerrero ran to the back door and started howling again. Then the cat suddenly rolled over on his side and played dead. Jack and Maria took the clue and dropped to the floor just as there were two quick gunshots followed by the roar of a large car engine. The bullets passed through the door and splattered the concrete on the opposite wall.

Jack exclaimed, "Yikes!" as he stood up. "That was a close call. Guerrero must be clairvoyant. The bad guys are upping the ante in a hurry. I've just done a new risk/benefit calculation about our launching an immediate retaliatory strike. Let's go wake Sleeping Beauty and spoil her dreams of a peaceful night of apareunia."

CHAPTER 33

DÉCOLLETAGE BAD DECISION

Before Jack and Maria could head upstairs, Reba came quickly into the kitchen with her pistol in her hand. "I heard two gunshots that woke me up. And I smell smoke. What's going on?"

Jack replied, "Somebody tried to burn the house down by igniting a big pile of rags on the porch that were soused with gasoline. We might all be crispy critters by now if Guerrero hadn't warned us by caterwauling. While I was putting the fire out, Super Girl dashed through the flames into the alley in time to see a figure jump into a car at the end of the alley that looked like a Cadillac.

"While we were discussing what to do, Guerrero started making a racket again by the door, then rolled over on his side and played dead. Maria and I both interpreted that cat move to mean 'hit the deck.' We were on the floor when two shots came through the door."

Reba said, "Sorry that I missed all of the excitement, but I took an antihistamine pill at bedtime and was really zonked out. I knew that you guys would protect me."

Maria spoke rapidly, "Let's have an adult conversation and decide how we should respond. I am not willing to play a sitting duck and wait for these narcos to capture us and deposit our bodies in the bay with lead feet. The best defense is almost always the best offense. I vote to find the Cadillac and take it out of action as an initial response."

Reba asked, "How do you plan to find the car in the first place? It could be anywhere."

Jack replied, "Maria is betting that the mob lieutenant is staying in the main hotel, and that his Caddy is in the guarded hotel parking garage."

Reba suddenly said, "Wait. Carmen told me yesterday afternoon that she had some hotel news to tell me that might be important. But I got so busy with preparing and serving dinner that I never got back to her."

There was the sound of a child crying coming from the direction of the staircase. Carmen came into the kitchen holding Nina, who was sobbing. Luis followed his mother and said as they entered, "The loud noises woke Nina up."

Reba walked over to Carmen, took Nina, and sat down with her, stroking her hair. "Everything is all right, Nina. You just heard a car backfiring in the alley." Nina slowly stopped crying.

Carmen said to Luis, "Please go to the refrigerator and fix a bowl of ice cream for your sister and you. Then you can sit in the dining area while we talk back here."

Once the children were gone, Reba asked Carmen, "What was the news from the hotel that you wanted to share with me yesterday afternoon? I'm sorry that I got busy and never followed up with you."

Carmen said, "I have a maid friend at the hotel whom I ran into at the market yesterday morning. She told me that some big shot was staying at the hotel in the top floor suite and that he was driving a fancy Cadillac. The man has a stream of women coming to his room at night. This may be the man who came here tonight looking for trouble."

"Did your friend have a name for the big shot?" Jack asked.

"She learned from the desk clerk that he registered as Ace Torres. But that may not be his real name."

Reba tried to stifle a yawn. "I'm betting things will be quiet for the rest of the night. My baby and I need more sleep. This mother-to-be is going back to bed."

Jack gave Reba a quick kiss and patted her tummy. "I'll try not to wake you when I come up. There are a few more things that I need to do down here."

* * * * *

By 3 AM there were two shadowy figures approaching the hotel from the rear. The man was carrying a heavy container. The woman had a low-cut top on and looked like she might be a late-night street walker. When the pair came close to the back of the hotel, the man stayed in the shadows while the woman walked up to the two-story parking garage and approached a young man sitting in a chair under a flickering sodium lamp with a rifle in his lap. She said something to the man, then pulled her top partway down and beckoned him to follow her. The man had only taken a few steps when something struck the back of his head forcefully.

Working as a team, the woman and her companion quickly had the guard hogtied with nylon rope and lying on his stomach with his mouth taped shut. They dragged him out of the light and then quickly entered the parking garage with the woman carrying the guard's rifle. A quick scan of the first floor did not show the Cadillac. But a dash up the stairs to the second floor rewarded them by revealing the car in a large spot in the corner marked 'Reserved for Suite only.'

Jack felt the hood of the car. "It's still hot," he whispered to Maria. Then he quickly jimmied the lock on the gas cap. He listened as he blew into the gas opening. "Lots of room in the tank. Good." Jack lifted the large container up and poured all of the contents into the gas tank. "Ace may have some travel problems in his future."

Jack and Maria exited the garage quickly and untied the guard who was still a little dazed. Jack picked him up and put him back into his chair as Maria was emptying the shells out of the guard's rifle into her hand. She threw the shells into a large clump of bushes and then gave the weapon back to the man.

Jack put a large hand on the neck of the guard, who was shaking with fright. He stared at the young man and said, "Let's all just forget what happened tonight. If you run your mouth, we'll come back, and we won't be so nice next time." Jack gave the man's neck an extra squeeze for emphasis. Then he and Maria quickly faded into the darkness.

CHAPTER 34

BELLING THE CAT

Jack and Maria looked a bit bleary eyed when they arrived in the kitchen at 6 AM for coffee and the pancakes that Carmen had prepared. Reba arrived shortly thereafter and sat down at the table. Maria looked at Reba and said, "You must be feeling better since you put on makeup and are back to your usual ravishing self."

Reba smiled and answered, "We all know that I am ravishing with or without makeup. But I do feel really rested after a good night's sleep—except for the interruption by the would-be arsonist and the gunshots. Which reminds me, did anything exciting happen after I went back to bed?"

Jack replied with a straight face, "Nope. We all just went back to bed and slept with visions of sugar plums dancing around in our wee heads."

Reba turned to Jack with a penetrating look and said, "Men never know how to lie well. Come on. Fess up. What mischief were you and Maria up to after I returned to my feather bed?"

Jack pointed to Maria and said, "That woman tempted me, and I succumbed. She insisted that we respond to the fire and the gunshots by sending a message to Ace. So, we moseyed over to the hotel parking garage and found his gold Cadillac at the back of the second floor of the building. I dumped two gallons of Clorox into the gas tank that was less than half full of gasoline."

Reba responded, "Clorox is mostly water. Are you sure that this will do any real damage to the car?"

Jack answered, "At first the car will run a little rough and start backfiring. But since there is so much strong bleach in the tank, damage to the fuel line and metal and rubber parts will happen rather quickly. Ace will never make it even ten miles out of town before his Caddy gives an agonal belch and dies forever."

Reba shook her head. "I doubt if a crime pro like Ace will be intimidated by losing his car. This will just make him madder than hell."

Jack said, "We already crossed the Rubicon when we labeled him human garbage and you shot his bodyguard. I have no doubt that he is terminally pissed and bent on revenge. We need to convince him and Rodolfo that they don't know who they are messing with and that we have massive backup power."

Reba frowned and replied, "And just how do we do that, master strategist?"

Jack shook his head. "Ah, Reba. You would have made a perfect wife for Doubting Thomas. You always underestimate the brilliance of your husband. Let me pump some more coffee into my veins before I unveil my master plan that even Genghis Khan would be proud to present."

Maria laughed and said, "It's getting deeper by the minute in here."

At that moment Hulga came in through the back door with B.A. trailing behind her. She surveyed the room and said, "I hope you guys had a quieter night than I did. B.A. sounded the alarm a little after 2 AM when some cretin tried to start a fire just behind the office. B.A. chased him down the alley and knocked him to the ground just before he reached a waiting car. The driver stuck a pistol out of the car and shot the man several times. Fortunately, no shot hit my dog. But the would-be arsonist was flat-out dead."

Reba asked, "What kind of a car was it? Could you tell in the dark?"

Hulga replied, "The driver had all of the lights off, but the roar when he took off after shooting the man sounded like a big V8 engine."

Maria asked, "Any ID on the victim?"

"No. His pockets were clean as a whistle. He looked pretty scroungy. I'm betting that he was a local druggie recruited for the job in exchange for some smack."

Jack said, "Well, at least the fellow is now in permanent drug rehab, either with St. Peter or the devil."

"Sit down and have some coffee and pancakes, Hulga," Reba suggested. "Genghis Khan is about to reveal his plan to strike the fear of God in all of the bad guys who would love to see us laid out on slabs." She turned to Jack and said, "We are all atwitter in anticipation. The floor is yours, mighty warrior."

Jack stuck one more bite of pancake into his mouth, followed by a swig of coffee and said, "My plan is not original. It started with Moses. As you Bible scholars will recall, God had Moses announce a series of plagues to encourage the Pharaoh to let the Children of Israel leave Egypt. My plan is similar in that we apply pressure to Ace and his buddies in similar fashion. Reba shooting his bodyguard was Stage One. Disabling his Cadillac was Stage Two. Stage Three will be when we have a friendly little chat with Ace in his posh hotel room."

Reba asked, "And who, pray tell, will go on this little mission? It sounds a lot like trying to bell the cat."

Jack replied, "One thing for sure is that no pregnant woman is going to make the cut for the assault team. Getting access to Ace's top floor suite with its own guarded elevator will take some planning. But I think that I have a brilliant idea if I can sell it to Maria."

Reba said, "Maria would be smart to say 'no' even before she hears whatever the cockamamie idea is."

Jack answered, "Ace is reported to have an insatiable desire for call girls. I don't think that he could resist having a beautiful, young woman brought up to his room for carnal pleasure."

Maria smiled and said, "Beautiful and young—clearly that describes me. I know how to play the temptress from my whorehouse days in Barlow. But I would have to kill that animal if he tried to touch me."

Jack said, "You would be taking a deadly little friend with you named Walther. And I would be providing backup security once you get into the room."

Carmen looked up from her cooking and said quietly, "I can tell Maria a sure way to get into Ace Torres' room."

CHAPTER 35

SHORT ON FOREPLAY

At 8 PM the next night a very shapely young woman arrived at one of the locked back doors of the main hotel in town. She was wearing a short skirt and a low-cut top that showed considerable cleavage. The woman was painted up like a professional daughter of the night with intense red lips and dark eyeshadow. She tapped lightly on the door and was admitted by a bellboy who looked cautiously up and down the dark hallway before motioning for the woman to follow him.

The two people entered a freight elevator that creaked and groaned as it carried them to the private top floor. There were only three large suites on that level. The main suite had a very impressive thick oak door with a large gold number one embossed on its face. The bellboy left the woman by the elevator and walked across the polished marble floor to the door and pushed the intercom button.

He spoke quietly into the microphone.

After a few minutes the door opened and a woman who looked like a walking advertisement for an overexuberant plastic surgeon came out casually pulling her bathrobe together in front. She cast a knowing eye at the young woman by the elevator, then disappeared into the door for the down staircase. The bellboy beckoned for the young woman to follow him into the room. Ace Torres sat on a large bed with tangled sheets wearing silk pajamas and smoking a cigar. He looked the young woman up and down and gave a slight nod of approval to the bellboy.

"Good job, Roberto. This chica is a knockout."

The bellhop smiled and replied, "I know how much you like young cherry girls like Carlita. You have a great night ahead of you."

The man stood up and reached into the nightstand, pulling out a wad of pesos that he gave to Roberto. The bellhop pocketed the money, then turned and left the suite, shutting the door behind him.

Ace Torres locked the door, then turned to the woman with a leer. "Come sit on the bed, Sweetie, and let's get to know each other better—much better."

The woman looked at Ace and said teasingly, "I'm not sure that I want to get to know you better unless you can promise me a whole lot of fun."

"Sweetie, fun is my middle name." Carlita did not move. Ace became visibly angry and said harshly, "Now get your ass over here and sit on the bed before I have to give you a fat lip, you whore."

Carlita shook her head. "You're a little short on foreplay, aren't you, Big Boy? I need to hear a few sweet nothings before I agree to come join you."

Ace stood up and strode over toward the young woman with one fist clenched. As he approached, Carlita pulled her Walther PPK out of her skirt pocket and pointed it directly at Ace's chest. "One more step closer and you will be stone-cold dead. I would rather die than let a dirtbag like you touch me."

Ace's eyes narrowed. He looked toward the nightstand.

Carlita said, "I would drop you long before you got near your gun in the nightstand. Don't make a fatal mistake. We have some talking to do. Why don't you take a seat on the bed while I unlock the door and let my friend join the party?"

Ace hesitated, then lunged toward Carlita with murder in his eyes. There was a quick gunshot as Carlita shot Ace in one of his thighs. He gave a little shriek and stopped and stared in disbelief as red circles began to stain his pajamas. "You bitch!"

Carlita said coldly with no emotion, "The next shot will be right in your pea-sized brain. You really are a dumb shit, aren't you, letting a pretend whore into your room. It's never smart to let your dick make decisions."

Ace staggered over to an expensive leather chair and slumped down into it. Carlita walked to the nightstand and collected a pistol out of the drawer. She then went to the door and unlocked it. Jack came in. He looked at Ace and said, "My, my. Looks like Mr. Big Shot got himself into a heap of trouble. We need to have a serious little chat about your future. So, listen up. I don't plan to repeat myself.

"First, you have no idea whom you are dealing with. We have more firepower than you and your thug friends could ever muster. Your new best friend Rodolfo Mendez has been benched for the season with injuries. Unfortunately, your personal bodyguard, Angel, took a bullet and just missed his chance to actually sing with the angels. And, now, you made a dumbass decision and got yourself shot. You bad guys are dropping like flies. So far, we have treated you bastards with kid gloves. Now we are getting ready to play for keeps. If you don't haul your fat ass back to Mexico City *muy rápidamente*, you will end up laid out in the local mortuary. If there is any more trouble in town, we will send a very experienced hit man to track you down wherever you are and end your miserable life. Do I make myself clear?"

Ace looked at Jack and snarled, "You are going to regret not killing me, because all hell is about to descend on you smelly gringos who think you are such hot shit."

Jack replied, "It's not too late to settle this matter right here. Perhaps if I throw you off the balcony the rush of night air will clear your head. It will be fun to see how high you bounce when you hit the pavement."

Suddenly Ace's bodyguard with a bandaged arm burst into the room and got off one wild shot before Carlita put a bullet into his chest. The big man stopped as if frozen in time, then vomited blood and collapsed onto the floor.

For the first time Ace Torres had a look of fear in his eyes. Jack walked over near him and said, "You amateur bad guys will never have as much firepower as the U.S. government. No way you win this battle. My beautiful friend and I will be leaving now. I would suggest that you call an ambulance for Angel and yourself. You better pray that you don't see either one of us again."

CHAPTER 36

WAITING FOR THE RAPTURE

Maria and Jack were back in the restaurant shortly after 9 PM. The dinner crowd had thinned out, and Reba was serving and running the cash register while Carmen was still cooking and preparing food. Hulga was begrudgingly loading the commercial dishwasher after scraping the plates. She looked up when B.A. gave a low growl as Maria and Jack came into the kitchen from the back door.

Hulga said with a slight smile, "The wandering adventurers appear to have returned unscathed." She paused, then added, "I'm hoping that sweet Maria did not have to take one for the team tonight and sacrifice her virginity to a low-life like Ace Torres."

Maria looked daggers at Hulga and retorted, "I've already shot one loser tonight. Perhaps you would like to be next."

Reba came into the kitchen and immediately assessed the situation. "Break it up, you two. I'm of a good mind to shove both of you into the pantry and lock the door and see who survives. We have trouble enough without my having to referee hen fights. Trying to survive is a full-time job for all of us. You ladies need to kiss and make up."

Both women scowled at each other, then looked away.

Reba turned to Jack and asked, "Were you able to exchange pleasantries with Ace?"

Jack nodded. "We have Carmen to thank for setting Maria, aka Carlita, up with a pimp in the hotel who escorted her up to the penthouse floor and into Ace's suite. Apparently, Ace got too amorous, and Carlita had to cool his ardor by putting a bullet into one of his thighs. After that little attitude adjustment, he and I had a friendly little chat about the wisdom of his getting his fat butt back to

Mexico City and never returning. Ace's tough guy act collapsed when Angel burst into the room and got off one wild shot before running into a bullet from Maria's trusty Walther pistol."

Maria joined in. "Jack told Ace that the U.S. government has more firepower than he could ever muster, and that we were through being nice guys. I'm not sure just how Jack plans to call in the U.S. feds if we get our backs up against the wall."

Jack replied, "I wanted to give Ace something to think about. The United States is very concerned about all the drugs coming across the southern border from Mexico. It is not unreasonable to think that there are U.S. agents throughout Mexico. I wanted Ace to think that we ourselves might be undercover agents with the backing of the FBI and CIA."

A few minutes later there was a knock on the back door. B.A. seemed unconcerned, so Reba opened the door without a pistol in her hand. Victor came in. "I will tell you some interesting news in exchange for a plate of your leftovers for a late dinner."

"Fair trade," Jack answered. "I bet Reba can find a few morsels for you. Let's hear the big news."

Victor sat down at the table and said, "I just got called to the hotel to pronounce a man with a bullet in his chest in Ace Torres' suite. Angel Cabral is no longer among the living. Ace himself had a wound in his left thigh that apparently missed the femur and any big blood vessels. He was not happy to see me and refused to let me look at his wound. I advised him to go to the ER at the hospital to get patched up and to have a tetanus shot. Ace sneered and said something about all hell descending on this city."

Reba sat a plate of broiled shrimp with black beans and rice in front of Victor. She asked, "Victor, do you think Ace and his bosses will decide that setting up a drug delivery system out of this town is not worth losing more men—or will they send heavy reinforcements?"

Hulga quickly said, "I can answer that from my experience with narcos in Detroit. If the big boys in Mexico City think that there is substantial money to be made out here, they will be happy to keep sending low-level stooges even if a number of them get offed."

Victor nodded in agreement. "Even though Rodolfo is out of action for a while, the drug heavies have the police chief and his men on their payroll. I expect that they won't give up on testing Rodolfo's bleeding vagina gambit as a way to get heroin into the States. One successful trip would deliver a huge profit. I feel certain that I'll be hearing from them again. Hulga, I hope that you and B.A. will continue to sleep at the office. It won't be hard for Ace's people to recruit another druggie with a gas can and a cigarette lighter in exchange for smack."

Jack said, "Since we won't have B.A. to help guard the restaurant, we will have to depend on our attack cat Guerrero. That feline is almost prescient in anticipating danger. Maria and I might have cashed in all of our cat lives the other night if Guerrero hadn't told us to hit the deck just before bullets came crashing through the back door."

Hulga shook her head and said, "I've heard lots of fairy tales in my day, but that one takes the cake. No way a stupid cat can give a warning like that." Guerrero's ears perked up and he sidled over to Hulga and began purring around her legs. Then without warning, the cat bit Hulga through her long pants. Hulga gave a little shriek and tried to kick the cat. But Guerrero was too quick and darted from the room.

Hulga was very angry and snapped, "The first chance I get, I'm going to wring that nasty little beast's neck."

Maria laughed and said, "Poetic justice, Hulga. Guerrero didn't like being disrespected. I bet if you locked the cat and B.A. in a closet, only Guerrero would come out."

Hulga shook her head. "Little Miss Smarty Pants doesn't know much about power rankings in the animal kingdom. One quick chomp from B.A.'s strong jaws and that stupid feline's mythical nine lives would disappear in a heartbeat. Guerrero would be sent on an all-expenses-paid trip to cat purgatory."

Jack smiled and said, "I have it on good authority that Guerrero is a Baptist—and Baptists don't believe in purgatory. Guerrero told me that he is waiting for the Rapture."

Hulga scowled and replied, "The BS in here is up to my knees. I'm heading for Victor's office for the night. Come on, B.A., let's get the hell out of here."

As Hulga started out the back door with B.A. behind her, Maria said, "Hulga, that cat has been acting strange lately. You better start the rabies shots tonight. They're supposed to hurt like hell."

Hulga turned around and glared at Maria and made an obscene hand gesture. Then she slammed the door as she and B.A. disappeared into the alley.

Maria smiled and said innocently, "That woman really needs to work on anger management."

CHAPTER 37

ANGER MANAGEMENT ISSUES

At 6:30 AM the next morning, Hulga and B.A. came through the back door of Ellie's Restaurant. Carmen was working at the stove, making cinnamon buñuelos for Luis and Nina, who were sipping orange juice at the table waiting for breakfast. Reba was sitting at a small desk in the kitchen making a shopping list for Carmen to take to the market when it opened.

Jack came into the kitchen, dripping sweat from a beach run just as Hulga arrived. "Any excitement at Victor's office last night?" he asked.

Hulga shook her head. "Totally boring. But I did have a near-orgasmic dream that Rodolfo tried to break into the office, and I sent him to hell with several perfect shots to the chest. It was such a disappointment to wake up. My only goal in coming back to Mexico was to exterminate the rat who ordered the restaurant fire that burned my poor uncle alive. Rodolfo is still among the living with only a leg wound and a broken thumb to pay for the murder. He needs to be very dead—and very soon."

Reba looked up from her grocery list. "Hulga, you need to play it smart or you may end up incarcerated for life in a dangerous Mexican penitentiary with more amorous girlfriends than you can handle. We are not opposed to eye-for-an-eye justice in a town where the law officers are criminals themselves. We all know that Rodolfo will never be convicted of murder in a place where the judges are as corrupt as the policemen."

Before Hulga could respond, there was a tapping on the back door of the kitchen.

B.A. showed no response, so Jack opened the door to let Victor come in. He was dressed in green scrubs with a few flecks of dried blood on the front. "It's been a long night," he announced. "I had to do an emergency C-section at 2 AM for a woman with placenta previa and severe bleeding. We had to give her four units of blood before I finally managed to get a finger in the dam."

"What about the baby?" Reba asked with concern.

Victor sat down at the table before replying. "The baby will be all right, but he tipped the scales at a hefty eleven pounds. His mother is overweight herself and will almost certainly become diabetic in the future."

Maria had come into the room during the conversation and put a cup of coffee in front of Victor. "Doc, you look like something the cat dragged in—and I don't mean Guerrero. This cup of coffee should wake you up while Carmen whips up some breakfast for you. If you are nice, I bet that she will start you off with one of the cinnamon buñuelos that she is making for the kids."

Victor smiled and took a sip of his coffee. "I haven't had a buñuelo since I was in grade school. My stomach is definitely interested." He paused, then said, "I saw an interesting sight as I was walking over here from the hospital. There was a fancy Cadillac being hoisted up onto a flatbed truck near the main hotel. The driver said that the engine apparently had seized up."

Jack shook his head. "Alas. It sounds like poor Ace Torres is now without wheels. I wonder if he was planning to be driven back to Mexico City to recover from his leg wound."

Victor said, "Apropos of the esteemed Senior Torres' recent misfortunes in life, I learned that he was seen in the hospital ER late last night by one of the interns. An x-ray showed a bullet buried in the quadriceps. The man wisely decided not to let the inept house staff take him to surgery. He settled for an antibiotic injection and a tetanus shot and stated that he wouldn't let any of the local clowns touch him."

Maria chimed in, "The poor guy may have to take the bus now that his big Caddy is out of action."

Hulga shook her head 'no.' "Ace is high enough in the crime syndicate that I feel certain his bosses will send a car for him or perhaps a small plane. But you can bet the farm that he will be replaced with someone even meaner. Ace's statement that all hell would soon descend on us is not to be taken lightly."

Hulga looked toward the door from the dining area as Guerrero the cat walked in with a supercilious look of "I own the place" on his face.

"There's that miserable excuse for an animal. Victor, tell these people that a scroungy alley cat like that one is bound to have toxoplasmosis and will infect them all. Toxoplasmosis in the brain is not a good way to leave this world."

Victor gave a small smile and replied, "It's not easy to catch toxoplasmosis from a cat. But since Reba is pregnant, she should avoid dealing with cat poop."

Reba sniffed and said, "As if a princess such as myself would ever deal with cat waste."

Guerrero walked over to Victor and purred as Victor stroked his head. Then the cat deliberately approached Hulga, stopped, and peed on her foot before arrogantly prancing away.

Maria laughed and said, "Hulga, I think Guerrero just gave you the middle finger."

Hulga was livid and screamed at B.A., "Kill that damn cat, B.A.! Kill it!"

But B.A., who was lying in the corner, did not move. Guerrero walked over to the dog, and the two touched noses. The cat then nonchalantly walked from the room.

Hulga was red in the face and hyperventilating. She screamed, "I've had about enough of this crap! You people are such pussies. I don't want your help in taking Rodolfo out for burning my uncle to death. I will take care of this problem myself while you people are trying to grow some balls!"

Hulga strode out to the back door and beckoned for B.A. to follow her.

Maria shook her head and said, "Like I said last night, this woman has anger management problems." She paused and then added,

"I wonder if Hulga has ever been with a man. Poor guy. He would probably have to tie a two-by-four to his butt to keep from falling in."

Reba shook her head and said, "Maria, that comment was unspeakably crude. Jack and I have taught you to be a good street fighter and how to use weapons. But we have been total failures in trying to give you some social polish. You really disappoint me."

Maria stayed silent for a minute, then tears filled her eyes. She said quietly, "You two perfect people have no idea what I endured as a slave in the Barlow whorehouse." She paused to wipe her eyes. "Every night I was just a product sold to nasty old men who paid to paw and rape me. I could tell you things that would keep you awake at night. Working as a 16-year-old in a whorehouse is not like spending six months at a Boston finishing school."

Maria bowed her head, then said softly, "You two are the only people I have ever loved. The last thing I want to do is disappoint you."

Reba went to Maria, hugged her, and whispered, "We love you, too, Maria."

CHAPTER 38

A BAD WAY TO GO

The rest of the day was uneventful, with busy lunch and dinner crowds at the restaurant. Hulga and B.A. did not reappear during the day. However, when Victor and Sofia dropped in for a late dinner, Victor reported that Hulga and the German Shepherd were already at the office for the night. He commented that Hulga seemed preoccupied and had no wish to engage in conversation.

When the doctor and his wife sat down to eat, Jack joined them with a cup of coffee. Reba, Maria, and Carmen were busy in the kitchen. Maria peeked into the dining area and came back and asked, "How many acres of skin does that woman need to expose? If the old statement that brain size is inversely related to cup size holds true, that woman will be lucky to have a brain the size of an English pea."

Reba laughed and said, "I have to challenge your thesis since you and I have been anatomically blessed, yet we are hardly dummies."

"True," Maria replied. "But neither of us feels compelled to be a traveling nudie show like Sofia. She's got Victor on such a short chain that his neck must have permanent bruises. And I'd be willing to bet a hundred dollars that she will say something nasty about the food before she leaves."

While Victor and his wife were having after-dinner coffee, Reba joined them and Jack at the table. Jack had just asked Victor for his prediction about a possible next move for Ace Torres and his narco buddies.

Victor hesitated, then replied, "I think Hulga has it figured out right. Professional criminals don't take threats lightly. It may not happen immediately, but it's almost certain that a massive retaliation is being planned. I keep wondering if we all should pull up stakes and disappear off the radar screen."

Jack and Reba exchanged glances. She gave a slight nod. Jack said, "Victor, I am not at liberty to tell you everything, but Reba, Maria, and I came to this town to do exactly that—disappear off the radar screen. Having people interested in trying to kill us is nothing new. We are not about to run again."

Sofia interrupted to say, "This is such a depressing conversation. I can't help but think that everything was safe in this town until you people arrived and stirred up trouble. Now poor Victor is afraid of his own shadow."

Victor stood up and said angrily, "That's enough from you, Sofia. You have no idea what you are talking about. Grab your purse. We are heading for home."

Sofia looked shocked and didn't move for a minute. Then Victor grabbed her arm, pulled her up, and guided her to the front door. Just before Sofia left, she turned and said to Reba, "Sweetie, your tortillas still need a lot of work."

After Victor and his wife left, Reba turned to Jack and said, "I don't believe it. Victor may not have cryptorchidism after all. At least one of them must have finally descended."

Maria had come into the dining area to see Victor herding his wife out the door. "What, pray tell, is cryptorchidism?"

Reba replied, "Jack and I spent a semester in medical school. But I can promise you that he has no clue what cryptorchidism is."

Jack smiled and said, "You lose, my wannabe doctor friend. Cryptorchidism means 'hidden testicles,' i.e., undescended testicles. The testes are up in the abdominal cavity during gestation, but normally move down into the scrotum after birth. If they don't move down early in life, there is infertility and a high risk of cancer."

Maria exclaimed, "Touché, Jack! Reba, the reason Jack is so smart is that he has a small cup size, which means his brain is huge."

Reba laughed and replied, "Descended testicles or not, I bet Sofia will make Victor pay a huge price for calling her out in public. Goodbye connubial privileges for at least six months—or maybe for life. Now we need to get the kitchen cleaned up and get some sleep before tomorrow arrives bright and early."

* * * * *

At 6 AM there was an urgent knocking on the back door of the restaurant. Jack was in the kitchen making coffee and went to the door with pistol in hand. "Who is it?" he asked, standing safely to the side of the door.

"It's me, Victor. You won't believe the shocking news that I have to tell everybody." Victor came in with B.A. at his side and paced nervously back and forth until Jack reappeared with Reba.

"You two better sit down for this one. Rodolfo is dead, and he died a pretty awful death. But let me start at the beginning. I got to the office very early to catch up on paperwork—and to get away from Sofia who is still fuming about last night. In any event, B.A. was at the office, but Hulga was gone. Shortly after that, one of my patients who knows everybody and everything that happens in town called me.

"The man told me that at about 1 AM there was a fire alarm from the hospital. The firemen saw smoke coming out of Rodolfo's room. They broke the door down and found Rodolfo ablaze in the bed. Someone had handcuffed his wrists and ankles to the bed frame. The firemen were able to control the fire and keep it from spreading. Rodolfo had third-degree burns over his body and was clearly dead. Then the fireman noted that someone had whacked off his private parts and left him to bleed out and burn to death."

"How awful!" Reba exclaimed.

Victor said, "There is more. The firemen found a piece of duct tape near the bed. Their speculation is that someone got into the room and overpowered Rodolfo and handcuffed him to the bed and gagged him with the tape. Then the person amputated his testicles and penis, soused him with gasoline, and ignited it. Apparently, whoever was in the room ripped the tape off Rodolfo's mouth since other patients on the floor heard horrible screams. That mystery person must have tripped the fire alarm on purpose as he or she left and disappeared into the night."

Jack shook his head in disbelief. "Yikes! What a horror show! A case of classic Old Testament eye-for-an-eye justice if there ever was one. This execution has Hulga's fingerprints all over it. She screamed at us last night that we were pussies and should grow some balls. How she could have engineered all of this without help boggles the mind."

Victor said, "One additional bizarre thing. Ace's Cadillac was towed to a locked storage garage. However, when the tow-truck person went to check on the car early this morning to make certain that it had not been stolen, he found a grisly surprise: bloody male parts were on the dashboard. And there was a scribbled note on a piece of cardboard that read, 'You are next.' Also, the car was still locked."

"Holy shit!" Jack said. "That might strike some fear in Ace's heart since he clearly has a lot of interest in a functioning dick. Victor, do you have any idea where Hulga might be?"

"Nothing certain," Victor replied. "But my guess is that Hulga hired a driver to take her to the closest border crossing after visiting Rodolfo. She's probably on the way back to Detroit. I don't think that we will ever see her again. But she sure stirred up a hornet's nest for the rest of us."

CHAPTER 39

A BUSHEL OF DYNAMITE

Carmen came into the kitchen just after Victor delivered his shocking news. She began silently making breakfast for the household. Victor smiled at Carmen and said, "If you ask me to stay for breakfast, I would be happy to accept. It's too early to go to the office, and my wife is still on the warpath at home."

Carmen smiled back and replied, "Doctor, of course you are invited. Our family owes so much to you for all of the healthcare that you have provided in the past without charge. I'm making omelets with corn tortillas stuffed with chicken, cheese, and vegetables. There will be more than enough for everyone."

By the time breakfast was ready, Maria had joined the group. Victor repeated his story of the brutal demise of Rodolfo for Maria. She gave a little gasp and said, "Holy crap! Maybe I underestimated Hulga. How she could pull this off without being caught or killed boggles the mind. But I must admit that emasculating Rodolfo and leaving his ding-dong and family jewels in Ace's car was a really nice touch—regardless of who did it."

Reba started to say something, but stopped short when she saw Luis and Nina entering the room for breakfast. The conversation quickly turned to more mundane things like the great beach weather and how well Ellie's Restaurant was doing. After breakfast Luis told his mother that he wanted to go to the park and play chess with the men who always arrived early with American money in their pockets for gambling. His mother gave him five American dollars and admonished him not to risk more than that amount.

Victor lingered for coffee. Once Nina went back upstairs to play with her dolls, Jack said, "Victor, I think that you are correct that the drug guys will return in force. But I think that we will have a few days of grace since with Rodolfo gone and Ace injured, they will need time to bring in new people and re-establish contacts."

Victor answered, "You may well be correct. The cartel people are smart and likely won't respond with a knee-jerk reaction and rush the cavalry in with guns a-blazing until they have considered all contingencies. But I feel certain that these professionals are not about to give up on convincing me to help them with their bloody body cavity plan to get drugs into the United States. I still think changing our identities and disappearing into a remote area might be our best chance for survival."

Reba shook her head and said, "We used the remote area gambit when we came here and started a new life. None of us would be willing to play that card again and keep on running."

Luis reappeared in the kitchen breathing hard. "Something I need to tell everyone. Just as I got near the park, a fancy Cadillac ambulance pulled up at the big hotel. Two men with guns got out of the ambulance and walked into the hotel. A few minutes later they came out again. The driver was pushing a wheelchair with a man in it who had a big bandage on his leg. Every time the wheelchair hit a bump, the man cursed loudly."

Jack interjected, "That had to be Ace Torres in the wheelchair being taken away for better care of the bullet in his calf. Did the man have a dark goatee and a big head of hair slicked back?"

Luis nodded yes.

Reba said, "I wonder where they are taking him. Tijuana would be the closest place in Mexico with good medical facilities."

Victor stood up, went over to Carmen, and put a hand on her shoulder. "Fantastic breakfast. Sorry that I have to head off to work and can't hang around for mid-morning tea and crumpets. If Sofia keeps yelling at me, I may have to start sleeping over here at night."

Victor turned to the people at the table and said, "I leave B.A. in your good hands. One of you should start bonding with him now that Hulga has disappeared. Super Dog needs to be exercised and worked with every day."

Maria raised her hand. "I'm something of a dog whisperer myself. I nominate the very talented and beautiful Maria Williams for that job."

She walked over to B.A., who was lying in the corner on full alert, and knelt down and started speaking softly to the German Shepherd. After a minute or so, B.A. rolled over on his back and let Maria rub his stomach. She smiled and said, "Done deal. I have become his best friend in the world."

* * * * *

The lunch crowd started arriving shortly after 11 AM, and by noon the serving area was almost full. But by 2 PM the dining room was empty, and cleanup time began. Just as the final dishes were scraped and stuffed into the dishwasher, there was a loud explosion that rattled the windows of the restaurant.

"That sounded like a dynamite blast!" Jack exclaimed as he rushed to the front door of the restaurant. He saw smoke rising from the downtown area of the town. "That was a huge explosion. I don't think wandering down there would be smart since there could be a follow-up bomb designed to take out people who rush to the scene."

Luis came running up and motioned for Jack to follow him into the kitchen. "I saw it all," he said between gasping breaths. "The Cadillac that was towed away yesterday was loaded back onto a different flatbed truck that I have never seen in town before. The driver had a pistol in a holder on his belt and looked really mean. Once he had the car on the truck and chained down, he went into the drugstore for a minute. At that moment there was a huge explosion that lifted the Cadillac high into the air. The car came down in burning pieces that set the truck on fire. There was a smaller explosion when the fire reached the truck's diesel tank."

Reba asked the group, "Any chance that the redoubtable Hulga has struck again? Maybe she isn't on her way back to Detroit after all."

Maria shook her head and said, "I'm not one hundred percent certain that we should credit Hulga with taking out Rodolfo and sending him to hell with missing male parts. And for her to pull off a spectacular encore like this major explosion overextends my credulity. You can't just walk up to Aunt Mary's fruit stand downtown and buy a half bushel of dynamite. Hulga may have the body of an NFL lineman, but I was never overly impressed with her brain size."

CHAPTER 40

WALLET CONUNDRUMS

The restaurant started filling up early, and the diners were all abuzz about the earlier explosion downtown. Someone floated the idea that the Cadillac was being repossessed and that the angry owner had wired the car with explosives. Other people who had seen the nattily attired Ace Torres around town pointed out that he looked way too rich to be paying for a car over time. Another person added that the owner of the car had been loaded into a fancy Cadillac ambulance earlier in the day by armed men and appeared to have an injured leg.

An elderly lady who had arrived in a wheelchair being pushed by her son heard some of the conversation from other tables after sitting down and suddenly announced loudly, "You folks are all wrong. That man who was driving the Cadillac is a big shot in a crime cartel. I can spot those people a mile away. Too bad he wasn't in the car when it exploded." This statement engendered more animated conversation at the tables.

In the meantime, Reba and Carmen were blurs of activity in the kitchen trying to fill all the orders in a timely fashion. Maria and Jack were waiting tables, with Jack dropping out to run the bar and the cash register as needed. As Jack passed by Maria, he pretended to wipe sweat from his forehead and said, "Where is Hulga when we need her? We are going to have to get more help."

The dining crowd had thinned out by 9 PM when Victor and Sofia arrived. Señora Hernandez was wearing one of her trademark super-cleavage specials and was also sporting an exquisite new golden chain around her neck with a large sparkling stone that nestled happily in the depths of her cleavage valley. Maria observed the couple arriving and went back to the kitchen to find Reba and Carmen.

Maria got their attention, then simply said "moo!" before turning around and returning to the dining area.

Victor and Sofia had a leisurely dinner and were still sitting at their table with coffee at the 10 PM closing time. Reba, Jack, and Maria joined them. Jack immediately asked, "O.K., Victor, who do you think loaded explosives into Ace's car and almost certainly tripped the blast off remotely?"

"Tough question," Victor replied. "If it really was Hulga who emasculated Rodolfo and then burned him up, she almost certainly would have skedaddled to the border immediately and not risked hanging around for a dangerous encore."

Maria shook her head and said, "Wait just a minute. If Hulga really executed Rodolfo and somehow got into his locked car to leave his private parts and a warning note on the dash, why couldn't she have planted explosives on a delayed timer in the car at the same time?"

"Possible," Jack responded. "But problem one would be how Hulga could get her hands on dynamite—and problem two would have been knowing how to set up a sophisticated timer system."

Victor responded, "I think some of you are selling Hulga short on brains. She was a very good student in school and has been in a top-notch police department for eight years. Hulga could easily have picked up some explosive skills from the department bomb squad."

Reba joined in. "Another real problem would be that if it wasn't Hulga who eliminated Rodolfo, are there any other likely candidates?"

"How about the big boys in the narcotic cartel that Ace represents?" Maria asked. "They wouldn't be above orchestrating a horrible death and body mutilation to scare off other wannabe drug dealers."

Victor said, "But it wouldn't make sense for them to leave an anatomy present and warning in Ace's Cadillac. He has to be pretty high up in the crime food chain. Sending a fancy ambulance with armed guards sure suggests that they value his services."

"Unless," Maria mused, "they were just driving the dirtbag out of town to quietly eliminate him for screwing up so badly in trying to take the town over from Rodolfo and his people."

Reba shook her head. "It's a real conundrum."

Jack had a small smile when he said innocently, "I thought a conundrum was what young men carry in their wallets to keep from getting girls pregnant."

Maria gave a hiss. "That junior-high joke was a groaner when George Washington was president."

Reba said, "Apologies, Victor, for my husband's arrested mental development in the eighth grade. He still adores flatulence jokes."

Jack said, "Just a bit of levity. But back to the serious matters at hand. I see no choice for all of us but to stay alert and armed at all times and wait for the cartel's next move. I'm guessing that we will have at least a few days of grace before all hell breaks loose."

Sofia gave a big yawn and did not cover her mouth. "It's time for my beauty sleep." She turned to Reba and said, "You are making slow progress with your food. In a few more months you should be up to a B grade as a chef. But every time I eat here, I still get acid reflux."

Reba came very close to responding, "I bet if you chewed your cud more thoroughly, your reflux would disappear." But she caught herself just in time and smiled and replied, "Sofia, I appreciate your honest criticism. I'll keep on learning from Carmen."

Victor stood up and said, "Let's all pray for a quiet night. Come on, Sweetie, time to head for home."

CHAPTER 41

EYE CANDY

Two days passed with no new excitement or danger. Ellie's Restaurant stayed busy and was popular among the locals as well as tourists. On the morning of the third uneventful day, Jack went running on the beach just after sunrise. Jack was moving at a good pace when a young man caught up with him from behind. The man paced Jack briefly, then smiled and said, "Bet that you can't beat me to the next mile marker"—and then broke into a fast sprint. Jack hesitated, then was immediately in hot pursuit. Both men crossed the marker at almost the same time, gasping for breath. They sat down on a stone bench and began to talk once they could breathe normally.

The young man extended his hand. "I'm Miguel Alonso, but my friends call me Mig. I hope that I didn't frighten you by coming up on you unannounced. You were moving at a very good pace, and I needed an incentive to really run hard."

Jack smiled and said, "I was glad to have someone push me. Do you live here in San Lindo?"

"No, I'm from La Paz, but am spending a few weeks here with my aunt."

Jack asked, "You look to be no older than twenty-two or twenty-three. Are you in university somewhere?"

Mig answered, "I just finished my first year of a master's degree at Tecnológico de Monterrey in engineering, but I am not certain if I want to continue. I'm thinking about studying for the priesthood."

Jack smiled and said, "Glad that you told me. I'll have to watch my language around you."

Mig shook his head and replied, "I'm hardly a saint."

The conversation continued, and Jack learned that Mig was planning to take a year away from the university. Jack thought for a minute, then said, "I'm about to make you a once-in-a lifetime offer that will be hard to turn down. How would you like a job at my restaurant as a bartender and bouncer? You certainly have the build to take care of any unruly customers."

Mig laughed, then looked Jack up and down and said, "You sure don't look like you need any help in the bouncer department. However, I did work part-time as a bartender at university and know my way around alcohol. And I have also spent a great deal of time training in martial arts."

Jack said, "You sound like a perfect fit. Give it some thought, Mig. If you decide you're interested, just drop by Ellie's Restaurant on the beach, and we can discuss salary and hours. Now that I have my breath back, I'm going to jog back up the beach and go to work. Thanks for giving me a good run."

* * * * *

The morning was a busy one in the kitchen preparing for lunch. Carmen had quickly proved herself invaluable in augmenting the menu with more unique Mexican dishes. She was a tireless worker and never complained. Carmen attended early mass faithfully on Sundays and gave Luis and Nina no choice about going with her. She once confided to Maria, "I am a very sinful woman and may never get out of purgatory."

Maria replied, "My grandmother dragged me to the Catholic Church when I was little. All the blabbering in Latin made me want to put my fingers in my ears. I'm not very religious myself, but why not go to confession and ask the priest for forgiveness? At least it may make you feel better."

Carmen shook her head and replied softly, "I am too embarrassed to tell anyone about the terrible things I have done."

Maria put a hand on Carmen's shoulder and said, "Tell you what, Carmen, some day we need to sit down and compare sins. I'm sure that I can make you feel like a saint once we talk. I bet that you haven't worked in a whorehouse or had to kill people."

Carmen crossed herself with a look of shock on her face. She stammered and finally managed to say, "Maria, I will pray for you."

Just after the restaurant opened for dinner at 5 PM, a young man showed up and spoke to Maria, who was seating customers and asked to see Jack. Maria went back to the kitchen and relayed the message. "Jack, there's a really good-looking man out front asking to see you."

Jack replied, "I think that must be the fellow I met on the beach running early this morning. His name is Mig Alonso. He's a university student visiting his aunt here in San Lindo. I offered him a job as our bartender. Looks like he may be here to accept."

Maria smiled and said, "That fellow is certainly eye candy with those dark eyes, wavy hair, and muscles. He's almost as handsome as you are, Jack."

Jack shook his head. "Maria, the man is way too old for someone who is only seventeen years old, even if he raises your pulse. Besides, he is planning on becoming a priest."

Maria gave a little smile and said, "I may be seventeen years old physically, but I am a lot older psychologically. And I am one hundred percent certain that I could torpedo those plans for the priesthood."

Jack laughed and said, "If he takes the job, Reba and I may have to get a restraining order to keep you from molesting the poor fellow. If it really is Mig out there, I will bring him back to the kitchen to meet everyone. I plan to tell him that you are my fourteen-year-old sister and are dead set on becoming a nun."

CHAPTER 42

CALL TO THE PRIESTHOOD

Jack brought Mig back into the kitchen and presented him to the group, giving him each person's name. "This handsome fellow is Mig Alonso who has agreed to serve as our bartender and also to be available to help me if any of our customers overimbibe and become unruly. He is working on a master's degree at Tecnológico de Monterrey in engineering. But he is taking a year off trying to decide if he is being called to the priesthood."

Maria cupped a hand to her ear, pretending to listen carefully, then announced with a smile, "I don't hear anyone calling him."

Mig laughed and said, "Maria, are you really only fourteen? You sure had me fooled. I am excited that you are thinking about becoming a nun."

Maria glared at Jack and replied, "Mig, Jack has won the Pinocchio Award three years in a row for telling lies. He could definitely benefit from spending several hours in a confessional booth and saying Hail Marys for the rest of his life."

Jack replied very seriously, "Apologies, Mig, for my little sister's rudeness. She spends so many hours in prayer each day that sometimes she acts a little wacky."

Carmen gave a slight gasp, then sealed her lips in a thin, straight line.

Maria shot daggers at Jack and started to retort but was able to hold her tongue briefly before blurting out, "If you ever do darken the church door, you might just be singing with the sopranos."

Reba intervened quickly with a friendly smile and said, "We love our Maria, but she may not be perfect material for becoming a nun.

Let us walk with you out to the bar and see your bartending and mixologist skills in action."

Mig turned out to be an ace behind the bar. He could make any drink a patron requested and was immediately a favorite of all the young ladies. Toward the end of the evening, an inebriated man got into an argument with his much younger female companion and slapped her face. Mistake. With no hesitation, Mig picked the man up, threw him out the front door, and returned to thunderous applause from the remaining diners. Maria, who was serving, passed by Mig as he returned to the bar area and said slyly, "Violence is never the answer, Father Alonso. I hope that you don't get defrocked by the Vatican."

By 9:30 PM the dinner crowd had thinned out. Victor and his wife arrived and took a table toward the back, ordering a light dinner. Sofia was wearing an arresting backless summer dress with her patented plunging neckline in front. Her hair was perfectly coiffed and was newly streaked with frosting. Victor ordered a bottle of expensive wine that Mig brought to the table with glasses. As he left the table, he couldn't resist taking a quick glance at Sofia's cleavage.

Maria sidled up to him when he returned to the bar and said quietly, "If your eye offends you, pluck it from your head." Mig looked at her quizzically. "Maria, just how old are you really? And why do you insist on needling me?"

Maria smiled and replied, "I'm actually one-and-a-half dog years old. Surely an aspiring engineer such as yourself can convert that to human years without a slide rule. And I keep annoying you since I am a confirmed wiseass—and since it would be a tragedy for a man as handsome as you not to procreate and enhance the human gene pool." Before Mig could respond, Maria smiled again and headed back to the kitchen.

By closing time at 10 PM, the dining area was empty except for Victor and his wife. Jack paid Mig for his night's work and let him out the front door before locking it. Then Jack and Reba joined Victor and Sofia for coffee at their table.

Jack asked, "Well, Victor, what do you think of our new combo bartender and bouncer?"

Victor replied, "I have known Mig Alonso for a long time. He frequently comes to San Lindo to visit his aunt. She has a successful gift shop on the beach called 'The Magic Seashell.' Unfortunately, she is one of the merchants who saw no way to avoid paying a weekly protection fee that cuts into her profits. Rodolfo may have gone to meet his maker, but the cartel people have sent a mid-level thug to keep the extortion money flowing in."

Sofia interjected, "Mig is really good looking. There are some interesting rumors about him in town."

Victor shook his head. "Sofia, you know there were rumors, no facts. People love to make up things. Mig is exceptionally nice and very bright."

Sofia continued, "All true. However, the daughter of Victor's patient who left the convent in town apparently got pregnant. Many people believe that Mig was the father."

Reba asked, "Was that where I got the nun outfit for my trip to the hospital to visit Reynaldo Huertas?"

Victor nodded yes, then said, "I personally doubt if Mig would have ever gotten involved with a young woman from the convent. Impregnating a nun would have to be at least a double mortal sin. Spreading salacious gossip is a full-time sport for too many women in this town."

Maria had joined the table for the last few comments and said, "I bet that Mig could talk the Mother Superior at the convent out of her britches."

Reba shook her head. "Our apologies for Maria. I think that we need to send her to Boston for a year at a high-price finishing school."

Sofia reached over to give Maria a congratulatory hand slap. "You nailed it, honey! I am in complete agreement with you."

"On to more serious matters, please," Jack said. "Any thoughts about what the next move of the cartel will be?"

Victor answered, "I believe that the cartel bosses will let violence calm down for a while. They won't want any more immediate sensational acts that might lead to the Federales coming to town to nose around. And you can be absolutely certain that the police chief wants to avoid any outsiders who might torpedo his lucrative agreement with Rodolfo's successors. But we are in the calm before the storm. Sleeping with one eye open remains essential."

Sofia tugged on her husband's arm. "It's getting late, and I need to get home and take some Pepto Bismol. That fish tonight had a funny taste."

Victor shook his head as he stood up. "My apologies to Reba and Carmen. I thought that the fish was outstanding. Prayers for a safe night for all of us."

After Victor and his wife left, Reba said tartly, "I hope that woman has explosive trots and projectile vomiting at the same time all night long. I have no idea how Victor puts up with her."

Jack looked at Reba and said with a smile, "Perhaps Maria and I can explain male hormones to you tomorrow using very simple terms."

Reba retorted sarcastically, "I'll need colored pictures and diagrams. Now let's all pitch in and finish the kitchen and head for bed. Pregnant women need more rest the further along the pregnancy is. I may decide to put a rocking chair in the kitchen in the morning and eat bonbons while assigning chores to you plebians as I rock and teach my baby to speak Russian."

CHAPTER 43

A GHOST

Just after the restaurant opened for lunch at 11 AM the next day, a tall American woman with a striking white forelock and dark green eyes came in and sat down at a table. She was wearing white shorts with a loose top. Her muscular calves suggested that she was a runner. Mig was at the bar and went to the woman's table and introduced himself and asked in Spanish what she would like to drink.

The woman replied in passable Spanish, *"Un Coca Cola and un menu, por favor, Señor."*

Mig smiled and replied, "Your Spanish is good, but I am fluent in English if that is easier for you."

The woman returned the smile and answered, "I learned most of my Spanish on the flight to Mexico from Virginia yesterday. So, English would be better. I am curious about the name of this restaurant—Ellie's. Do you know why the owners picked that name?"

Mig shook his head and said, "I just started working here yesterday. When one of the owners comes out, you can ask the husband or the wife."

Things were usually slow before noon, so Mig ended up taking the American woman's order and bringing her a hamburger and French fries. As she was eating, a muscular man wearing a bright orange Speedo and a partially unbuttoned floral seersucker shirt that exposed a hairy chest came into the restaurant. He had a small fanny pack that he was wearing incongruously in front just above his Speedo. He looked around, then walked directly to the table where the woman was and sat down.

The woman looked up and said, "There are plenty of open tables. I did not ask you to join me. Please move. I have no interest in talking with a stranger."

The man stared at the woman and did not budge. Then he said, "Honey, I can tell by looking into your eyes that you are very lonely. What say you buy me lunch, then we can go to my hotel room, and I'll show you my collection of Speedos."

The woman looked straight at the man and said firmly, "If you don't get your butt in gear immediately, I'll have to help you. And it won't be pleasant. You need to go to your room, take a shower, and use a lot of soap. You smell."

The man snarled and stood up. "I'll just pick you up and take you to my room, you bitch!"

As the man moved toward the woman, Mig intervened and said, "Leave the woman alone, friend, unless you want to deal with me."

The man laughed. "All of you stupid college students think that you are such hot shit. Go back to the bar and hide before you get hurt real bad, asshole."

The woman stood up. "Mig, I can handle this all by myself. But thanks for trying to protect me."

Mig was undecided for a moment, but something in the woman's voice made him move back.

The woman took a step toward the man in the Speedo and said quietly, "OK, super stud. Let's see you try to pick me up."

The man lunged at the woman. She moved deftly to the side and gave him a hard slap on the face.

He roared, "Big mistake, you whore!" The enraged man rushed at the woman who grabbed one of his arms, wrenched it behind his back, and shoved him to the floor.

She looked down at the man and said quietly, "Let's just call it even. If you get up nicely and head for the door, I won't have to send you to the hospital."

The man stood up slowly and took a couple of steps toward the door. Then he whirled around with a revolver in his hand. "Guess who's in charge now, bitch. If you play nice and walk out the door with me, nobody will get hurt. My car is in the parking lot. We can take a drive along the beach. Maybe we can stop and collect seashells."

The woman stared at the man and said quietly, "You really are dumb, aren't you? I'd rather be dead than go anywhere with a smelly greaseball like you."

The man's face became red and the veins in his neck started to bulge. He said between clenched teeth, "Since you attacked me, it will be self-defense when I put a bullet in your brain."

Mig started to come back from behind the bar, but the woman said, "No."

Suddenly, the woman ducked as she grabbed a water glass off the table and hurled it at the man. He shot wildly as the glass struck him in the chest. The woman moved with lightning speed, knocked the gun from the man's hand, and butted him in the chest. He staggered backward, then crashed to the floor as the woman broke a chair over his head.

Mig was watching in disbelief from behind the bar. Jack heard the commotion and stuck his head into the dining area. His face paled, and he immediately ducked back into the kitchen. Reba looked up and asked with concern, "Jack, are you OK? Your face is white as a sheet. Did you just see a ghost out there?"

"Worse," he answered. "Much worse."

CHAPTER 44

SPECIAL PLASTIC SURGERY

Jack walked over to Reba and said grimly, "Our old CIA contact Becky Reagor is out there big as life, and she just disabled some goon in a Speedo who is lying on the floor with pieces of a broken chair all around him. So much for living a quiet life after all of our enemies were sure that we were all blown to smithereens when my crazy uncle's compound in the Texas desert exploded. As owners, I think one of us is obligated to go out there and show some concern for the injured man."

Reba answered, "You, Maria, and I all look very different from the last time Reagor saw us. Maybe if you go out there and stick with Spanish and pretend not to know English, she won't recognize you."

"The man on the floor is out cold. I need to call an ambulance and get him hauled away before the lunch crowd starts arriving. Maybe I can pull this off since my hair is now a different color, the beard is new, and I am super tanned. You and Maria need to stay hidden. Three of us together would be a dead giveaway."

Jack walked into the dining area, approached Reagor, and addressed her in Spanish. "Good morning, Señora. I understand that the man on the floor had an accident and needs an ambulance."

Mig interrupted in English to say, "Jack, this woman does not speak Spanish."

Jack looked at Mig intently and replied firmly in Spanish, "Please translate for us. My English is terrible. Tell the woman that we are very sorry for the disturbance and that her meal will be on the house. Also, let her know that we can safely secure the gun on the floor. I will call an ambulance for the injured man."

Mig translated in English, and the woman nodded in agreement. She looked at Jack with no sign of recognition and said, *"Muchas gracias. Are you one of the owners of Ellie's Restaurant?"*

Jack replied, "Como?" as if he did not understand the question in English. Mig intervened and said, "Yes, Jack and his wife Reba own the restaurant."

Before the woman could ask any more questions, Jack quickly told Mig to take the American woman's order. "Please tell her that if there is any way we can be of help, just let us know. And explain to her that I am going to the back now to send for an ambulance."

An ambulance arrived quickly. The attendants put the comatose man on a stretcher and seemed to have no curiosity about his accident.

Mig served as the waiter and brought the woman her food when it was ready. She ate leisurely and seemed in no hurry to leave. By this time Maria had been informed that Reagor was indeed at the restaurant. She, Reba, and Jack agreed to stay out of sight and pray that the woman would leave soon without recognizing any of them.

Mig came back into the kitchen and said, "People are starting to arrive for lunch. I can't handle everything by myself. But—My gosh! You should have seen that American woman in action! I have never seen anyone fight like that. She must be some sort of martial arts teacher. She really wiped out the jerk wearing the 'look at me' Speedo."

Maria said, "I'll go out and start taking orders with my hair pulled down over part of my face, and I'll try to stay away from Reagor's table. If I have to use English, I'll make it sound like I'm a Berlitz English class dropout."

Reagor dallied over her food, then ordered coffee and dessert. She finally motioned for Mig to come to her table and asked for her bill. He advised her that the owners absolutely would not let her pay to make amends for the troublesome man in the Speedo who tried to attack her. Reagor expressed her appreciation, then left the restaurant.

Maria saw her leave and reported back to Reba and Jack. "Thank God!" exclaimed Reba. "If Reagor knew that all three of us had survived the mega explosion in the desert, it would be very hard for her not to share the miraculous news with the director, as well as Maria's runaway friends in the Barlow whorehouse, Linda Kay and

Ryn. The girls have been living with Reagor and her husband in Virginia for over a year now."

Maria said wistfully, "I would love to see Linda Kay and Ryn again. We went through hell together in Barlow."

Jack replied firmly, "Maria, we have enough enemies here in Mexico that want to kill us. The last thing we need is for the KGB and the Chicago crime syndicate to learn that somehow we survived when Uncle Wilbur's compound exploded like a hundred tons of dynamite."

As soon as the restaurant closed at 2 PM, everyone pitched in for cleanup and to start preparing food for the dinner crowd. The restaurant was busy by 6 PM with mostly tourists. It was almost 8 PM before the locals started to drift in. Mig gave a last call for alcohol just before 10 PM, which started clearing out the late diners. Just as Mig was about to lock the front door, the American woman who had been there for lunch returned with two young women.

The American said, "Sorry to be so late. We just got out of a movie, and my girls really want to try your sopapilla cheesecake before bedtime. We won't stay long."

Mig seated the three of them, then went back to the kitchen with their orders and informed Reba and Jack that the American martial arts expert had returned with two young females.

"That has to be Linda Kay and Ryn," Maria said.

"Our cover is in real danger of being blown," Jack said with obvious concern. "The KGB has long tentacles. If they learn that we are alive, it wouldn't take them long to show up. Let's stay out of sight and hope that the three of them don't linger over dessert."

While the girls were eating their sopapillas, Reagor suddenly stood up and walked back to the kitchen. Reba looked up from the sink with a start and asked, "Can I help you?"

Reagor smiled and replied, "I'm sure you know this town well. Can you recommend a good plastic surgeon here? I know that surgery is much less expensive in Mexico than in the States."

Reba hesitated, then replied, "Can I ask what kind of procedure you are interested in?"

Reagor replied, "It's kind of private—but I'm looking for a surgeon who can remove my penis." Jack, who was loading the dishwasher, gave a little gasp.

Reagor walked over to Reba and gave her a big hug. "I knew who Woody was the moment I saw him, and the same for Leta. Twenty years in the CIA taught me a lot more than just how espionage works. It was an incredible shock when Jack came out to talk to me after I took care of the smelly Speedo man. At first, I thought I was seeing a ghost. And just for the record, Jack, your Spanish was not nearly good enough for you to be the native speaker you pretended to be."

Jack laughed and said, "Touché. Let me pay Mig and send him on his way. Our helper Carmen went upstairs to tuck her children in for the night. Why don't we all join Linda Kay and Ryn at a table out front and do some serious catching up?"

CHAPTER 45

FROM THE TEXAS DESERT TO MEXICO

Linda Kay and Ryn were absolutely shocked to see Leta when she came out to their table. There were hugs and tears before the three of them went upstairs to Leta's room for some privacy. Jack, Reba, and Reagor sat at the table with cups of coffee. Reagor started the conversation. "The whole world was certain that you two and Leta, or should I say Maria, were blasted into tiny bits when the entire compound became rubble in the blink of an eye. How in the world did you escape and end up here in Mexico?"

Jack and Reba exchanged glances. Then Reba said, "Jack, Wilbur was your crazy uncle, not mine. You can explain."

Jack paused as if to collect his thoughts, then began. "Becky, you know a lot of this story, but here is a thumbnail sketch. First, let me reiterate that my Uncle Wilbur was beyond brilliant despite having paranoid schizophrenia. He was absolutely certain that German agents were after him. Wilbur built an amazing survival compound out in the Trans-Pecos desert with secret underground rooms and a host of lethal booby traps. Once Ava and I received death threats while at CIA Camp Peary, we asked you and the director to help us escape to my uncle's compound in hopes of disappearing into the desert and getting off the radar of both the KGB agents and the Chicago mafia, who were determined to capture and kill us as painfully as possible.

"You provided new documents to change my name from Woody Stressel to Bob Smith and Ava Volkov's name to Mary White. Then the CIA provided a nondescript van for us to drive from Virginia to Texas. When we reached the compound, we found only a young woman named Leta Mitchell. We learned that Wilbur had rescued her from a whorehouse in Barlow, where she and two other young runaways were being forced into prostitution. Leta finally confessed that she and my uncle became lovers. Wilbur died in bed during sex with Leta. She panicked and buried him at the back of the compound.

"As you know, Leta turned out to be Mensa smart. She was terrified that the people from the whorehouse might find her and drag her back. Ava and I decided to make Leta self-sufficient and taught her martial arts and how to handle weapons. She was fearless and turned out to be a huge asset when the mafia boys located us at the compound. Along the way, the three of us rescued Leta's friends Linda Kay and Ryn from the whorehouse. You and your husband were kind enough to take them in as part of your family in Virginia. Our plan to disappear into the desert turned out to be a definite failure since killers hired by the Chicago crime group tracked us to the compound. Once the United States Protective Service pulled all of their agents, the reincarnated Randy Williams and some of his closest killer friends made an assault on the compound with more bad guys than we could handle."

Reagor interrupted. "I cannot tell you how bad the director felt about letting the head of the Protective Service abruptly yank his men from protection duty at the compound. When the director and I visited the smoldering compound ruins, he got very emotional, blaming himself for your deaths."

Jack replied seriously, "It was just a matter of time until the crime goons overpowered the small Protective Service contingent, who literally hated being assigned to duty out in the barren desert. One of the guards actually told us that none of them would mourn if all of us got wiped out."

Jack continued, "You know most of the story from that point on, except for what happened just before the compound exploded so spectacularly. Sticking with our current assumed names, Reba, Maria, and I were trapped in a small room in an underground area of the compound with the mafia thugs placing dynamite just outside the room. Wilbur had set up an amazing defense system with a panel that controlled many areas of the compound. One button was marked 'Armageddon,' and we suspected that this button was to be pulled only as a last resort. Just before the dynamite was set to explode, Maria pulled the Armageddon switch. The floor simply disappeared beneath us, and we started falling down into an endless black abyss. We must have all blacked out.

"I cannot begin to explain what happened next. We opened our eyes and found to our surprise that we were all alive and intact in a well-lit space that suggested an underground silo. There was a large leather briefcase on a table with small gold initials—W.N. Inside were very explicit instructions for making a new passport for Wilbur with a sophisticated printer and camera that were in the room. It was obvious that someone had set up an incredible system for my uncle to vanish from the compound in a dire emergency."

Reagor had been listening intently. She interrupted to ask, "Did you know whose initials were on the briefcase?"

Reba responded, "Maria was actually the one who suggested that W.N. stood for William Norton, the construction engineer who helped conceive and build Wilbur's amazing compound. When the project was finished, Wilbur apparently murdered Norton to make sure the secrets of the compound were never shared with the Nazis who Wilbur was certain were planning to kill him. Norton himself was reputed to be a genius. Our guess is that it was he who designed the escape plans."

Jack said, "It was quickly obvious to us that Norton had arranged a very complex escape system for Wilbur, including how to make a new passport and providing explicit instructions on how to enter Mexico undetected and take over an old restaurant in San Lindo that had gone bankrupt. Norton somehow managed to purchase the restaurant and also hide huge sums of Wilbur's money in the building. Once we made our own new passports, I became Jack Roberts, Ava was Reba Roberts, and Leta became Maria Williams. The instructions told Wilbur that after entering Mexico illegally, his new passport would simply serve as future identification for him."

Reagor shook her head. "My gosh, your story is almost beyond belief. I am all ears. What happened next?"

Jack continued, "We took an elevator up to the ground floor and found a shed with a complicated dial compound lock. I was able to crack the lock. Inside was an old Suburban with the battery on trickle charge. The engine fired up immediately, and we headed out to California. The instructions on how to enter Mexico undetected near San Diego were perfect. I always carried a stack of Wilbur's hundred-dollar bills in my pants. This cash came in very handy since it allowed us to purchase a Jeep from a sleazy used car lot in Tijuana and drive to San Lindo. Like in the desert, we planned to disappear into Mexico and lead quiet lives. But no such luck."

Reagor said, "It seems like running a restaurant in a sleepy Mexican beach town would be a perfect cover. What went wrong?"

"Plenty," Reba chimed in. "The start of the problems was when the crooked police chief's son tried to pull Maria's skirt down out on the street one day. She had to yank his shoulder out of place and give him a major testicular contusion. Then we refused to pay some local slimeball criminals $200 a week to keep them from burning Ellie's Restaurant down. Trouble mushroomed when a drug cartel decided to move in and use this town as a staging place for getting drugs into the United States."

It took another hour to bring Reagor fully up to date about all that had happened since Wilbur's incredible escape plan brought the survivors out of the desert compound explosion and conflagration to a small Mexican beach town. Maria and her friends also had plenty of catching up to do and only came to the kitchen once to grab some Cokes.

Reagor marveled, "If only Ellie were still alive, she could write a fantastic novel based on your experiences to date. I noticed that Leta, I mean Maria, is getting more and more striking as a young woman."

Reba replied, "Maria has been well trained, and I would put her up against anybody that she might meet on the street. She seems to have eyes for Mig, the handsome fellow who let you and the girls into the restaurant tonight. He supposedly is thinking about becoming a priest. We are hoping that he doesn't try to take advantage of her."

Reagor smiled and said, "Not a chance in the world. When I was dealing with the rude jerk in the Speedo, I couldn't help but notice that Mig couldn't take his eyes off the large bulge in the man's scanty swimsuit. I think Maria is safe unless she changes her name to Fred."

CHAPTER 46

HULGA-MIA

There was a moment of silence at the table. Then Reagor shook her head and said, "I saw a lot of unbelievable things during my twenty years in the CIA, but your story tops everything. And, unfortunately, it sounds like your troubles are far from over. Getting on the bad side of the narco boys is a huge problem. They are ruthless killers and have lots of assets. This Hulga Larsen woman sounds like she must have received a large genetic dose of testosterone as well as estrogen. Are you two convinced that it was Hulga who burned up and mutilated Rodolfo Mendez?"

Jack nodded and replied, "Hulga was very angry with us for not moving fast enough in helping her avenge her uncle's death after Rodolfo and his men burned down her uncle's restaurant with him in it. The last time we saw Hulga, she was furious and called us pussies who needed to grow some balls and vowed to take care of Rodolfo herself. The way he was executed suggests that the perpetrator was incredibly angry. Hulga might just as well have carved her initials on Rodolfo's chest before she soused him in gasoline."

Reba added, "I have to agree with Jack, but it's hard to explain how Hulga was able to get into Rodolfo's room, kill him, and then escape, apparently undetected. A huge woman like her carrying a man's bloody penis and testicles in a bag would be hard to miss. Then, there is the problem of how she got into a guarded car storage facility at night to leave a charming souvenir on the dashboard and also plant explosives with a time-delay switch. Maria insists that Hulga is not nearly smart enough to pull that off. The two of them have been at odds ever since Hulga arrived."

Jack said, "And the fact that Hulga disappeared the same day Rodolfo's burned body was found sure suggests that she did the deed and then escaped back into the United States."

Reagor said, "Let me offer an alternate hypothesis just for fun and see what you think. Assume that the cartel higher-ups decided that an injured Rodolfo was no longer useful to them. Creating an absolutely gruesome death for him might serve as a powerful warning to any other possible interlopers not to challenge the cartel. Being burned alive and emasculated would be a very strong deterrent."

Reba asked, "If that were true, what happened to Hulga? She had a strong relationship with the guard dog B.A. It's hard to believe that she would abandon the animal. Maria is good with animals and took over the care of B.A. But the dog still mopes around."

Jack added, "I've been trying to understand what benefit Hulga would have seen in blowing up the disabled Cadillac of the mid-level crime person Ace Torres. He obviously would not be driving a car that she knew would have to be towed after Maria and I wiped the motor out with some midnight mischief. If Hulga did execute Rodolfo, it seems obvious to me that she would have been smart enough to head for the border immediately and not take the risk of hanging around to leave a surprise present in Ace's car, as well as wiring the Caddy to blow up at a later time. It just doesn't make sense."

Reagor listened intently, then asked, "Are you guys absolutely certain that Hulga is not still in the country hiding out somewhere?"

Jack and Reba exchanged questioning glances. There was a pause, then Reba replied simply, "No. We're not sure of anything."

There was a pause, then Jack said, "Becky, you've given us a lot to think about. I'm still amazed that you and the girls would magically appear in San Lindo of all the vacation spots in Mexico."

Reagor replied, "Linda Kay and Ryn are out of school for the summer. I told the girls if they made good grades this last school semester, I would bring them to a beach town in Mexico. My cousin visited San Lindo a year ago and told me that the beach was beautiful and that the town was not overrun by tourists. I probably shouldn't tell you this, but my cousin is younger than I am and is a free spirit. She told me that she met some incredibly handsome man here and spent some amazing nights with him. He was Mexican and had a strange name that I can't remember."

Reba looked at Jack, then asked, "Could his name have been Mig?"

"That's it!" Reagor said. "How in the world did you come up with that name?"

Jack answered, "The handsome fellow who let you and the girls into the restaurant tonight is Miguel Alonso—also known as Mig. He is our newly hired bartender and bouncer. Maria has eyes for him, and we were afraid that he might take advantage of her. But you assured us that Mig is interested in men. Sounds like this alleged candidate for the priesthood swings both ways."

Reagor replied, "Now, I have to tell you the rest of the story. After coming home from Mexico, my cousin had to take two weeks of heavy-duty penicillin. Maria needs to keep her distance."

"Yikes!" Reba said. "It may be time for a mother-daughter talk for me with Maria. But I'm sure that after spending several months in forced prostitution in the Barlow whorehouse, there is no great wisdom that I can impart to Maria about the hazards of casual sex."

Reagor replied, "Obviously true. But I need to add that this Mig fellow told my cousin with a straight face that using protection was a mortal sin for a good Catholic like himself. He also crossed himself every time they ended up in bed together."

Reba shook her head and said, "Handsome, yes. But also a dirtbag."

Jack replied, "Mig's a great bartender, and he's eye candy for all of the women who come in. He would be hard to replace. I think once Reba discusses that Mig is a poster boy for spreading gonorrhea, Maria's IQ will overrule any hormonal rush."

Reagor said, "Maria is a very smart young woman. I don't think that you two need to worry about her. But, as to the question of where Hulga actually is now—I still have connections. Tomorrow I can find out if Hulga has crossed the border legally back to the United States. But for now, I need to collect my girls and head for the hotel. How about my coming in for an early lunch tomorrow after my girls head for the beach again?"

CHAPTER 47

THE PENICILLIN CLUB OF MEXICO

Shortly after 10 AM, Reagor reappeared at the restaurant. Maria met her and took her back to the kitchen. Carmen was serving breakfast for her children, Luis and Nina, who had slept in. Maria introduced Carmen and the children to Reagor. Reba looked up from the dishwasher that she was emptying. "Becky, I trust that you and the girls had sweet dreams at the hotel."

Reagor answered, "After all day in the sun yesterday, the girls were out like a light just as soon as their heads hit the pillows. I had to wake them at 9:00 for breakfast. After we ate, they were eager to get back to the sand and water. The girls are hoping that Maria can join them at the beach once the noon rush is over at the restaurant."

Jack emerged from the pantry with a large bag of corn flour on his shoulder. He smiled at Becky and asked, "We've all been on tenterhooks to learn what you found out about Hulga."

Becky answered, "Hulga absolutely has not crossed back into the United States legally. So, either she is still in Mexico or she somehow managed to slip across the border. I'll know later today whether she is back in Detroit or not. My bet is that Hulga is still in Mexico, hiding out."

Luis finished his French toast and went over to his mother and whispered in her ear. She gave him several one dollar U.S. bills and told him to be careful.

Jack explained, "Luis is really good at chess. He goes to the town square and plays with people much older than himself for money. Most days he returns with more cash than Carmen sent him out with."

Luis slipped out of the back door with a thumbs-up sign. Carmen took Nina back upstairs to play with her dolls.

Reba said, "Well, if Hulga is still in Mexico, that raises all sorts of interesting questions. If she was the one who burned Rodolfo up and mutilated him, her whole purpose for returning to Mexico should have been accomplished. Why take the risk of hanging around until the feds show up? It won't take a genius to connect Rodolfo's assassination with an angry niece who made no secret of her desire to avenge the death of her uncle."

At this point, B.A. wandered into the kitchen. He stopped short and gave a low growl when he saw Reagor. Maria went over to B.A. and said quietly, "It's OK, B.A. Becky is a friend." After a moment, the dog walked over to the corner and lay down. Guerrero the cat arrived shortly thereafter. After looking all around the room, Guerrero walked over to the dog and sat by him. Reagor looked at the cat and asked, "Is that the mouser for the restaurant? He and the dog seem to be buddies."

Jack smiled and answered, "Guerrero is a pretty special cat. He saved Maria's and my life by warning us to drop down before bullets came through the back door."

Reagor shook her head. "That sounds like something from a fairy tale. Every cat I have ever known has been totally self-centered and arrogant."

Jack said, "Scout's honor about Guerrero saving our lives. I found him starving in an alley and brought him home. I think the cat must have ESP. Hulga loved the dog, but absolutely hated the cat—particularly after Guerrero peed on her foot. It is really strange that Hulga would abandon B.A. and just disappear."

"Becky," Reba said, "I had trouble sleeping last night worrying about the fact that there are now three people who know for certain that we survived the huge explosion and fire at the compound. I am confident that you and the girls will be careful, but a slip of the tongue could alert the KGB and/or the Chicago crime group that not only are we alive, but we are in Mexico and very vulnerable. We already have enough bad characters eager to kill us as it is. I want to live at least long enough to bear Jack's child."

Reagor replied, "The girls and I will have sealed lips. We are all total unknowns here in Mexico, so I think it would be hard to connect us to the tragically deceased compound victims."

Carmen returned to the kitchen and began grilling shrimp and stirring a huge pot of black beans. Reba looked up and said, "We all need to get hopping. The early lunch crowd will start filtering in as soon as we open at 11 AM."

Reagor quickly responded, "I'm really good in the kitchen. Let me pitch in and help. I know that you must be short-handed without Hulga. Just assign me a task, and I will exceed your expectations. I've had enough beach sun already to make me a future dermatologist's annuity. The girls promised to show up for a late lunch, so I might as well become part of the kitchen team until then."

Mig came in through the back door and flashed a smile at Maria, who returned the smile. He announced, "The best bartender in town has just arrived. We sold a lot of booze last night. I hope that you guys have restocked. I'm going to head on out to the bar and get set up. These tourists don't wait until sundown to start their heavy drinking."

Maria said, "I'm going to begin putting napkins and utensils on the table. I can also keep an eye on the future priest and make certain that he doesn't take money from the cash register to send to Rome."

Mig laughed. He flashed another smile and said, "Maria, it would be my pleasure to have your beautiful company in the dining area."

Once Maria and Mig left, Reba remarked acidly, "We need to hang a big sign on that man's crotch that reads '*Peligro.*' No question that Maria has been smitten. Reagor, I think that Mig's fascination with the jerk's Speedo last night was more out of jealousy than lust. I need to have a serious mother-daughter talk with Maria before she joins the Penicillin Club of Mexico."

CHAPTER 48

A COMMAND PERFORMANCE

Lunch at Ellie's was busy, and having Reagor as an extra hand was a godsend. She quickly adjusted to helping fill orders in the kitchen and took over the cash register when Mig became very busy taking care of drink orders. Just before 2 PM when the lunch crowd had almost completely disappeared, Linda Kay and Ryn arrived and sat down with Reagor for a late lunch. Maria joined them. Mig came to the table to meet the two new girls and dazzled them with his Hollywood smile and good looks.

When Mig left to finish cleaning up the bar, Linda Kay said, "That is a really handsome man. I haven't had the remotest interest in a male ever since we escaped from the Barlow whorehouse. However, I might just make an exception for Mig."

Maria laughed and replied, "He's mine. I saw him first."

Reagor paused as if trying to decide exactly what to say, then simply remarked, "Let me caution you three young women, before you all go into ovarian flutter over Mig, that all that glitters is not gold. Perhaps the fact that he says he is considering becoming a priest should be viewed more with suspicion than admiration."

Ryn chuckled and said, "Becky, I think you're just jealous that you are too old for him!"

Reagor smiled and replied, "A word to the wise is sufficient. Let's talk about what you girls want to do this afternoon. I spoke with a man on the beach this morning at a parasailing place. He said that he can easily take three people up at the same time with one of his large canopies. Maybe Maria would like to go up with you two girls."

"Sounds great!" Maria exclaimed. "Count me in. I'm sure I can be spared for an hour this afternoon at the restaurant."

After lunch Reagor walked with the three young women to the parasailing place and paid for them. She then went back to the hotel and spent some time on the phone. By 4 PM she was back at the restaurant to help with dinner preparations.

Shortly after arriving, Becky motioned for Reba and Jack to join her at a table in the empty dining area.

Once everyone was seated, Becky said, "I have some perplexing news. My very good sources tell me that no one named Hulga Larsen ever worked for the Detroit Police Department. Also, no one there has ever seen a six-foot-two Amazon woman weighing over two hundred pounds. It would have been hard to forget seeing Hulga. How did you learn about Hulga's background?"

Jack replied, "We have become friends with a doctor in town named Victor Hernandez. He has known Hulga for a number of years. She often visited her uncle in town who owned a restaurant. Victor knew Hulga's background well. He told us that Hulga had been on the Detroit police force for almost ten years and currently was on the SWAT team. Hulga also talked about her police work."

Reba said, "Things just don't add up. Hulga's uncle, like us, refused to pay a weekly extortion fee to a group of local thugs. They burned his restaurant down and immolated the poor man at the same time. Rodolfo Mendez, was the man who was just set afire and mutilated in his hospital bed, was the leader of the local gang. Hulga held Rodolfo responsible for her uncle's death and swore to avenge it."

Jack said, "I see no reason why Victor would lie to us. Of course, it's possible that Hulga concocted an elaborate story and sold it to Victor. But why would she do this?"

Reagor replied, "If we stick to just what we know, I think it is safe to say that Hulga Larsen is still in Mexico and, for unknown reasons, created a past history that is a fabrication. We don't know for certain that she killed Rodolfo Mendez. We also don't know if Hulga was the person who placed explosives in the Cadillac of Ace Torres, who is part of a drug cartel planning to move into this area."

Before anything else could be said, Luis came into the dining area with a sealed envelope. He came to the table and said, "It happened again. I was playing chess with a stranger in the square. I beat him and won five American dollars. But I had the sense that he might not have been trying his best. After the game, he gave me a twenty-dollar bill for delivering this envelope to Jack."

Jack said, "It's déjà vu all over again. Remember that Ace Torres also paid Luis to deliver a message to us. Luis, was the man who gave you the money today well dressed like Señor Torres?"

"No. This man had one eye that turned out, and his clothes were not super clean. But he did not look like one of the beggars who are often in the square trying to get money."

Luis handed the envelope to Jack, who held it up to the light. "Nothing suspicious. So, I'll go ahead and open it."

Jack extracted a monogrammed sheet of thick paper. There was distinct English writing in an excellent hand. Jack laid the paper down on the table for all to read.

My Dear Mr. Woody Atwood,

Congratulations to you, Ava, and Leta for surviving the horrendous explosion at the desert compound in Texas. Your escape to Mexico was brilliantly engineered, if I do say so myself. Fortunately, I am one of the very few people who know who you people really are. Were I to share this information with certain interested parties in the United States, I think that your lives would be in immediate and severe danger. Even a cat has a limited number of lives. May I respectfully say that you three people are running out of lives very quickly.

The purpose of this letter is to advise you that we have some mutual interests that need to be discussed. My group is in a position to protect you, your pregnant wife, and Leta. Of course, this would have to be a quid pro quo situation. May I suggest that you visit me at my hotel tonight after the restaurant closes? How about 10:30 PM? Simply present yourself at the front desk and identify yourself as Jack Roberts, and you will be escorted to my suite. And please don't make the mistake of arriving armed.

Best regards,

Armando Cabral

CHAPTER 49

A HOBSON'S CHOICE

There was a moment of silence around the table. Then Jack said, "Sounds like a command performance to me. But I'm sure that whatever quid pro quo arrangement this drug cartel boss suggests will be nothing that we would even remotely consider. Señor Cabral will be asking for nothing less than our souls."

Reba shook her head and said, "This may be a trap to kidnap you. Our child is going to need a father, assuming we live that long. My vote is to ignore that note."

Reagor spoke. "The fact is that the cartel can kidnap any one of you almost at will if they choose to do so. All of you are vulnerable every time you go out on the street. And, of course, Cabral could send several of his armed heavies to the restaurant and take you by force. I agree with Jack. He doesn't have a real choice here."

Maria joined the table and heard only Reagor's comment. She asked, "Who, may I ask, has only a Hobson's choice? In the interest of your enlightenment, may I remind all of you that Thomas Hobson owned a livery stable in London in the late 1880s. He had an absolute rule that any customer wanting to rent a horse had to take the horse nearest the door or get no horse at all. So, who has no choice here?"

Jack replied, "Maria, we appreciate your attempt to educate illiterate rubes such as ourselves. However, if you read the letter on the table that Luis just delivered, you will understand my so-called Hobson's choice."

Maria scanned the letter quickly and gave a quiet "yikes." She paused, then said, "I think that Jack has to play this straight. Cabral seems to be very high in the cartel food chain. He's bound to have tight security."

Jack said resolutely, "I am definitely going to meet Cabral. We all may have more cat lives remaining than he thinks. But for now, the restaurant opens in 45 minutes for dinner. We need to pitch in and be ready for any early customers."

Ellie's was busy earlier than usual. Mig was soon spending so much time making drinks at the bar that he had to call on Reagor to take over the cash register. However, by 9 PM the dining area was starting to thin out. Victor Hernandez and his wife Sofia arrived and were seated by a smiling Mig, who took a long look at Sofia's impressive décolletage. Reagor was still at the cash register and saw the pair as they walked in. The next time she went back to the kitchen, she found Reba and asked, "Who is the lady who just came in who looks like a walking advertisement for the La Leche League?"

Reba laughed and said, "That can only be Sofia. She is the wife of the doctor we spoke about. Her special purpose in life seems to be exposing her prodigious chest anatomy for all of the world to see."

"That has to mean that her husband is Victor Hernandez, the doctor who shared Hulga's apocryphal past history with you. I would like to meet the two of them. You can introduce me as a friend from the United States here on vacation."

The dining room was empty by 9:45 PM. Jack paid Mig and told him that he was free to leave a little early. Mig blew Maria a kiss as he left through the front door.

She responded with a big smile. Reba, who had joined Victor and his wife at their table, gave a frown of disapproval. "The chances of Mig ending up as a priest are about the same as my growing a male appendage."

Sofia nodded in agreement. "That man is just too delicious to waste his life being celibate. The word around town is that he has broken a number of hearts—including married women. Your little Maria better be careful before she joins Mig's long list of conquests. She seems to have the hots for him."

Reba beckoned to Reagor, who had just finished closing the cash register. Becky came over to the table. Victor stood up, and Reba introduced Reagor to him and his wife as a friend from the States who was in San Lindo on vacation. Becky smiled and shook hands with Victor and nodded to his wife before sitting down. Jack came out of the kitchen with cups of coffee on a serving platter and joined the group.

Victor looked at Reagor and asked, "So what do you think of our beautiful little beach town?"

Becky replied, "One of my cousins visited here last year and raved about the weather and the beach. San Lindo is just as wonderful as she described it. And my cousin took a very special souvenir back with her."

Before Victor or his wife could ask about the souvenir, Jack stood up and said, "I need to take Victor with me to the kitchen to share some male secrets while you ladies get better acquainted. We won't be gone long."

Sofia quickly replied, "Jack, any bedroom secrets that you can share with Victor would be appreciated. He is desperately in need of new material."

Once Jack and Victor reached the kitchen, Jack pulled the letter from Armando Cabral and gave it to Victor to read. After Victor read the letter, he gave a low whistle.

"Cabral is very high in the drug cartel hierarchy. I am surprised that he would get involved in what would seem to be a small potato effort to get heroin across the border using the novel idea of faux bloody vaginas as a transport vehicle. One of my medical school classmates in Mexico City has seen Cabral as a patient and says that he is smart and very polished."

Jack hesitated, then said, "Victor, Reba, Maria, and I trust you completely. But there are a couple of questions I have to ask you. First, how does a local physician such as yourself have access to guns, a smoke bomb, and detailed information about local and national criminals? And, second, we have learned from a very reliable source that Hulga was never on the Detroit police force, nor have people on the force seen any giant woman like her. Also, she never crossed back into the United States after the brutal death of Rodolfo unless she did so illegally."

Victor was silent for a few moments, then said, "Jack, there are some things that are best if you don't know at this time. All I can say is that you can trust me completely, just like I trust you, your wife, and Maria. And as far as going to see Armando Cabral, I don't think you have any choice but to comply."

CHAPTER 50

CHOPIN'S *NOCTURNE NUMBER TWO*

At 10:15 PM, Jack slipped out of the front door of the restaurant and headed for the main hotel in town. There were still groups of happy tourists on the streets and in the bars. Jack mused that people on vacation in Mexico seemed to share the common misbelief that they are immune to the effects of heavy alcohol consumption. Toilet hugging was a ritual for many of them in the early morning hours.

Jack unobtrusively made certain that he was not being followed since he assumed that Cabral traveled with substantial security and might be monitoring his activity.

Once he reached the hotel lobby, he went to the desk. There was an attractive woman there who smiled and asked if she could help him. Jack identified himself.

The woman could not conceal a quick flash of fear that crossed her face as she pushed a button on a small intercom system under the desk. *"Un momento, por favor, Señor Roberts."*

A tall, muscular young man wearing a dark suit materialized from the room behind the desk. He motioned for Jack to follow him to the elevator. The man did not speak and his face remained expressionless. Jack thought to himself, "A stereotypical killer if I have ever seen one." Jack could see the bulge of a gun at the man's waist and could not keep from wondering how many notches might be on the pistol.

The elevator reached the top floor where there were three large suites. The man pointed to the same suite that Ace Torres had occupied. He did not budge as he waited by the elevator. Uncertain what to do, Jack hesitated, then walked over to the heavy, walnut-paneled door and pushed the bell. A voice came over the intercom.

"Right on time, Mr. Roberts. I like punctuality. The door is now unlocked. Please come in."

Jack opened the door and stepped inside. The room had undergone a quick transformation after its previous occupant had left. There was a new expensive carpet on the floor that no longer had blood stains. Another change was the presence of a black Steinway grand piano in the center of the main room.

Armando Cabral sat at the piano. He was a tall, strikingly handsome man wearing a velvet smoking jacket with perfectly creased white trousers. There were a few early strands of gray in his flawlessly coiffed hair. Cabral stood up and walked over to Jack and extended his hand. The aroma of an expensive cologne preceded him.

"It is so nice of you to accept my offer for a little discussion tonight, Jack. I am optimistic that we can come to an agreement that will be mutually beneficial. But before we talk, please sit on the couch. I will play a bit of Chopin's *Nocturne Number Two in E Flat* to get us in a relaxed mood."

Once Jack was seated, Cabral began to play. His fingers nimbly skimmed over the keys with a touch that had to be the product of hundreds of hours of practice. Cabral closed his eyes as if lost in a reverie and continued to fill the room with beautiful music. When the piece was over, Jack spontaneously rose to his feet and applauded.

Cabral walked over to a circular antique table and motioned for Jack to join him.

Once they were seated, Cabral poured two tulip glasses of cognac from a bottle on the table and offered one to Jack. "I wonder if I am about to be poisoned" Jack thought to himself. But there was no way that he could refuse the drink. Both men raised their glasses. Cabral smiled and said, "*Salud, mi amigo.*"

The liquor burned going down Jack's throat. He thought to himself, "If there's strychnine, I'll know pretty quickly."

Cabral sensed Jack's discomfort and said reassuringly, "No poison, my friend. I learned long ago that if a person needs to be eliminated, the act should be done in a way that makes it an object lesson for other people who might challenge you. Poison is a girl's way of taking care of a problem."

Jack replied, "Well, that is certainly reassuring. You play the piano like a concert pianist."

Cabral said, "That is what my mother wanted for me, but I grew tired of starving. When the opportunity for a better life came my way, I could not turn it down. With a great deal of hard work, I rose quickly in my new profession. Jack, you need to understand that the only reason there are people who supply drugs for your country is the insatiable demand from customers. The laws of supply and demand clearly apply. If there were no demand in your country, I would be forced to return to my former life as a musician."

"Mr. Cabral, I know that you did not have me come tonight just to exchange pleasantries. What type of quid pro quo do you have in mind?"

"Jack, Jack. Please don't be so impatient," Cabral said with a smile that showed his perfect teeth. "All in due time, my friend. Let me explain that those of us who control the drug market are generally refined, well-educated people. Just like any good business, we keep close records of distribution, profits, and losses. The unpleasant parts of the business we leave to well-paid underlings. We never get our hands dirty. And we are very charitable to people in the towns and villages where we operate. Each year we provide almost one million dollars for healthcare and schools."

Jack said, "With all due respect, dealing drugs is a dirty business. Your drugs kill thousands and thousands of people every year."

Cabral shook his head. "Jack, you have such a provincial view. How many people die each year from traffic wrecks, gun violence, and smoking? Drug use is really not that different. And a lot of people who die from a drug overdose are nonproductive citizens who are a burden on society. The loss of these weak people is actually a positive thing. Their demise is simply a classic example of survival of the fittest."

Jack shook his head. "This sounds like Hitlerian eugenics at its very worst. I'm not certain what you want me to do for you, but I am certain that my answer will be no."

Cabral answered, "It would be a real pity for a person as talented and smart as you are to make an unfortunate decision that will endanger your pregnant wife.

"Let me explain some things clearly. I know that you, your wife, and Leta were high-value targets for the KGB as well as a large crime syndicate in Chicago before your unbelievable escape from the desert compound that blew up into smithereens. All your enemies were convinced that you three were dead. How very convenient for all of you."

Jack said, "I cannot deny anything that you said. But if you knew our record well, you would know that we all have several of our cat lives remaining. We are not afraid of you or the thugs that you employ. It's time for me to leave. You make me want to puke."

Cabral's face hardened. "Jack, I am a civilized man and will let you walk out of here unharmed. Please realize that you are worth much more to me alive than dead. I can sell your location to some of my friends in Chicago for a huge amount of money. They will be thrilled to learn that your capture and torture are easily within their grasp. The KGB promised them over a million dollars at one time to capture you and your friends and film your extreme torture and slow death. There are some very wealthy people in the Middle East who will pay a fortune for such exotic snuff movies. The torture of a beautiful, pregnant woman will raise the selling price to the sky."

Jack stood up and said, "Cabral, you are evil incarnate. I suggest that you stuff that Steinway up your fat ass."

Cabral stood up with a smile back on his face. "That was a very ungentlemanly thing to say, Jack. And, besides, it's an anatomical impossibility. Let me simply say that I plan to come to your restaurant at 10 AM tomorrow with a concrete proposal to save your life and the lives of your wife and Leta. Unless you want to have to witness your wife being raped by goons, then having body parts whittled off, you will need to consider my offer carefully. And, of course, the *pièce de résistance* for the video will be when your child is removed piece by bloody piece from your screaming wife."

CHAPTER 51

SEWER SCUM

It was 11:30 PM when Jack let himself in the back door of Ellie's Restaurant. When Reba saw him, she ran across the room and hugged him. There were suddenly tears in her eyes. "I was so worried," she said softly. "I was afraid that Cabral might kill you or capture you to use as a bargaining chip."

Jack gave Reba a kiss and said, "You never used to worry about me like this. It's a shock to see the toughest woman I have ever known actually cry."

Instead of getting angry as Jack expected, Reba held him tighter and said, "Getting pregnant has messed up all of my hormones. I'm carrying your baby, and I want to be certain that when this child comes, I don't have to show him or her a photograph instead of a real father."

Jack paused a moment and then said slyly, "Are we sure that this baby is really mine?"

Reba pushed him away and snapped, "It's not yours. I had a quickie in the barn with one of the security guards at your crazy uncle's compound. And he is so much better as a lover than you are."

Before she could continue, Jack pulled her back to him and said, "I'm sorry, Sweetie. That was a bad joke. But, if the child is incredibly handsome and smart, we'll know for certain that I'm the father."

Reba shook her head and said, "Jack, we both know that you spent a lot more time in college pursuing busty sorority girls than studying. So, this literary allusion will likely escape you. But you need to read some Greek tragedy and learn about hubris."

Reagor spoke up, "Enough quarreling, children. Jack, we are eager to know what special proposition Cabral had for you."

Jack replied, "Well, nothing Cabral said made me feel very secure about being around to see my brilliant offspring. I have no idea how he learned who we are, but he knows that Reba, Leta, and I survived the explosion in the desert compound and are here in San Lindo with new identities. He's coming to the restaurant at 10 AM with a take-it-or-leave-it offer. If I refuse, he plans to let his crime buddies in Chicago know that we are alive and easy pickings here in Mexico."

Reagor interrupted to say, "I can assure you that there could be no leak from a U.S. government agency. You three were officially dead. Forensics managed to find only a few blobs of charred human flesh and bone after the raging fire was finally extinguished. No ID was even remotely possible."

Jack continued, "Cabral said that while we were still alive, the KGB had promised the Chicago group one million dollars if they could capture us. The plan was to make videos of each of us being slowly mutilated and killed. Such videos are said to sell for hundreds of thousands of dollars to perverted oil barons in the Middle East. Having a pregnant woman star in one of the films would raise the price even higher."

Reba said, "So the trump card Cabral has is the threat to share our location with the Chicago killers. No doubt he plans to sell information to them for a huge profit. Did he tell you what you would need to do for him in exchange for his silence?"

"No. He plans to let me know that when he comes to the restaurant tomorrow morning."

At that moment Maria, Lynda Kay, and Ryn came into the kitchen. Maria had a black eye that was almost closed shut.

Jack looked at Maria and asked with great concern, "Maria, what happened to you—and whom do I need to kill?"

Ryn said excitedly, "You should have seen Maria in action. Three low-lifes attacked us as we were walking home from the movie. One of them sucker punched Maria before she knocked out his front teeth and kicked the crap out of him. Becky has been working with Linda Kay and me on street fighting, and we took care of the other two. But suddenly several more sewer scum arrived and started talking about raping us."

Maria interrupted to say, "First, I'm fine. The asshole who punched me was the police chief's son, who will need major medical attention. When at least seven or eight more men appeared out of an alley to join the party, I pulled out my pistol from the waist holster and promised to kill the first person who came near any one of us. Some cretin announced that women never have enough balls to shoot anyone and lunged at me. I shot him in the crotch. His screaming and writhing and bleeding on the ground spooked the other cowards, and they beat a hasty retreat."

Linda Kay said very seriously, "I had a flashback of all the times the three of us were literally raped when we were forced prostitutes in the whorehouse in Barlow. I must have had an adrenaline rush since I picked up one of the men and threw him into a brick wall. I could have killed him without even a twinge of regret."

Reagor shook her head. "Things really ran off the rails tonight. I don't think Linda Kay and Ryn should be walking in town or at the beach without my being close by."

Jack asked, "Becky, you should have a weapon. The three of us carry at all times."

Reagor hesitated, then replied, "Actually, I do have a bit of personal firepower."

Reba looked shocked and asked, "How in the world did you get across the border with a weapon?"

Becky answered, "I'm taking the Fifth on that question. The girls and I need to head for bed. We'll be perfectly safe walking to the hotel. We'll come back in the morning. I want to be here when Cabral arrives just in case he brings a lot of heavies with him."

Jack said, "I forgot to tell you that Cabral has a Steinway grand piano in his suite. And the man can play like a true concert artist. Unfortunately, when our discussion became heated, I suggested a new anatomical location for his piano."

CHAPTER 52

TAKE IT OR LEAVE IT

Luis was perched on a stool by a window upstairs facing the street. Jack had promised him five American dollars to serve as a lookout for the arrival of Armando Cabral. Reagor was in the kitchen helping Carmen and Reba prepare food for lunch. Maria was also upstairs and armed. One minute before 10 AM, Luis stomped hard on the floor. When Reagor heard the sound, she slipped out of the back door and into the alley.

Jack, who was setting tables in the dining area, walked to the front door and waited for the chime to ring. As Jack was opening the door, Carmen left the kitchen hurriedly and headed up the back stairs to be with her children.

Cabral was wearing a light summer suit with an open collar that showed a dense growth of curly chest hair. He had a large diamond pendant around his neck.

Cabral smiled at Jack and said, "I, like you, am a punctual man. May I please come in?"

"Of course," Jack replied. "There is a table in the small alcove to the back. We can talk privately there. Would you like coffee?"

Cabral answered, "Thank you for your kindness, but I am something of a health freak. I never touch caffeine or alcohol. But a bottle of sparkling water would be nice."

Jack retreated to the kitchen and returned with the water. Cabral held the bottle up to the light, then took a large swallow.

"No poison, Scout's honor," Jack said.

Cabral smiled again. "I'm not worried. And in case you are concerned, I am not armed. There are no men outside waiting to rush to my aid if problems arise. Jack, I trust you, and you need to trust me. I can make your life and your friends' lives safe and very, very comfortable. The alternative would be very unfortunate indeed."

Jack replied, "So, let's hear it. What would I have to do to enter into the nirvana that you describe?"

"It's really very simple, Jack. I know a great deal about you. You and your wife were real CIA heroes for your country. There are few people as skillful as you are at weapons, street fighting, and tactical planning. I mentioned that there are unpleasant parts to our business that are handled by people we hire. But these people are often clumsy and indiscreet in taking care of the tasks that they are assigned. Some of them are so indiscreet that we have to fire them."

Jack asked, "May I assume that 'fire them' means kill them?"

"Oh, Jack, that is such a cold way to describe a necessary part of our enterprise. Let's just say that such people simply cease to thrive."

Jack asked, "Enough candy coating. What do you want me to do for you in exchange for what you describe as a very secure life?"

Cabral's face hardened a bit. "All right. Here is the proposition that you cannot afford to turn down unless you want to witness your beautiful wife and Leta being raped by countless scumbags and then slowly dismembered. And, of course, this would all be professionally filmed for sale to perverts around the world. I know that you would not want this to happen. After Ava and Leta are finally dead and through screaming, it would be your turn to work for an Oscar."

There was an ominous pause. Then Cabral continued harshly. "If you agree to join our company, your job would be to eliminate people we ask you to take care of. We would expect you to do this profes-sionally and cleanly, with no slip-ups. You could continue to live a normal life with your family in San Lindo and run the restaurant."

Jack said, "In other words, you want me to be a hired killer."

Cabral shook his head. "Jack, you have such a crude way to describe a very rewarding profession. You may ask why we would be willing to pay you so well when there are many people out on the street who would work for us very cheaply. The answer is that there are going to be big hits in the near future of people who are well protected. We will need someone very smart to plan and carry out these missions. I am convinced that a man of your experience and talent would be a perfect fit for the position."

Cabral paused to read the disgust in Jack's face. Then he continued. "I would guess that you would have jobs assigned to you no more than once or twice a month. We would pay you ten thousand American dollars for each successful job. The fee could go up for a judge or police chief. All travel would be in Mexico, and there would be a generous travel allowance."

Jack stood up. "Cabral, despite all of your cologne, fancy clothes, and smooth talk, you are nothing more than a disgusting piece of human shit. I would never agree to do anything for you. You make me feel dirty. Now get your nasty ass out of here before I decide to help you fail to thrive."

Cabral also stood up. He snarled, "You just signed a death warrant for all of your family. As soon as I am back in the hotel, I will be on the phone to a friend in Chicago. I'll ask them to be certain to have Technicolor film in the camera and a good sound engineer when they arrive in town."

Cabral pulled a snub-nosed revolver out of his pocket. "If you weren't so valuable to me alive, I would put a bullet right into your small brain. I seriously overestimated your intelligence."

At that moment Reba walked into the room with a pistol in her hand. "Cabral, I am a much better shot than you are. If you don't immediately drop your weapon, we are going to need to call a hearse for you."

Cabral's hand wavered, then there was a clang as metal hit the floor. He smiled at Reba and said, "I am looking forward to seeing your movie. It would be nice for you to keep your hair fixed and your womanly parts tidy. The film crew will be here before you know it. Remember to scream as loudly as you can for the sound technician."

With this, Cabral headed for the door. He stepped into the street and moved toward the black Cadillac parked in front of the restaurant. There was the sudden report of a high-powered rifle, and the man's head disintegrated with a geyser of blood shooting straight up into the air.

CHAPTER 53

A BULLET AND A SHOT OF WHISKEY

There was a black Cadillac limousine with darkly tinted windows with the motor idling parked in front of the restaurant. The driver took one glance at his exsanguinating boss, gunned the engine, and screeched forward with the tires spraying gravel. A second shot rang out and shattered the rear window of the car. The vehicle lurched to one side and smashed into a light pole and burst into flames.

Jack ran out of the restaurant and sprinted toward the burning vehicle. Just before he reached the car, the gas tank exploded, sending shrapnel in all directions. Jack felt a sharp sting on his arm followed by a jet of blood. It was too late to help the driver since the Cadillac had become a blazing inferno. There was the sound of a siren in the distance. Jack took the alley back to the restaurant to make himself a less-inviting target in case the shooter might be looking for another target.

Reba had come out of the front door of the restaurant following the first shot. She saw Jack head for the alley after the car exploded and was waiting for him at the back door. Reba saw his arm and gasped, "Oh, my gosh! Your arm is really bleeding. What hit you?"

"Must have been a piece of shrapnel from the Caddy when it blew up. There is bound to be some metal in my arm. Dr. Reba, if you will be kind enough to put a compress on the wound until the bleeding stops, then you can dig the piece of metal out."

Reba grabbed a clean dish towel and applied pressure over the wound to stanch the flow of blood. She asked with concern, "Don't you think you should go to the ER and get an x-ray and a tetanus shot?"

Jack shook his head. "No way I'm going to let one of the third-year medical students in the ER mess with my arm. I'm up to date on tetanus toxoid. Just give me a shot of whiskey and a bullet to bite on like in the movies, and you can dig away. You can boil some water and sterilize a pair of needle-nosed pliers."

By this time Maria and Carmen had gathered around Jack. Carmen hesitated, then said, "Why not call Dr. Hernandez and have him bring some proper instruments over?"

"I'll call now," Maria volunteered and headed for the phone.

There was the rising sound of a siren that passed by the restaurant with the engine roar of a diesel fire truck. The siren descended in pitch and then was silent.

Almost immediately a new siren began to wail in the distance.

Jack said, "That's bound to be Chief Cardenas or some of his pretend policemen heading our way. Someone must have called in about the gunshots and the body lying in front of the restaurant. I hope they don't make a four-hour crime scene. A body with its head blown off lying in a huge puddle of blood will not serve as an enticing aperitif for any of our potential lunch customers."

The compress worked well to stop the bleeding. Reba took a tentative look at the wound. "I see a glint of metal. May not be too hard to pull the shrapnel out. What brand of whiskey do you prefer, Jack—and what caliber bullet?"

Within a few minutes, there was a tapping on the back door. B.A. did not growl, so Maria felt safe opening the door to let Victor in. He headed over to Jack and said, "Your high-dollar surgeon has arrived. But first I need to know if you have health insurance or if you plan to pay cash."

Jack smiled and replied, "I'm hoping for some pro bono service in return for all of the free food we have supplied for you."

Victor nodded and said, "Fair enough. Now let's put your arm up on the table on this sterile gauze pad. I'll clean the wound up with some Betadine that will sting like hell. But we all know what a tough guy you are."

Victor put on gloves and poured Betadine into the wound. Jack's eyes narrowed, but he did not move or utter a sound. "Now I need to put on my operating loupes and turn the light up in the kitchen."

Victor blotted the wound with a gauze stick. "I can see the end of the metal. This should be a piece of cake." Victor took a pair of forceps and carefully put them into the wound. "Get a grip on your sphincters, Jack, because here goes."

With a deft move, Victor extracted a blackened piece of metal and laid it on the gauze pad. "Just like delivering a baby," he said with a smile. "Now I need to close the episiotomy with a couple of stitches."

Jack said with pretend seriousness, "Great job, Doc! That didn't hurt as much as my circumcision. Of course, the surgeon didn't need a loupe for that procedure."

Maria laughed and said, "Jack you must not have looked up the meaning of 'hubris' like Reba asked you to do."

Reba shook her head and said firmly, "Enough about Jack's anatomical fantasy world. Victor, any idea who blew Cabral's head off and shot his driver?"

Before Victor could answer, there was another tapping on the back door. Carmen let Mig in. He saw Jack's arm and said, "I'm going to have to ask for hazardous duty pay to keep on working in this warzone. There's a man with almost no head remaining lying in a lake of blood out front and a burning car just down the street."

Reba asked, "Mig, did you hear the shots that were fired?"

"Yes, I was leisurely walking to work when there was a single shot, followed a few seconds later by a second shot. The sounds seemed to come from the direction of the cathedral. A person in the bell tower with a high-powered rifle and scope would have had a good view of the street in front of the restaurant."

Jack asked, "Any idea who might have been the sniper?"

"Not a clue," Mig responded.

Jack looked at Victor, who responded, "There are a number of possibilities. One thought might be a rival narcotics group initiating a turf war."

Victor used two stitches to close the shrapnel wound and put a bandage on the arm. "Unless gangrene sets in and your arm falls off, you should be as good as new in a couple of weeks."

"Many thanks," Jack replied. "That surgical feat is good for a deluxe meal for two at Ellie's fine restaurant and bar."

Before Victor could respond, there was a sudden pounding on the front door and a voice shouting, "Police! Let us in before we break the door down!"

CHAPTER 54

SATI

Jack went to the front door and opened it. Police Chief Miguel Cardenas rushed in with several uniformed men behind him. The chief pointed a finger at Jack and screeched, "There's a dead man in front of your restaurant! We think that you shot him! My men are going to search this place for illegal weapons."

Jack said calmly, "Surely you have a search warrant. May I please see it?"

The chief sputtered, then replied, "We're getting it."

Jack smiled and said, "No search warrant, no search. Now if you and your men will kindly leave the restaurant, we can avoid any unpleasantries. And you may want to know that our employee Mig Alonso was walking to work when the shots occurred. He reports that the sounds came from the direction of the cathedral. You may want to check out the bell tower for casings. I would be nervous if I were you. Two cartel higher ups have been murdered in your fair city. The Federales are likely to come nosing around soon."

The chief's face grew red, and the veins on his neck popped out. He looked at Jack with intense loathing, then headed for the door and motioned for his men to follow him. Jack returned to the kitchen and found Reba and Maria with guns in their hands. "Happy to know that you guys had my back. The creepy chief and his men have left. It was in another life, but a woman once told me that the police chief in a small town couldn't find his own butt in the dark with both hands. That description is perfect for Miguel Cardenas."

There was another tap on the back door from Reagor. She came in and said, "I sure missed all of the excitement when I went back to the hotel to check on the girls who decided to sleep in today. There are a lot of policemen out front with a body with its head blown off. I am assuming that the body is that of Señor Cabral, and that his days of playing the concert piano are over."

"True," responded Reba. "He'll be playing only dissonant notes in hell. Small loss for the world. And Cabral's driver was shot as he tried to speed away. The Cadillac limousine plowed into a light pole, burst into flames, and then exploded. Jack had run out to try to save the driver and got a piece of shrapnel in his arm when the gas tank exploded. No good deed goes unpunished. Fortunately, Super Doc Hernandez was able to fix Jack up."

Maria chimed in, "I looked out and saw the car in flames. The Caddy served as a funeral pyre for the driver. Which reminds me—I've been wanting to suggest to Reba and Jack that they draw up a will that specifies 'sati' for the wife if Jack goes first."

"Sati?" Jack asked.

Maria nodded with a small grin. "Sati is an old custom from India that when a man died, his body would be burned on a large funeral pyre. Once the flames were red hot, the wife would voluntarily jump into the flames so that she would be available to serve her husband in the afterworld."

"Don't hold your breath on that one," Reba snapped. "Those women never voluntarily jumped into the fire. They were all drugged up and then hurled into the flames screaming bloody murder. But I'm sure Sofia would be happy to do such a noble thing for a husband as wonderful as Victor."

Victor laughed and replied, "She wouldn't even be at my funeral. Sofia would be too busy speaking with my life insurance agent trying to get the payout expedited."

"Returning to the real world," Jack said. "Victor, what happens next in our tragedy play?"

Victor paused, then said, "I think it depends on who the shooter was. If it was a rival cartel, this may cause Cabral's group to back off to avoid a bloody turf war. On the other hand, if the sniper was local, all hell may descend on us in the immediate future."

Reba noticed that Mig had been listening intently to the conversation. She said abruptly, "We have to open up for lunch in fifteen minutes. Mig, you need to get the bar ready, and the rest of us need to hit the kitchen. We can play 'Who do you think it was?' when lunch is over."

Maria smiled at Mig and said, "I'll go with Handsome and get all the table places ready."

As Mig left the kitchen, Reagor detained Maria and whispered in her ear, "If you can't control your raging hormones, you better hope that you don't have a penicillin allergy."

Maria had a puzzled look on her face as she left the kitchen.

Jack, Reba, and Carmen walked back to the kitchen. Jack immediately plopped down into a chair and announced, "After my near-death experience, I'll need to serve as a consultant and not a worker bee for at least three weeks."

Reba walked over to Jack and patted his head. "Poor baby. After your life-threatening injury, I'm going to insist that you sleep on the couch by yourself to protect your injured arm."

Jack stood up quickly and said, "I'm feeling much better already."

CHAPTER 55

TRUE AMAZON WOMEN

Surprisingly enough, having a dead body in front of Ellie's Restaurant seemed to serve as an attraction, even after it was covered with a tarp. Lunch was exceptionally busy, and tongues were wagging about the crime scene as well as the burned-out Cadillac limousine just down the street. Finally, just before 1 PM a police hearse arrived to remove Cabral's body, which had started to attract a swarm of flies.

Victor breezed in just before closing time for lunch and saw Reagor sitting alone. He asked if he could join her, and Reagor nodded. Once Victor sat down, he turned to her and spoke in English. "I was a little nervous about joining you since I heard about what happened to the man in the yellow Speedo who tried to become your dinner companion. May I ask how you learned to be so efficient in neutralizing creeps?"

Reagor smiled and answered, "I might have to kill you if I told you that, Dr. Hernandez."

Victor was a bit taken aback, but smiled in return. "Please call me Victor. I'm only a doctor in the office or at the hospital. At home I'm pretty much just a houseboy for my wife."

Reagor laughed and replied, "Please call me Becky. You are clearly a favorite of Jack and Reba. I have been amazed to learn of all the problems and dangers they have encountered since opening their restaurant. The travel guides I read before coming here described San Lindo as a picturesque beach town on the Baja Peninsula. There was not one word about murders or drug cartels."

Victor nodded. "This town was almost perfect until a few years ago when the criminal riff-raff started moving in. The police department and the local judge have all been bought and paid for. San

Lindo has become like a Wild West town in the 1800s in your country."

Becky said, "Two men have been shot down in cold blood here in the last few weeks. You would think that the federal government might want to come in and clean things up."

Victor shook his head. "Cartel profits are so huge that all levels of the government and federal police have been compromised."

Becky asked, "Any idea who shot Cabral and his driver?"

Victor paused, then said, "A couple of possibilities come to mind. One would be Hulga, who disappeared after Rodolfo was burned to death in his hospital bed. Hulga always made it plain that the only reason she came back to Mexico was to settle the score with the people who killed her uncle. Perhaps she went loco after taking Rodolfo out and decided to hang around and become a one-person vigilante committee."

Becky replied, "I really regret never meeting the infamous Hulga. She must be quite a female specimen."

Victor nodded and said, "A true Amazon."

Maria was passing by the table and heard Victor's comment. She paused and said, "Not to intrude, but I would like to point out that Hulga could not be an Amazon."

Victor smiled at Maria and asked, "And why not, my Mensa girl?"

Maria replied, "True Amazon women in Greek mythology only had one breast—and I'm pretty certain that Hulga came equipped with two."

Reagor said, "That's new information to me. Why only one breast?"

Maria replied, "The Amazons were ferocious warriors. At a young age all girls had their right breast cauterized since not having this appendage would make it easier to draw a bow and handle a spear."

Jack had walked up to the table in time to hear Maria's last remarks. "Man!" he exclaimed. "And Maria accuses me of having a portable BS machine. The woman is confabulating again."

Before Maria could launch a withering retort, Reba came up to the table and said, "We are all caught up in the kitchen, and Mig has only a couple of people still at the bar. Jack and Maria, let's sit down and take a well-deserved break. My baby is starting to make my legs swell if I stand too long."

Once everybody was seated, Reagor volunteered, "Victor and I were just discussing who might have been the marksman who took out Cabal and his driver. Victor has made a case for Hulga as a possible assassin. He analogized Hulga to an Amazon woman. Maria stopped by at that point to provide us with a gratuitous historical discussion of why Amazon women have only one breast."

Maria said, "I was just providing kernels of wisdom to the great unwashed."

Victor laughed. "Maria, you are a feisty young woman yourself—perhaps an Amazon woman in training."

Maria responded with an emphatic "nope" and pointed at her chest and said "two."

Reagor asked, "What was the second possibility that you were going to suggest, Victor?"

Victor replied, "The distance from the cathedral to the front of the restaurant is roughly 250 yards. Hitting Cabral in the head with one shot, and then taking out the limo driver in an accelerating vehicle with a second shot, would take an expert with a good scope. This makes me wonder if the gunman was a hired gun from another drug cartel that has eyes on this town as a transportation hub and wants to scare away any competition."

Jack added, "There was also a significant morning sea breeze that the marksman would have to correct for. A casual marksman could never have pulled off two such perfect shots."

Victor said, "I have an interesting tidbit to share. Looks like the police took Jack's comments about the cathedral to heart. A very reliable source told me that Mendez and his pretend police officers found two AR-15 shell casings in the bell tower of the cathedral. There are always priests around in the cathedral. It's hard to think how a stranger with a gun could get up into the bell tower, which always has a locked door—and then escape without being seen."

Maria said softly under her breath, "Unless…"

CHAPTER 56

TESTOSTERONE CRISIS

The afternoon passed quickly since there was a great deal to do in preparation for what promised to be a large dinner crowd. The violence that had previously taken place inside the restaurant as well as the assassination of Cabral in front of the restaurant had actually served to make Ellie's a preferred dining destination, particularly for young locals who liked the element of danger.

Carmen had become increasingly valuable and now ordered all of the food and did most of the cooking. Reagor had quickly learned to help in the kitchen as well as wait tables and operate the cash register. For the first time ever, there was a line of people waiting to be seated by 7:30 PM. The patio was finished, but there were not enough staff to open it for service.

After a frantic evening, the serving area was mostly deserted by 10:30 PM. Many of the patrons had headed to one of the local nightclubs for more alcohol and live music after their meal at Ellie's. Jack, Reba, and Reagor were taking a break in the kitchen and having some late dinner. Linda Kay and Ryn were in the main dining area and had just ordered dessert. When Maria brought the girls their flan de coco, she sat down at their table to visit. Mig kept looking over at the young women.

Ryn laughed and said, "Poor Mig is having a testosterone crisis. It might be fun to help him out."

Linda Kay shook her head and replied, "Count me out. Becky told me Mig has the wandering penis syndrome and reportedly sent an acquaintance of hers back to the States with a bad gonorrhea infection. But he sure is good-looking."

Ryn looked at Linda Kay and said, "Chicken." Then she gave Mig a big smile and beckoned for him to come join them at their table.

Mig looked undecided for a moment, then nodded and came over and sat down.

Ryn pushed her flan plate toward Mig and asked, "Would you like a bite?"

Mig replied graciously, "Thank you, but I am in training for a marathon in the fall and avoid all sweets."

Ryn mischievously replied, "The word on the street is that you don't avoid sweet women."

Mig laughed. "Never believe what you hear on the street. Actually, I'm planning to become a priest."

Linda Kay joined in. "Mig, you're going to set all the young ladies' hearts a-fluttering in the parish. There's bound to be some knockout woman who comes to you for counseling whose real goal will be to make you break your vows of chastity. Is it safe to assume that since you are seriously considering becoming a priest, you have been saving yourself for the church and are a virgin like all three of us are?"

Maria had a sudden coughing fit that gave Mig a chance to compose his answer. He was obviously a bit uncomfortable. "That's a very personal matter that is between me and the Lord. I respectfully decline to answer."

At this point Mig quickly stood up and said, "Excuse me, ladies. I need to get back to the bar. It looks like the last remaining couple in the restaurant wants one final drink before hitting the road. I have enjoyed your company."

* * * * *

Jack, Reba, and Reagor were still sitting in the kitchen talking after their late meal.

Carmen had been an amazing one-person clean-up crew and had gone upstairs to join her children for the night. The group had been discussing whether the death of Cabral and his driver would deter the cartel brain trust in Mexico City from continuing their push to take control of San Lindo or just incite them to bring in the heavy artillery.

Reba said, "Well, if there is any good news, Cabral was eliminated before he could sell the information that we are actually alive in Mexico to his crime brothers in Chicago. I never want to see anybody as malicious and evil as Randy Williams on our trail again. When last seen, he was soaked in gasoline and all aflame before falling down the paternoster shaft. I am not in the least ashamed to admit that his screams of terror were music to my ears. That monster for sure got his direct ticket to hell punched and didn't even get to sniff purgatory."

Jack hesitated before he said, "There's one large fly in the ointment. Cabral was offering me a deal to keep him from selling our location to the crime syndicate that Randy Williams was a part of. Cabral insisted that he could be trusted and that he was unarmed when he came to the restaurant. Then, the lying SOB pulled a pistol on me. I wouldn't trust a sleazeball like Cabral any more than I would trust a condom with twelve holes in it."

Reba shook her head. "Jack, surely you could have come up with a better analogy than that. I often wonder whether Maria or you are in more need of an emergency deportment intervention."

Jack replied, "Sorry. I'll work on developing some goody-two-shoes analogies that are not offensive. However, I would bet a small fortune that Cabral had sold our information long before he asked to talk with me. We better hope that we all have a plethora of cat lives remaining, because we are sure as hell going to need them."

CHAPTER 57

A LOVE NOTE

Luis came back to the restaurant from playing chess in the town square well before lunch time. He walked up to Jack, who was resupplying the alcohol for the bar, and held out an envelope. "Some man in a big Lincoln paid me ten American dollars to deliver this envelope to you. But I wonder if he made a mistake since the envelope is addressed to Atwood Stressel, not Jack Roberts."

As he looked at the envelope with beautiful cursive writing in English, Jack experienced an immediate fight-or-flight reaction with a spike in heart rate and faster breathing. Reba came into the room and saw Jack immobilized with an envelope in his hand. She said jokingly, "You look like you are in shock. Is that a love note from one of your old college sweethearts letting you know that her three-year old son looks more and more like you every single day? Perhaps that was the time you used the condom with the 12 holes in it."

Jack shook his head. "Not a joking matter. Luis just brought me this envelope that a stranger in town paid him to bring to me."

Reba took the envelope and looked at the name on the front. "Shit. Someone knows your real name. That rat Cabral obviously sold us out even while he was pretending to bargain with you. Our lives just suddenly became a lot more complicated and dangerous."

Luis came back into the room with a bottle of Coke that he had taken from the refrigerator in the kitchen. Jack asked him, "Luis, what did the man who gave you this envelope look like?"

Luis responded, "I was playing a game of chess in the square with an American tourist when a long black Lincoln pulled up and stopped. The chauffeur rolled down the window and motioned for me to come over. As I got near the car, a rear window opened and the passenger held the envelope out with a ten-dollar bill. He said in a very raspy voice, 'Kid, take this to Jack Roberts. And don't screw things up.' I took the envelope and the money. The car immediately sped off."

Reba asked, "What did the man look like?"

Luis replied with a shudder, "The man looked like he belonged in a horror movie. He was wearing large dark glasses, but his lower face was terribly scarred, as was the hand that held the envelope."

Jack gave Reba a look of great concern and said softly, "Surely it's not possible…." He paused, then gave Luis five dollars from his pocket. "Thank you, Luis. Go back to the square and make some more money."

Jack and Reba sat down at a table. Jack looked at the envelope, then ripped it open. Inside was a single sheet of expensive paper with very clear writing.

My dearest Woody,

How strange it is that we meet again in Mexico. I cannot tell you how excited I was when I received the call from Armando Cabral that you, Ava, and Leta were in fact alive in San Lindo. My friends and I have really big plans for the three of you. We will be getting together soon for a very memorable reunion. But, first, we need to wait just a bit for the cinematographer and sound technician to arrive. I cannot tell you how wonderful it is that Ava is pregnant. Not only will she be an erotic star in the film, but the child will also have a spectacular role when our perverted surgeon performs a live C-section with a Swiss army knife. I am so excited that I can hardly wait!

Fondest wishes,
Randy

P.S. You three are not the only people blessed with multiple cat lives. And fear not. We will be watching you day and night to keep you safe until movie time.

Reba and Jack sat in shocked silence. Then Jack asked, "How did the SOB survive being burned alive and falling down the paternoster shaft with spikes at the bottom? I wonder if the person in the car was really Randy."

Reba replied, "The scarring sure sounds like how bad burns would heal. We need to get together with Maria and Reagor and decide how to survive. Reagor should grab Linda Kay and Ryn and run before things spin out of control. We still have our cyanide pills stashed away." She teared up. "I don't want to lose this child, and I don't want to be raped by animals and cut up into small pieces."

Jack had a grim look on his face as he said, "We need to go on the offensive and not just wait here until Randy and his goons storm the restaurant. If I'm going down, I want to take out as many of those assholes as I can. Extinguishing Randy's last cat life would be a good start."

CHAPTER 58

DISCOUNT BREAST IMPLANTS

Jack and Reba were still sitting at the table with the letter in front of them when Reagor arrived to help with lunch. The grim expressions on Reba and Jack's faces told her that something was very wrong. Reagor came quickly to the table. Without a word, Jack pointed to the letter. Reagor scanned it quickly, then sat down. After a moment she said, "The odds against you three are getting way too great. Let me talk to the director and see if we can pull you out of here and get you to a safe house somewhere until we can all figure out what the best next step should be."

Jack answered, "Becky, you need to grab Linda Kay and Ryn and get the hell out of here before you get sucked into this mess. Reba, Maria, and I are not going to keep on running. We like San Lindo, and we enjoy having this restaurant."

Reagor replied, "What about Reba's baby? Doesn't he or she deserve the chance to live?"

There was a moment of silence. Then Reba said, "Becky, you can see what the director suggests, but there is no guarantee that we will follow his advice. I would give anything if Jack and I could just be normal people instead of fugitives with a mob of people hell-bent on capturing and torturing us."

Reagor closed her eyes as if deep in thought, then asked, "Can I take this letter?"

"Sure, take the damn letter," replied Jack. Then he added angrily, "Are you planning to keep it as a memento after Randy and his friends carve us into little pieces?"

Reba interrupted, "Jack, don't be ugly to Becky. She's trying to help us."

"I know, Reba. Sorry, Becky. But staying always armed and sleeping with one eye open really wears a person down after a while."

Reagor stood up and put the letter in her purse. "I need to run a quick errand before I come back to help in the kitchen. Try not to get into trouble while I am gone." She walked briskly to the front door and stepped out into the street.

Reba and Jack went back into the kitchen to help prepare food for lunch. Maria was busy making a large bowl of salad with pecans and mango slices. She looked up and said, "Carmen ran back to the market to buy some more shrimp. Some of the shrimp in the refrigerator had a bad smell."

Reba said, "Maria, you need to know that Luis just delivered a letter to Jack that a man in a black Lincoln handed to him out of the car window. He instructed Luis to deliver it to Atwood Stressel. Luis said the man's face was very scarred. The letter was signed Randy Williams and promised to capture and torture all of us just as soon as the cinematographer and sound engineer get into town. And we are being watched at all times."

Maria immediately replied, "That rat Armando Cabral blew our cover. Our first goal should be to take out Randy Williams for good this time."

Jack said, "Maria, Reagor thinks the CIA director could arrange for us to be taken out of here and put in a safe house somewhere while we decide if we would be willing to change our identities again and relocate to some god-awful third world country."

"Not for me," Maria answered firmly. She paused, then added, "But then I'm not pregnant."

Reba stood up and said, "Let's all pitch in and get ready for the lunch crowd. We can sit down and have a strategy session with Reagor this afternoon."

About ten minutes later, Carmen came in through the back door with some fresh shrimp. As soon as she put the shrimp on the counter, she went over to Reba and whispered something into her ear. Reba's eyes widened with surprise.

Lunch was busy, and having Reagor and Mig to help made a great difference. When the main lunch rush was over, Reba beckoned for

Jack to follow her to the pantry. "Carmen whispered something very interesting in my ear when she returned from the market with the new shrimp. She said that as she passed by one of the coffee shops on the way home from the market, she noticed in a booth way in the back that Reagor and Sofia were in deep conversation."

"That's sure odd," Jack replied. "What could the two of them possibly have to discuss? Unless, of course, Reagor wanted some advice about getting discount breast implants before leaving town."

Reba laughed. "Reagor would be the last person on earth to plop down money for a boob job. I can think of no topic that those two women could possibly share an interest in. Maybe Sofia was asking if Reagor could ship her some extra-strength smart pills from the United States when she returns home."

Jack smiled and replied, "No magic IQ pills are going to help poor Sofia. As my very astute scoutmaster once told me, 'You can't make chicken soup out of chicken poop.'"

Reba nodded in agreement and said, "Let's get back to work and finish in the kitchen so we can sit down with Maria and Reagor for a strategy session before it's time to get going for the dinner crowd."

When the two walked back into the kitchen, Carmen was preparing to dump a large plate of the bad shrimp into the garbage. Reagor saw this and quickly said, "Hang on a minute, Carmen. I bet Guerrero would love that shrimp. Cats are like billy goats—they will eat anything."

Jack shook his head and said, "Reagor, you don't know much about aristocratic felines. Guerrero wouldn't touch that nasty shrimp with a ten-foot pole. Put the plate on the floor, and you will see."

Reagor took the plate and set it down near Guerrero. "Time for a wonderful feast, little buddy."

The cat walked slowly over to the plate, sniffed, then raised a hind leg and peed on the shrimp.

Jack smiled and said, "Impeccable taste, Guerrero. Your imported caviar from premium Black Sea sturgeons will be ready soon. But, first, we humans need to have an important meeting about cat lives. Please feel free to join us and share your feline wisdom."

CHAPTER 59

AN UNUSUAL DEMISE

Reba, Jack, Maria, and Reagor sat down at a table in the empty dining area. Jack started the conversation. "Now that Randy Williams and some of his Chicago friends are here in San Lindo, our lives have become much more complicated and perilous. We don't know if they have any connection with the drug cartel people out of Mexico City who have been sniffing out San Lindo for a drug distribution center. Perhaps the cartel people would be happy to let their U.S. crime brothers do the dirty work of killing all of us. That would let the Mexican thugs walk in to San Lindo unopposed."

Jack continued, "We really have a simple binary choice: Do we run or do we fight? If one does a risk/benefit analysis, the obvious answer is to pull up stakes and let the CIA pluck us out of here and relocate us in a safer place."

Maria impatiently interrupted to say, "I am not in favor of tucking tail and running. If we do stay here, our only hope to stay alive is to have a strong show of force and kill Randy once and for all—and then wipe out his thugs one by one."

Reba hesitated, then said, "Maria, that sounds heroic. But one immediate problem is that we have no idea where Randy is. I think it is safe to say that he is not staying in one of the beach hotels. No doubt he does have men here to watch us and make certain that we don't escape. You all know that I am a fighter, but I'm really torn about whether to fight or run since I'm pregnant. This baby means a great deal to me. I don't want Randy and his goons to force me to watch as they rip this child out of my belly in small pieces with cameras running."

Reagor spoke. "There is no question to me what you three should do. You should let me talk with the director about extricating you

ASAP while you still have all of your body parts. But in all fairness, I have to share with you some new information regarding where Randy might be staying. I took the letter from Randy when I left this morning and asked Sofia to meet me."

Reagor took the letter out of her purse and put it on the table. "Does any one of you see anything on the letter other than the words that might be important?"

No one spoke for a couple of minutes while they all studied the letter. Then, Maria picked the piece of paper up and held it up to the light. She turned the sheet over. "Ah!" she exclaimed. "Now I see it. This is a high-grade piece of stationery that has very subtle embossed initials in one corner. The initials are J.E.M."

Reagor said, "Correct, Maria. Now what do you make of all this?"

Maria answered, "This piece of paper is too expensive to come from a hotel. Expensive embossed stationery like this had to have come from a business or private home owned by a wealthy person."

Reba volunteered, "Perhaps Randy borrowed this piece of stationery from a place that he was staying and wrote on the back side to make the embossed initials less obvious."

"Right on target," Reagor said. "I asked Sofia to meet me at a coffee shop to see if the initials meant anything to her. One look was all that she needed to say, 'Those initials stand for Juan Eduardo Medrano.' I learned that he was a very wealthy banker in Mexico City who grew up in San Lindo. When he retired, he moved back to San Lindo and built a mansion on a hill overlooking the bay. His first wife died, and Medrano had a hasty courtship with a young and beautiful exotic dancer. The man died in his honeymoon bed. The rumor was that the dancer lured him into some sort of kinky sex that involved her choking him to heighten orgasm."

"So, what happened to the dancer?" Maria asked.

Reagor answered, "The dancer had insisted that Medrano set up a trust fund for her as a condition of marriage. She pocketed a tidy one million dollars after his death and moved on to the next sucker. The bulk of his estate went to his only child, a son who has lived in New York City for years. There was a fund set aside to take care of the estate in perpetuity with a full house staff and also to care for

Medrano's four beloved Bengal cats. The son seldom visits in Mexico, but will occasionally lease the mansion to wealthy people."

Jack said, "This means that there is a good chance that Randy Williams leased the mansion and is staying there. No doubt there is a basement that will be absolutely perfect as a torture and filming room. I think some of us need to visit Randy and welcome him into the community."

Reagor said, "That would be super high risk. Williams is bound to have a goon squad that protects him. Also, if you leave the restaurant, you can be certain that you will be followed to make sure that you don't try to flee before your filming date arrives."

Jack replied, "I'm very good at picking up tails and making certain that they disappear. Obviously, neither Reba nor Maria could shadow me since they would attract their own surveillance people. I would need a shadow who is very experienced in espionage and who would attract no suspicion."

Reagor said, "Don't look at me as a potential volunteer. I think your chances of being able to actually get to Randy, eliminate him, and escape would be slim indeed. Jack, you have the right to choose to put yourself at risk, but you have no right to put your future child in grave danger."

Jack asked, "Do you know if Sofia has ever been to the Medrano mansion?"

Reagor hesitated. "I don't want to betray a confidence. But I can tell you that Sofia knows the mansion very well."

Jack asked, "Does that include the master bedroom?"

Reagor replied, "I'm taking the Fifth on that one."

SECRETS

There were so many dinner arrivals that evening that a decision was made to open the patio and turn on the overhead coolers. Linda Kay and Ryn were thrilled to be asked to wait tables in the patio and deliver food. Just as the dinner crowd was starting to thin out, Victor and Sofia arrived and were given a prime table in a small alcove off the main dining area. Sofia did not disappoint with an arresting floral print cotton twill midi dress with a plunging neckline. She and Victor lingered over their meal and then had after-dinner drinks followed by cappuccino.

Reagor sat down at their table when the dining area was almost empty. She smiled at Sofia and said, "That is really a beautiful dress, Sofia. It looks like it was designed expressly for you."

Sofia answered, "Thank you, Becky. But just like all of my dresses, this one needed a major tailor job to really enlarge the bodice. And after all that work, I still can barely fit into it. Sometimes I wish that I were a 35B instead of being so large." She paused, then added with a large smile. "Not really. I would never have trapped Victor with those measurements, would I have, Dear?"

Victor said with a perfectly straight face, "Everybody knows that I married you for your brilliant mind, Sweetie, not your body. While you ladies continue your discussion of body parts, I'm going back to the kitchen to talk with Jack."

Once Victor left, Reagor became very serious. "Sofia, there are some really bad people in town who want to kill Jack, Reba, and Maria. The information that you gave me today regarding Juan Medrano and his mansion was very interesting. We have reason to believe that one of the killers may be staying in the mansion. It would be a huge help if you could tell me everything you know about the property and the house. Perhaps you can sketch a floor plan on this napkin and show all of the entrances."

Sofia hesitated, then said, "I'll only help you if you promise not to say a word of this to Victor."

Becky responded, "Victor will never know even one word of what you tell me. What I learn from you may save the lives of Jack, his wife, and Maria. This is really important."

Sofia appeared to be weighing things in her mind. Then she began to talk. "When I was fourteen, I got a summer job working for Señor Medrano as a kitchen girl. He entertained a great deal and had incredible parties. Medrano was very handsome and utterly charming. One day he found me alone in the kitchen and convinced me to go with him to his bedroom. Although I was only fourteen, I was already a woman. To make a long story short, he seduced me."

Reagor said with concern, "That's not seduction—that's rape. Did you tell your parents or the police?"

Sofia shook her head. "Of course not. I enjoyed every minute of it. Juan was an incredible lover and very gentle. I learned so much from him. His wife died shortly thereafter, and he and I spent a lot of time in that fancy master bedroom. When Juan married that whore exotic dancer, I was very upset. Then the bitch killed him. My parents didn't understand why I cried so hard at his funeral."

Sofia became slightly tearful and wiped her eye with her dinner napkin. Then she continued. "I know every inch of Juan's mansion. He liked weird things and had a collection of shrunken heads from Africa. But the strangest thing was a real naked woman who had been preserved by a taxidermist. Juan kept this specimen in a locked room where he had a collection of weapons and all sorts of explosives. I asked Juan once who the woman was, but he became angry and said it was none of my business."

Sofia and Becky continued to talk for a long time until Victor and Jack came out of the kitchen and joined them at the table. Victor asked, "Well, did you ladies finally finish discussing body parts, shoes, and fancy clothes?"

Sofia glared and answered, "One thing you can be sure of is that we never discussed men who have preternatural talents in the bedroom."

Jack laughed and said, "Sofia, speak for yourself. Hopefully, Reba wouldn't agree with you."

Victor replied, "Apologies for my wife. It's that time of the month for her, and she can really get catty." Before Sofia could respond, Victor took her hand and said, "It's bedtime for me, Dear. I have a woman in labor at the hospital who may need a C-section before morning. I am hoping to grab a few winks while I can before the phone rings at 2 AM."

As Victor and Sofia got to the door, Sofia turned around and said, "Jack, be sure to tell Reba that she and Carmen need to do a lot more work on the tacos al pastor. There was not nearly enough cilantro or pineapple."

After Victor and Sofia left, Reba and Reagor joined Jack at the table. Linda Kay and Ryn had bought a Monopoly board in town and talked Maria into joining them at a table in the kitchen. Jack looked at Reagor and said, "You two ladies spoke for at least 45 minutes. Did you learn anything else about Juan Medrano's mansion that might help us if we decide to drop off a welcome basket at his door step?"

Reagor answered, "I learned things about Medrano and his palace that are hard to believe. Sofia was a veritable fountain of knowledge. Juan Medrano was a bizarre man who lived in a mansion that Jack's crazy uncle in the desert would have absolutely loved. Hang on to your hats—I have a great deal to tell you."

CHAPTER 61

FIGHT OR FLIGHT

After Victor and Sofia left, Reba joined Jack and Reagor at the table. There was a moment of silence, then Becky said, "Sofia and I had a fascinating discussion. I quickly learned that she is really not as IQ deficient as she pretends to be. Suffice it to say that she knows the Medrano mansion inside and out. She also knew Señor Medrano very well."

"Knew in the biblical sense?" Jack asked.

Reagor replied, "Not to betray Sofia's confidence, I shall have to leave the answer to that question to your imagination. But I can say that she started working in his mansion when she was fourteen years old and spent a great deal of time there for several years on and off. I learned that Medrano was something of a weirdo who collected shrunken heads and also had a nude woman preserved by taxidermy in a locked room with weapons and explosives."

"Yikes!" Reba responded. "Medrano sounds almost as strange as Jack's crazy uncle with his fortified desert compound."

Reagor continued. "Look at this napkin and you can see the entire layout of the Medrano mansion that Sofia sketched. She really has artistic talent. All the entrances and exits are shown, as well as a secret entrance with a punch-key lock that Sofia often used to visit Medrano. The entrance leads to a small suite separate from the main house and accessible from the inside by a disguised sliding wall panel. I think it is safe to assume that Medrano, like many wealthy Mexican men, had a number of female friends apart from his wife."

Jack asked, "Did Sofia actually have a job at the mansion?"

Reagor replied, "She started out as a kitchen helper at age fourteen. Medrano quickly spotted her and became her, shall we say, mentor."

Reba said, "Becky, we know that you were a high-level espionage agent for the CIA for a number of years. There were strong rumors that we heard at Camp Peary that you were at one time considered the most skillful assassination expert in the entire agency. Understandably, you cannot comment on that rumor. But just assuming that your job was to get into the Medrano mansion, eliminate him, and escape alive, how would you do it?"

Becky frowned, then said, "Let me reiterate that the best chance you two and Maria have to still be alive with all your body parts intact a week from now is to let me have the director arrange a quick extraction back to Camp Peary. You would be safe there until you decide whether you want to be relocated to another foreign country. If Randy Williams and his professional sadists capture you three, it won't be pretty."

Reba replied, "Granted, none of us want to die while being slowly hacked to bits. If I were not pregnant, I would be just like Maria— 'Let's go kick ass.' But the further along my pregnancy is, the less able I will be to help take out the bad guys. I've learned that maternal instinct is real, even for women as tough as I am.

"I'm now more concerned for the safety of the creature developing in my uterus than I am for my own life."

Jack moved his chair closer to Reba and took her hand. Then he said, "Becky, what we will decide to do is still up in the air. However, I really want to hear what your strategy would be to take out Randy Williams given the information that Sofia provided."

Becky hesitated, as if undecided whether to comply with Jack's request. Then she answered slowly, "If Williams were known to leave the Medrano mansion on occasion, I would simply find a safe vantage point with a long-range rifle and scope and wait until he exposed himself. But I suspect that he is happily hunkered down and safe, using his flunkies to go out for food and other necessities. That leaves the difficult option of getting into the house without being shot, finding Randy, eliminating him as quietly as possible, and then escaping. Not an easy task by any means."

Jack waited expectantly, then said, "Please don't leave us hanging."

Becky paused, then said, "This is against my better judgment." She hesitated again, then slowly spoke. "I would enter the house late at night using the private door and hope that the combination on the lock to the private trysting suite remains the same since Sofia last used it. If not, lock-picking skills would be necessary. Once in the suite, I would use the sliding panel to enter the main house. If I were discovered at any point by a guard, I would be prepared to take him or her out with a pistol with a silencer. Using information from the house map that Sofia provided, I would head for the main bedroom, thinking that Randy would be asleep there."

Jack interrupted, "The only weapon that you would take would be a pistol?"

Reagor shook her head. "I would go loaded for bear with a stun grenade as well as a regular grenade. And I would take two pistols with a lot of kick, as well as some extra ammo. A guard in front of the bedroom door would have to be neutralized.

"If the bedroom door were locked, I might have to shoot out the lock, which would not be ideal since this would awake anyone sleeping inside. And let me say at this point that having an armed second person might mean the difference between living and dying."

Reba commented, "The important question is whether eliminating Randy and maybe a few of his slimy friends would give us any protection at all. Now that our location seems to be public knowledge, the KGB and Chicago mafia, as well as the Mexican narcotics cartel, all have a vested interest in killing us. The KGB will never forgive one of their trained agents like me for helping the CIA. It's easy for me to say that if we are trapped in a hopeless situation, I would take my cyanide pill. But the child in my tummy just gave me a first kick today, and he or she would vote 'no' against this dual suicide."

Reagor gave a slight smile. "Does that mean that I can call the director and talk about an extraction ASAP?"

Jack replied, "I agree that you can talk with him about logistics, but no action until Reba, Maria, and I—as well as baby Herkimer—sit down for a discussion."

Reba was annoyed and quickly said, "First, you have no idea whether our child is a boy or a girl, and, second, I wouldn't name a pet rat Herkimer."

Jack replied, "Sorry, Honey. This was not a good time to give your chain a gentle tug. But determining how to stay alive is a lot more important than picking a name for our baby. We should be safe for another day or two. It's very unlikely that Randy would orchestrate a frontal assault here at the restaurant. Their plan almost certainly will be to grab us one by one with as little drama as possible when we venture out in public. We'll have Carmen do all of the shopping and stay holed up here."

Reagor said, "I will need to tell the director when I can give him a definite yes or no. Arranging a safe extraction will take a little time and preparation."

Jack answered, "You need to know that this won't be an easy decision. All of us are tired of running and assuming new identities. I promise that I will have a definite answer for you by tomorrow at noon."

Reagor agreed. "That will work. But I hope that you both know that there is really only one right decision. Better to be alive and safe at Camp Peary than to become stars in one of Randy's torture movies. Don't forget that Randy promised to give your unborn baby a starring role in the cinema."

Reba gave a little shudder and teared up.

CHAPTER 62

HELL'S GATE

Reagor stood up and said, "Time to collect Linda Kay and Ryn and head back to the hotel. I'll come back around lunch time to let you know what I have learned from the director about getting you people out of here with no missing body parts."

Reagor walked into the kitchen but came back almost immediately with alarm showing on her face. "Linda Kay and Ryn are gone!"

Jack asked, "What do you mean gone?"

"Maria is still in the kitchen. She said after playing Monopoly for a few minutes there was a tap on the back door from Mig who wanted to take all the girls for an ice cream cone at a nearby street vendor wagon. He promised that they would be back in twenty minutes. Linda Kay and Ryn were eager to go. But Maria decided to stay behind to help Carmen finish cleaning up."

Jack rushed into the kitchen and out the back door into the alley. He immediately saw a note pinned to the outside of the door:

You people are so stupid. We will be in touch tomorrow with a deal that you won't be able to turn down. Don't worry about the young women. We will keep them fully entertained—if you know what I mean.

Jack gave the note to Reagor, who had followed him back into the kitchen. She scanned the note quickly and softly said, "Shit. I should have been smart enough to see this coming. Once I took care of that slimeball in the yellow Speedo, I lost all hope of anonymity. This changes everything. I wonder why B.A. didn't bark when someone pinned the note on the door."

Maria replied, "That's an easy one. It had to have been someone the dog knows well that kept him from barking. It's obvious that Gonorrhea Mig lured Linda Kay and Ryn outside to let them get kidnapped. He then came back and pinned the prepared note on the door. The strange thing is that the cat Guerrero went to the back door and howled shortly after the girls left with Mig."

Reagor sat down in a chair and closed her eyes briefly. Then she raised her head and said, "There is no point in trying to find Linda Kay and Ryn tonight. They could be stashed away anywhere. They might even be on the floor of a panel truck heading out of town as we speak. But I would be willing to bet a great deal that they are prisoners in the Medrano mansion. It's obvious that Randy plans to use the girls as bargaining chips to get the three of you. We have to rescue the girls and wipe out Randy Williams once and for all before we can get out of this place. I have a great deal to do between now and morning."

Maria shook her head and said, "My poor friends. This is probably going to be a whole lot worse than being back in that whorehouse in Barlow. One other thing we need to do is to find Mig and cut his balls off."

* * * * *

Carmen left the restaurant early the next morning to shop at the market to resupply the kitchen. Reba had fully informed her about the missing girls and the note on the door. Carmen returned an hour later with boxes of groceries precariously balanced on a large pull cart. Once she had stored all of the food and supplies, she found Reba and whispered in her ear. Reba nodded and gave Carmen a hug.

There was a knock at the front door, which Jack answered, gun in hand, after B.A. had sniffed at the door and showed no concern. Reagor came in. Her eyes were red either from little sleep or crying, but she had an angry look on her face as if she had adopted a new persona.

Reba came into the room and walked up to Reagor. "Becky, sit down with us and at least have some coffee. You look like you have been up the whole night."

"I couldn't begin to sleep. Linda Kay and Ryn are like my daughters. They have made so much progress since you, Jack, and

Maria rescued them from being forced to work in that hell hole whorehouse in Barlow. I blame myself for letting them get captured."

Reba replied, "Let me give you a bit of good news. We know where the girls are. This morning Carmen ran into one of her friends downtown who works at Medrano's mansion. The woman told Carmen that she heard the sound of a truck last night and looked out to see a panel truck drive into the motor court. The driver and another man got out and dragged two women who were blindfolded into the house through a door that my friend didn't know even existed. So, unless they have been moved, Linda Kay and Ryn are being held in the Medrano private suite."

Suddenly there was a rumble in the direction of town.

"What the hell was that?" Jack asked. "That sounded like a major explosion. The last thing any of us want to do is run out into the street to see what's going on and get grabbed by a team of Randy's goons. Let's have a bite of breakfast and see how Becky thinks we should proceed. We are pretty well stuck until we hear from Randy and learn about his offer that is 'too good to turn down.'"

Reagor nodded in agreement. "We need to wait at least until darkness before making our move."

Shortly after 10 AM, Victor tapped on the back door and was let inside the kitchen. He was wearing green scrubs with blood flecks on the shirt and was breathing heavily. "I'll trade you some hot news for a Coke and one of those corn tortillas Carmen is turning out." Once Victor had swallowed half the bottle of Coke in a giant gulp and inhaled a tortilla, he was ready to talk.

"One of my old patients who works at the main hotel came by to tell me about the explosion there. Last night a black Suburban drove up with two mean-looking men and lots of camera and sound equipment. The men had one of the bellboys help them lug everything up to one of the top floor suites and tipped him fifty American dollars. Then they gave him another ten dollars to park their Suburban safely in the parking garage."

Jack interrupted to say, "Looks like the camera and sound crew has arrived. That may speed things up."

Victor said, "There's more to the story. This morning the same bellboy helped the men load all of the equipment back into the Suburban and asked him for directions to the old Medrano estate. The driver ran back into the hotel to change some American dollars for pesos. Right after he left, there was a huge explosion that lifted the truck up into the air. It flipped upside down and burst into flames. There was no way to save the passenger who burned to death screaming. The Suburban and equipment were a total loss."

Reba said, "What a pity that our potential Oscar-winning performances have been delayed. Becky, does this change any of your ideas about the rescue mission tonight?"

"We have to go tonight. I shudder to think what those animals might be doing to Linda Kay and Ryn." Her face hardened, and she added, "I swear those bastards are going to pay. There'll be a rush of new admissions at hell's gate before the night is over."

CHAPTER 63

PAID LEAVE

Victor smiled at Carmen and pointed at his mouth. She returned the smile and brought him another hot tortilla. Victor engulfed the second tortilla and finished the bottle of Coke with one giant swallow. He stood up and said, "I need to get back to the OR. There's a woman in labor who likely will need a C-section. I'll keep my ear to the ground for any more breaking news. All of you people would be well advised not to go wandering around the town."

After Victor left, Jack said, "Having to bring in new cameras and sound equipment may delay Randy's plan to become the Cecil B. DeMille of torture movies. I wonder if the deal that we supposedly cannot afford to turn down will be altered by the explosion."

Reba replied, "I, for one, or should I say for two, am not planning to play even a cameo role in any of Randy's cinematographic triumphs. We need to eliminate that monster once and for all."

Maria said, "Today was the second unexplained car explosion. I'm having trouble conjuring up an image of any local person who could pull this off. But there sure seems to be some mystery person working on our behalf."

Jack responded, "Well, Hulga remains unaccounted for. But it is hard to believe that she would hang around after she took care of the person responsible for the death of her uncle. She just disappeared into thin air. And we still have no idea why Victor and she would spin the false tale about her being on the Detroit police SWAT team. Things just don't add up."

Reba added, "And how can a busy doctor like Victor magically come up with guns and explosives on short notice? Sometimes I find myself wondering if Victor is playing us for fools."

Jack replied firmly, "We definitely can trust Victor. In all modesty, I have the rare gift of being able to read people accurately at the first encounter. As an example, when I first saw Reba across the cadaver table in med school, I knew that she would fall hopelessly in love with me."

Reba shook her head. "What a giant crock of BS. I only agreed to see Jack as an act of kindness. And then he cruelly took advantage of me," she added with a slight smile.

Jack said, "I'm tempted to come right over and pinch your nose, but it's growing so fast that I might poke my eye out."

Maria interjected, "Here we are all worrying about whether we will still be alive in the next 24 hours, and you guys are still quibbling about who seduced whom."

Before Maria could finish, Reagor walked briskly back into the room. "I just got off the phone with Sofia. She has agreed to come to the restaurant to answer any questions about the layout of the Medrano mansion. She should be here in fifteen minutes. We need to know the geography of the grounds and house to the nth degree. Things may happen really fast tonight."

Twenty minutes later Sofia arrived. Amazingly enough she was well covered and not wearing a scanty top to display her favorite assets. She willingly sat down with the four of them and fielded a stream of questions about the floor plan of the large house and the surrounding grounds. After thirty minutes she looked at her watch and announced that she had to leave for a hair appointment and was quickly gone.

Reba said, "Sofia is not as dumb as we all thought. Maybe brain size is not inversely related to cup size."

Reagor commented, "We got a great deal of helpful information. I was amazed that she knew the location of the main circuit breaker and also remembered the combination to the private entrance after all these years."

Jack replied, "Agreed. But if the combination of the door lock has been changed, it could take me several minutes to pick it. The fact that the door opens to a short hallway with a right turn should give some cover to whomever enters that way. It also would be nice to know if the doors to the mansion are wired with an alarm system. If we are still planning to rescue the girls tonight, I should make an earlier visit to determine if the old combination still works and if there is an alarm system."

Reagor said, "From what Sofia told me during our private chat, Medrano had several armed guards at all times. He may well have considered having an alarm unnecessary. But before we can firm up our strategy for tonight, we need to see what proposition Randy Williams has cooked up."

Lunch time came and went with no message from Randy and no new events. The restaurant was only moderately busy and was empty by 2 PM when the front door was locked. While the after-lunch cleanup was going on in the kitchen, Carmen revealed that one of her friends who is on the Medrano mansion's permanent house staff came by and shared some news. The people leasing the mansion paid all of the staff for a week in advance and told them that they would not be needed for the next seven days.

Jack said, "It's obvious what that means. Randy has a new film and sound crew on the way and wants complete privacy for his forthcoming torture movie tour de force."

B.A. suddenly became on high alert and went quickly to the front door where he gave a growl. Jack followed him with a pistol in hand. He looked through the peephole and saw an old woman who looked like a street person. "What do you want?" Jack asked. "If you come to the back door, we have some food left over from lunch that we can give you."

The woman answered, "I don't need any food. Some man near the marketplace hired me to deliver this envelope to Woody Stressel. He paid me more pesos than I have seen in a long time. Are you Señor Stressel?"

Jack answered affirmatively and cracked the door enough to take the envelope. He relocked the door and went back to the kitchen. "OK, ladies. Here is the message that we have been waiting for all day. Let's all sit down, and I will open the envelope to see if we get to pass Go and collect one hundred dollars or not."

CHAPTER 64

ONE HECK OF A DEAL

Jack opened the envelope and took out a piece of stationery identical to the one Randy had used for the first note. "Not much imagination here. Randy used the same high-dollar stationery from the Medrano estate. I'll go ahead and read this out loud so we will all have the content simultaneously."

A special good day to all of you expats in sunny Mexico. Now that all opening pleasantries of civil discourse have been honored, we will get down to business immediately. At the outset, let me point out what a weak hand you people hold with no face cards and no aces. In striking contrast, in my hand I hold two perky young women who have stated a strong preference not to have roles in my upcoming movies. I shared with them some of my favorite film clips from my days at the medical school crematorium. These young ladies just want to get back to the safety of the good old USA as quickly as possible. And this is certainly a possibility. Neither I, nor the KGB, nor our cartel friends have any fight to pick with them.

Here is the deal that I am offering, which you should jump at while there is still time. I will return the two young women unharmed in exchange for Señor Stressel, Señora Volkov Stressel, and Señorita Mitchell. True, not exactly quid pro quo, but the best deal that you are going to get. And let me point out that in my strong hand are a number of experienced killers who are just salivating at the mouth for a chance to get to know the two young women a great deal better. It would be a pity for that to happen. Never forget that we have you under constant surveillance. There is no way you can escape. I promise that we will get all of you one way or another.

Out of the goodness of my heart, I will give you 24 hours to respond to my kind offer. If you agree to my terms, the three of you are to walk out into the alley behind the restaurant at 3 PM tomorrow afternoon with your hands above your heads and no weapons. There will be a black Suburban for you to enter. Please don't do anything foolish. There will be a number of armed men in other vehicles parked in the alley. What happens if the three of you don't show up? It will not be pretty. First, I will advise my men that they can amuse themselves with the young women in any creative ways that they might choose.

But we will be certain to keep the girls alive to feature them as co-stars in the impending movies with the three of you. You have no idea how much money people in the Middle East will pay for these movies. I have a buyer who is willing to pay one million dollars to see a baby removed from the belly of a woman using just a Swiss Army knife and pliers. Of course, our price includes Technicolor and advanced sound to capture all of the screams.

Think carefully, my good friends.

Randolph Williams

There was a moment of silence. Then Jack said, "These people are animals. Tonight will be our only chance to rescue Linda Kay and Ryn and wipe out the rat nest. As soon as it is fully dark, I need to get on the estate grounds and find out if the old combination works on the punch lock and whether the doors are alarmed."

Reagor said, "Jack, how pray tell do you plan to leave the house without one of Randy's surveillance goons grabbing you? If you take your Jeep, you can be certain that you won't get far before getting rammed off the road and captured. Maybe Victor can be of assistance since he seems to know everybody in town."

"He should be out of the OR by now. I'll give his office a call." Jack walked to the phone and dialed. He then began to have a long conversation in a low voice. When he got off the phone he said, "Later tonight three of us need to get to the estate undetected. Victor has a solution, but it will only work once. He has a friend who operates a private garbage pickup company that actually services the Medrano estate. The trucks often run late at night. Victor can have his friend drive one of the trucks down the alley at whatever time we suggest."

Reba interrupted. "You said three people, which obviously excludes me. An extra body with a gun might save some lives."

Jack replied, "Sweetie, you are now five months pregnant with ankle swelling by the end of the day and constant fatigue. We can't risk you and the baby."

Reagor added, "Reba, I have made arrangements that if we don't come back, you and your baby will be extricated as an emergency and taken across the border to a safe house. With your fatigue, you would only slow us down if you insist on joining us. You have to be reasonable."

Reba started to object, then teared up. "I used to be the best damn woman fighter on two feet, but now I've been turned into a blubbering ninny."

Jack walked over to Reba and hugged her. "You will have a job to do while we are gone. It is certainly possible that Randy might send a probing mission to emphasize the fact that his people are watching our every move. You will need to stay armed and awake with B.A. at your side in case trouble erupts. And, one thing I failed to mention is that the driver's brother will occupy the other seat in the cab of the garbage truck. We three will be riding in the smelly back. I think we are going to have to scrub plans for my early scouting mission and pray that we can get into the house without alerting Randy and his band of thugs."

Reagor said, "Jack, tell Victor to have the garbage truck in the alley at 1 AM. Now let's sit down and go over the strategy again for rescuing the girls and killing all of the cockroaches in the house."

CHAPTER 65

FREE DRINKS–AGAIN

After a lengthy discussion and a detailed review of Sofia's sketch of the floor plan of the Medrano mansion, everyone pitched in to get ready for the evening dinner crowd. Jack had suggested closing the restaurant for the night to allow more time for preparation for the rescue mission. But Reba had quickly pointed out that Ellie's was almost certainly under surveillance and shutting down might arouse suspicion.

Not having Mig to handle the bar was an immediate problem, but Reagor stepped in and quickly showed her skills as a bartendress and mixologist. If she was worried about her girls, she never showed it. One of the customers had come into the restaurant already well lubricated. After downing a couple of shots of whiskey at the bar, he moved over and sat by a young woman who was having a sandwich. She was wearing a beach robe that the man began to tug at. The woman tried to slap him, but he grabbed her wrist.

Reagor immediately came from around the bar and ordered, "Leave that woman alone, or you will have to deal with me. It's time for you to head for home, Bozo."

The man snarled and said, "Says who? No bitch tells me what to do."

Reagor gave him a cold stare and said quietly, "This bitch does."

The man released the woman's wrist, then stood up and pulled a long stiletto out of his belt. "How would you like for me to slit your throat, you whore?"

Reagor announced in a loud voice for all to hear, "No need for concern, people. This will be over in the next few seconds." She approached the man, and when he slashed at her, Reagor disarmed him with one lightning-quick move and yanked his arm behind his back with a loud crack of breaking bones.

The man began to curse. "You broke my arm, you bitch."

Reagor gave the broken arm a large yank to dislocate the shoulder before releasing the arm. The man began to scream.

Reagor announced, "We are really sorry for the disturbance, friends. As soon as I help this gentleman outside, I'll open up the bar for free drinks until closing." After saying this, Reagor grabbed the man's long, greasy hair and dragged him to the front door, shoving him into the street with a swift kick to the butt.

The rest of the evening was uneventful. Once the front door was locked, there was a quick clean-up of the dining area and kitchen. Carmen went upstairs to check on Luis and Nina while Maria fed B.A. and Guerrero late suppers. Then Maria went over to Reba who was sitting in a chair with her feet propped up. "Reba, I want to go over the commands for B.A. just in case you need his help tonight while we are gone. He knows you well, and I feel certain that he will respond to commands from you."

Jack commented, "We'll be meeting the garbage truck in the alley in less than three hours. Let's hope that it's not too smelly. I learned from Victor that his friend who is the driver will give us the code to the back gate of the estate when he lets us out there. We should be able to slip up to the entrance to Medrano's mistress suite in the darkness."

Maria asked, "What about guard dogs?"

Jack replied, "Once Medrano was dead, the need for tight security was gone. His two guard dogs were sold. And I don't think a short-term lease person like Randy would need dogs when he has his own security men. But we'll have to wait and see if there are any outside guards. My guess is that Randy feels safe at the estate and won't be expecting any unfriendly visitors."

There was a tap on the back door. B.A. was near the door and sat perfectly still. Maria opened the door carefully and saw Victor standing there with a wooden chest with wheels and a pull handle. He dragged the chest inside and said, "A few provisions for your excursion tonight."

Reagor came into the kitchen, walked over to Victor, and asked, "Were you able to get everything on my wish list on such short notice?"

Victor smiled and replied, "Of course, Becky. I always aim to please."

Becky lifted the heavy chest with little effort and set it on the table. She undid the latch and opened the lid. Inside were several pistols, a rifle with a scope, ammunition, and a variety of grenades. Becky reached into the chest and fished out a pair of goggles.

"Night vision goggles. Perfect, Victor. The local Five and Dime is going to have to restock after your visit tonight. I'm going to take these goggles and go upstairs and check out the street and alley for anybody watching the restaurant. We need to be certain that there is no snooper in the alley when we load into the truck."

Reba asked, "Victor, weren't you afraid that some of Randy's men might try to kidnap you on the way over tonight?"

Victor answered, "I had a patient who drives a city cab pick me up at the back of the office. He drove an erratic route until I was certain that I was not being followed. The alley was pitch black, so I felt pretty safe—but I did have a little friend with me." He lifted his shirt to show a small pistol tucked in at the waist.

"The driver will be back in exactly 20 minutes, which will give me just enough time for a large piece of Carmen's pecan pie and a glass of milk."

Maria answered, "Your pie and milk are on the way. And we won't tell your wife."

Just as Victor was putting the last piece of pie into his mouth, Reagor came back into the kitchen. "There is definitely a watcher in an old pickup truck parked at the end of the street." She took the rifle out of the chest and sighted down the barrel. "I'm just going to make certain that our little friend doesn't get bored."

There was the low sound of a motor in the alley. Victor stood up and said, "Time for me to head for home. I'll start an abbreviated novena for you folks' safety and the safety of the girls."

Just as Victor stepped into the alley, there was the sharp crack of a rifle from upstairs.

CHAPTER 66

OLFACTORY ADVENTURES

Reagor came back into the kitchen with the rifle in hand. She put the weapon down on the counter and said, "I feel certain that our little friend wet his pants when the bullet came crashing through the windshield of his car."

Maria asked with obvious disappointment, "Why didn't you do the world a favor and put a bullet through the scumbag's head?"

Reagor replied, "The man was bound to be some low-level hire. Eliminating him would serve no useful purpose. Later tonight is when we start exterminating vermin."

Reba stood up and walked over to look into the wooden chest that Victor had brought. "This is all first-class stuff. Reagor, how can a busy doctor in a small beach town in Mexico have immediate access to so much fire power?"

Reagor simply replied, "Life is full of mysteries. Now let's go over once again how we deal with any possible guards outside of the house. We want to avoid using guns if at all possible. If you look in the bottom of Victor's surprise chest, you will find two piano wire garrotes with handles. Jack and I will each carry one. Taking someone out with a garrote is much quieter than firing a weapon."

Jack said, "Having an overall strategy is important, but on-the-fly tactics will determine if we will be successful in rescuing the girls, finally putting a silver spike through Randy's heart, and escaping intact."

Maria asked, "Assuming we get Linda Kay and Ryn out of the house, how are we all going to get back to the restaurant?"

Jack said, "Simple. The man with the garbage truck will wait for us outside the back gate. He'll know that if we are not back in forty-five minutes, there is no point in him waiting any longer. Becky's extraction plan for Reba will be activated by morning, and she and the baby will be safe."

Reba bit her lip and tried not to tear up.

Shortly before 1 AM, Reagor, Jack, and Maria had gathered in the kitchen. They were all dressed in black and each had a small backpack. Guerrero walked over to the door to the alley and began a low growl. "Truck's coming," Jack said matter-of-factly. B.A.'s ears perked up, and he walked over to the door and gave a single low bark. The sound of a truck motor approaching slowly became audible.

Jack opened the door and said, "OK, guys, time to load up." There was an old deuce and a half military truck with an open back containing a number of garbage cans idling in the alley.

The three black figures quickly sprinted to the back of the truck and hoisted themselves into the cargo bed. Jack tapped the back window of the cab, and the truck started slowly moving down the alley.

"Pee-ew!" Maria exclaimed softly. "It smells like we all just fell down a latrine."

Reagor cautioned, "We need to all flatten out in the bed of the truck and keep quiet. This truck is going to pass through town before it heads up into the hills. No telling where Randy has people staked out."

Once the truck left town, it was quickly on an uneven dirt road that bounced the rear passengers up and down. Maria said in a low voice, "Good thing Reba didn't come. She would have broken her water for sure."

As the truck climbed, the lights of the Medrano estate slowly came into view. The driver soon took a side road lined with coastal chaparral and desert scrub that led within a hundred yards of the massive front gate. He continued along the periphery of the property on a narrow unfinished road that dead-ended near the back gate.

The driver killed the headlights and turned the big diesel engine off thirty yards from the gate. There was a sliver of moon in the sky that provided just enough light to reveal three shadowy figures melting into the darkness. They moved silently until they reached the gate. Jack used a flashlight covered with a black cloth that gave just enough illumination to see the large combination lock on the tall iron gate. He plugged in the numbers from the scrap of paper that the driver had given him and pulled on the hasp. It did not move. Jack pulled much harder. Nothing. He spun the dial to clear the lock, then partially uncovered the flashlight to study the piece of paper again.

Reagor, who had been watching intently, pointed to the last number on the paper and raised two fingers. Jack nodded. He had initially read the number as a three. Jack re-entered the correct numbers and was then able to open the lock easily. The gate was very heavy, and it made a grinding sound as it was pushed part-way open, causing Jack, Reagor, and Maria to freeze. Then they saw the beam of light from a high-powered flashlight coming in their direction. Reagor motioned everyone away from the gate just before the beam of light fixed on it. She took her backpack off and reached inside and pulled out her piano-wire garrote.

A large man appeared who was cautiously moving toward the gate with a flashlight in one hand and a rifle in the other. Jack, who was off to the side of the dirt road that led from the gate to the house, gave a loud cough. The guard whirled toward the direction of the cough. Reagor had the piano wire around his neck instantaneously and bent over with the gasping man on her back. The guard gasped and spewed blood out of his mouth as the wire shut off all blood to the brain and crushed his trachea. It was over quickly.

Jack closed the gate and reached through the bars to reset the lock. Then he dragged the body several feet off the road into the scrub brush. On the way back to the road, Jack tripped over a solid object in the dark and fell face forward. Using the guard's flashlight, he identified a strange wheelbarrow with a giant front wheel. Jack lifted the wheelbarrow handles and found that it could be moved easily over the hard-packed road inside the gate. He hesitated, then immediately loaded the body of the strangled guard into the wheelbarrow and rolled it to where Reagor and Maria were standing waiting for him.

Jack asked Reagor quietly, "Did you bring any grenades?"

Reagor gave a thumbs-up sign. Jack pointed at the body of the lifeless guard sprawled over the wheelbarrow with a fixed, sardonic grin of death on his bloody face. Reagor looked perplexed for a minute. Then, with a look of understanding, she extended her left hand face down and made a fist with the other hand, placing it under the first hand. Then Reagor suddenly jerked the upper hand up into the air. Jack nodded in agreement.

CHAPTER 67

DATE NIGHT

As the three black-clad figures moved closer to the house, they encountered periphery lights that made their approach more dangerous. Reagor and Maria left the road and sought the cover of local vegetation. Jack was forced to stay on the road to continue pushing the wheelbarrow carrying the dead body of the guard whom Reagor had garroted. Flickering lights suddenly appeared in the distance on the periphery road that the truck had taken to reach the area near the back gate.

Maria whispered, "That looks like car headlights. It has to be someone who knows the roads and is expected. Let's backtrack and hide out by the gate. Someone has to get out to open it. If we are really lucky, there will only be the driver in the car."

Jack said to Reagor, "My turn, Becky. Let me have one of the garrotes out of your backpack. It will be your turn to cough."

Maria quickly responded, "Let's be a bit more creative. My vote is to let me stand in front of the gate with my top pulled part way open. Working on the assumption that the driver is a normal man, this will distract him much better and for longer than a cough. When the driver gets out, I can explain that my blind date forced me out of the car when I refused to cooperate with his advances. By this time, Jack will have the garrote in place, and the driver will be on the way to a rendezvous with the devil."

Reagor nodded and said, "Good idea, Maria. Also, this will distract anyone else in the car long enough for me to take care of them."

Jack pushed the wheelbarrow with the body in it off the road, and the three of them retreated to the gate. Jack opened the lock, then closed it when everyone was outside. He hid in a clump of brush with the garrote in hand. Becky took the other side and waited with a drawn pistol. As the vehicle came closer, Becky announced in a stage whisper, "The headlights look like the pickup truck I shot the windshield out of."

As the truck approached the gate, Maria unzipped her top and stood in front of the gate waving her hands. The driver slowed down, then stopped ten yards in front of the gate and put on the high beams.

"Please help me!" Maria yelled. "My boyfriend dumped me out here."

The driver's side door opened, and a short Mexican man stepped out. He looked Maria up and down, then smiled and walked toward her. When he was near, he said, "This is really my lucky day," and reached out to open her top more. That was the man's last act on earth. Jack hoisted the man into the air with the piano wire around his neck. Once the man's legs stopped kicking, Jack lowered him to the ground, then dragged the body off into the brush.

Reagor said, "That is definitely the man who was watching the restaurant. The shattered windshield tells the story. This is a real stroke of luck. Now we have a vehicle that will be recognized by people in the house. Also, we can put the wheelbarrow and the body in the back of the truck."

Maria asked, "Why are we lugging that stupid wheelbarrow and dead body around?"

Jack replied, "Elementary, my good Watson. We know from Sofia that the hidden entrance leads into a short hall with a right-end turn that opens into Medrano's passion pit. We have no idea who might be inside that large room. We can leave the body in the wheelbarrow and place a hand grenade under it just as we shove the wheelbarrow into the room. The body and the bottom of the thick metal wheelbarrow will block the shrapnel and not run the possible risk of killing or injuring Linda Kay and Ryn. But the explosion will definitely shake up anybody in the room and give us the upper hand."

Jack then said, "Maria, you drive, and Reagor can ride shotgun. I'll jump up into the back and be ready to load the wheelbarrow with the body when we get to it."

The truck with Maria at the wheel proceeded slowly once it was past the gate. Jack tapped the back window when the truck reached the place where the wheelbarrow had been hidden off the road. He hoisted the body, now with a macabre protruding purple tongue, up into the truck. The wheelbarrow followed.

Reagor motioned for Jack to come to her window. "Jack, Maria shouldn't drive. If anybody at the house is watching the truck arrive, they will be looking for a man at the wheel—not a woman." Jack nodded and slid into the driver's seat. Maria and Reagor climbed into the bed of the truck and flattened out. The truck was ancient and ran roughly with occasional backfires. Jack eased the pickup into the courtyard at the back of the house. Just as Jack killed the engine, a guard approached the truck with a pistol in his hand. "Is that you, Reynaldo? What happened to the windshield?"

When the man headed for the driver's side of the truck, Reagor raised up from the bed of the truck and fired once with a pistol with a silencer on it. Her aim was perfect and the bullet passed through the man's heart. He had a sudden look of utter disbelief on his face before blood started pumping from his chest. The guard staggered once or twice, then collapsed to the ground.

Reagor and Maria vaulted out of the bed of the truck with pistols in their hands and took cover behind a large tree at the edge of the courtyard. Jack eased out of the driver's seat and moved to the opposite side of the parking area, armed and ready. The three people watched the back of the house intently, ready to fire if the gunshot had attracted any unwelcome friends of the guard who was lying by the side of the truck in a widening circle of blood.

The courtyard itself was not lighted, but two of the doors at the back of the house had small sodium vapor lights that gave an eerie yellow illumination, which did not penetrate far into the darkness. After a tense five minutes, Jack walked cautiously over to Maria and Reagor. He whispered, "That back-firing truck saved us. People inside must be used to its sounds and did not recognize a gunshot. I'm going to slip over to the north side of the house and find the secret door and see if Sofia's old code still works."

Just as Jack was about to move, there was a beam of light from the opening of one of the rear doors. A man stepped out with a rifle in his hand and walked toward the truck.

Maria gave a gasp of recognition. "Holy shit! It's that bastard Mig!"

CHAPTER 68

UNHEALTHY AIR

Mig walked up to the truck, then saw the dead man and whirled around with his rifle raised. He was peering nervously into the darkness when Jack tackled him from behind and knocked the rifle from his hand. Maria raced to help and forced her hand over Mig's mouth so he could not yell. Reagor quickly arrived with a thick cloth and duct tape to gag the struggling man. While Jack and Maria kept Mig pinned down, Reagor pulled out a 50 cc syringe from her backpack and drew it full of air. She then palpated to find an arterial pulse in Mig's antecubital fossa.

With the care of a surgeon, Reagor carefully inserted a 21-gauge needle that she had placed on the syringe into the artery. Once a small amount of bright red blood backed up into the syringe, Reagor pushed the plunger and forced all of the air into the artery. After a few seconds Mig ceased his voluntary struggling and began having focal seizures. He vomited forcefully and streams of green fluid leaked around the gag. The man arched his back with one final gasp and then lay still.

Maria whispered, "Not with a bang, but a whimper, for poor old Gonorrhea Mig. Too bad that there's not enough time to send him to the underworld as a gelding."

Jack said quietly, "I am going to roll body number one up to the door to Medrano's private love nest. Hopefully, the old door code that Sofia gave us will still work."

Jack pushed the wheelbarrow quietly across the motor court and disappeared behind a wall on the north side of the large house. Maria followed silently behind him at a distance, while Reagor stayed near the truck and watched the back of the house carefully. Jack eased the wheelbarrow and body into a small alcove with a door disguised to blend in with the house. Jack pushed the numbers that Sofia had shared. There was a slight whirring sound, but nothing moved. No door knob was present.

Maria walked up behind Jack and made a pushing sign with one palm. Jack pushed the door, but nothing happened. The second time he pushed harder, and the door opened slowly inward. Jack eased the wheelbarrow and its passenger into the hallway and stopped to listen. All was quiet. There was a small light fixture in the ceiling with a low-wattage bulb that gave feeble illumination. Jack walked slowly to the end of the short hall and peered carefully down the right-angle continuation. There was a door at the end that was closed. Sofia had not mentioned a second door.

* * * * *

After Jack, Maria, and Reagor slipped out of the back door to climb into the garbage truck, Reba locked the door. She then walked with B.A. to the front of the restaurant and looked out of a window at the street outside. All was quiet, with a few tourists still wandering around with drinks in hand. Reba checked to be certain that her pistol was fully loaded. She had a strange premonition that she would need the weapon before the night was over. Guerrero was unusually restless and kept going to the front door, then walking back to the kitchen.

The sudden shrill ring of the restaurant phone startled Reba. She hesitated, then picked up the phone and said 'hello.' There was the sound of heavy breathing on the other end—then a hang-up. Five minutes later the phone rang again. Reba ignored it. Shortly thereafter there was an insistent knocking at the back door. An urgent voice said, "It's Victor. I'm being chased! They are going to kill me right here in the alley if you don't let me in!"

The voice did not sound like Victor, and B.A. obviously thought that the person at the door was a stranger since he was at the door barking loudly. Reba went to the door and said loudly, "Hang on, Victor! I'm opening the door." Then she coolly shot through the door just above waist level. There was a loud scream followed by pounding on the door—then it was quiet.

Carmen rushed into the kitchen. "Reba, what's happening?"

Reba answered, "Someone tried to break in the back door. I shot them. Something tells me that we will have more visitors soon. Carmen, do you know how to fire a gun?"

Carmen did not answer immediately, then answered. "I know a great deal about guns, but I am not sure that I could ever bring myself to shoot a person."

Reba went to a drawer in the kitchen, pulled out a pistol, and tossed it to Carmen, who caught it expertly.

"Carmen, these evil people who are trying to capture Jack, Maria, and me want to film us being tortured and having body parts cut off before killing us. If they get inside to get me, you can be certain that they will also take Luis, Nina, and you. And there is no question that they would love to film a four-year-old girl being raped and then sliced into pieces."

Carmen's eyes teared up. Then she sighted down the gun and said, "My husband had a Walther PPK like this, and I have shot it many times."

There was a sudden crash as the back door was forcibly pushed in. Two men burst into the kitchen with guns drawn. Carmen instantaneously whirled and put a bullet right into the forehead of the first man. B.A. leaped and knocked the second gunman down. Reba screamed "kill!" and B.A. ripped the man's throat out.

"Bravo!" Reba said as she looked at Carmen. "You handled that gun like an expert."

Carmen had a grim look on her face when she replied, "No one is ever going to hurt my children."

There was a moment of quiet, followed by the roar of an accelerating truck that crashed into the front door and shook the entire building.

"Good Lord, protect us!" Carmen exclaimed and crossed herself as she raised her pistol.

CHAPTER 69

OLD FRIENDS

Reagor crossed the courtyard slowly and stood in the vestibule outside Medrano's trysting boudoir while continuing to survey the area behind her.

Jack came out to join Reagor and explained about the second unexpected door.

There was a whispered conversation, then Jack went to the end of the small wall to keep an eye on the courtyard while Reagor entered the hallway. She nodded to Maria, then brushed past her and walked carefully to the newly discovered second door. Reagor took a stethoscope out of her backpack, placed it on the door, and listened.

Lighting was very poor. Reagor felt along the door until she encountered a knob and tried gently to twist it. It would not move. Reagor then tapped very lightly on the door. The sound told her that the door was hollow. She went back to the door and motioned for Jack to join her. He listened as she whispered in his ear, then nodded in agreement.

Jack turned to Maria and told her, "Becky says the door is hollow, and that if you and I push the wheelbarrow very hard we should be able to get at least the front part of it into the room. But we won't have much time. Becky brought a hand grenade that has an eight-second timer after the handle is released. We'll have to poke the grenade under the body and race it down the short hall into the door.

"Then we run like hell and hit the floor right after where the hall has the right-angle turn. Becky will stay back to guard the door, then she'll join us—hopefully, inside of the love suite."

Jack looked at the body draped across the wheelbarrow that was starting to show livor mortis blood patches. He nodded at Maria, then pulled the pin on the grenade and shoved it under the man. He and Maria began their race down the short hallway pushing the wheelbarrow. The front of the ungainly vehicle smashed into the door and forced it partially open. Jack and Maria barely had time to sprint back to the bend in the hall and dive to the floor before there was a deafening explosion that filled the hallway with smoke.

Just as he and Maria were standing up, the staccato sound of gunfire was heard from outside. There was a loud bang as the heavy entrance door was slammed shut. Jack peered toward the door— Reagor was gone. The explosion had turned the wheelbarrow upside down on top of the shredded body. Globs of flesh were stuck to the ceiling. Jack and Maria, with weapons in their hands, wedged themselves past the wheelbarrow and squeezed through the partially open door into the Medrano pleasure suite.

There was considerable smoke in the large bedroom. Linda Kay and Ryn were huddled in one corner with terror in their eyes. They were wearing the same clothes they had on when captured, but their clothes were ripped with buttons missing. Ryn had bruises on her face, and Linda Kay had a swollen lip.

No one else was in the room.

"Oh, my God!" screamed Maria. "What have these animals done to you?"

Linda Kay and Ryn began to sob and ran over to hug Maria. Jack immediately turned and squeezed by the overturned wheelbarrow and ran to the entrance door which was now shut. There was no handle on the inside, and the door would not budge even when Jack used his shoulder to push hard on it.

Jack came back where Maria and her friends had sat down on the king-size bed. "Looks like we are trapped in here," he said. "I know that it will be hard for Linda Kay and Ryn, but we need to know everything that happened after you left the restaurant with Mig."

Linda Kay immediately stopped crying and was all business. "Ryn can chip in as she sees fit, but here are the facts. That rat Mig tapped on the back door of the restaurant and promised to take us for a quick ice cream cone. But before we had walked to the end of the alley, Mig pulled a pistol and threatened to kill us on the spot if we screamed or didn't follow his instructions. A panel truck came down the alley and two men jumped out and helped Mig force us into the back. We were blindfolded and driven over some bumpy roads to this place. The men led us down a short hallway and shoved us into this room and disappeared."

Ryn added, "They warned us that if we took our blindfolds off, we would be killed. Linda Kay and I had no idea where we were and whether there might be other people in the room. After ten minutes when nothing happened, and there were no sounds, we slipped our blindfolds off and discovered that we were in this fancy bedroom with no windows. We tried the only door and found that we could not open it."

Jack said, "This is important. When the men left you, did you hear a door closing?"

Linda Kay answered, "I am sure that there was no sound of a door closing. But there was a strange sound like something sliding."

Jack said, "Please go on with your story. Any detail could be very important."

Ryn teared up and almost broke down. She breathed deeply several times and then, with effort, regained her composure and slowly began to speak. "After an hour or so, Mig came back into the room using the door that you blasted open. There was a huge man with earrings and a tattoo on his face carrying an expensive camera and tripod. Behind the camera guy there was a short person with a blind eye who was rolling a stand with some type of sound equipment. All three men were armed.

"Mig ordered us to sit on the bed. He said that he had been promised some fun time with Linda Kay and me in exchange for helping us be captured." At this point Ryn choked up and could not speak.

Linda Kay continued. "To make it short and sweet, Mig raped both of us multiple times while his cameraman was filming. He told us that if we did not cooperate fully, we would be shot with no warning. I cannot tell you some of the awful things he made us do."

Ryn was able to speak with difficulty and said hesitatingly, "Mig promised that he would be back later to share us with some of his friends. But so far nobody has returned."

Jack asked, "The three men came in through the only obvious door to the room. Did they leave the same way?"

Both girls nodded yes. Ryn said, "Same way, and they locked the door behind them."

Jack replied, "There is a very heavy main door to the outside at the end of the hall. I checked it. The door is locked with no obvious way to open it from the inside."

Maria pointed to the ceiling. Jack looked up and nodded. "We are miked. But so far, we have told no secrets."

There was a swishing sound, and a curtain on the wall opened to reveal a thick glass plate. On the other side was the leering face of a horribly scarred man.

He formed a crooked smile with his deformed lips and said, "Keep talking. I just love secrets."

CHAPTER 70

MOUNTING BODY COUNT

The large truck was moving at a high rate of speed when it hit the restaurant's front door, sending fragments of wood and metal flying across the room. Three armed men jumped out of the truck and quickly canvassed the area. Two of them headed for the kitchen, while the third man found the stairs and bounded up them. Thinking ahead, Reba had turned one of the metal tables in the kitchen on its side just before the crash. Carmen was paralyzed with fear and stood immobile in the middle of the kitchen. "Find cover!" Reba screamed just as the first armed man burst into the kitchen and fired at Carmen.

The shot hit Carmen in the shoulder, and she groaned and fell to the floor. The shooter had three seconds to look for other people before Reba eliminated him with a perfect shot to the chest. He screamed and did an agonal pirouette before collapsing. The second man was more cautious and peeked through the kitchen doorway. Seeing his companion on the floor, he quickly retreated.

"Down!" Reba screamed. B.A. was just a blur as he shot out of the kitchen. Reba dashed into the serving area and found the second man struggling on the floor with B.A.'s jaws firmly attached to the arm with the gun. Reba kicked the gun out of the man's hand. There were two quick staccato sounds of gunfire from upstairs. "Merciful God!" screamed Carmen from the kitchen. "My kids are up there." She ran into the front of the restaurant with blood oozing from her shoulder and a gun in her other hand and headed for the stairs.

"My job!" Reba shouted as she grabbed Carmen and sprinted for the stairs. Reba yelled over her shoulder, "Shoot the bastard if he so much as moves a muscle." Reba was taking three steps at a time when a man spurting blood from his neck and chest stumbled down the stairs, almost knocking her over. Luis came behind the man with a gun in his hand. Before Reba could respond, there was the sound of a gunshot in the serving area, followed by a scream.

Fearing the worst, Reba raced down the stairs and leaped over the body of the hemorrhaging man and rushed back to where Carmen was watching the shooter being held down by B.A. The man was writhing on the floor with blood spurting from his neck. Carmen stood over him with her pistol still pointing at his head.

Carmen blurted out, "He pulled a knife and stabbed B.A. I shot him in the chest just before the dog ripped his throat out." She paused as if remembering, then screamed, "My children!"

Luis walked into the room, still holding a pistol. His mother shrieked and ran to him. "Is Nina all right?"

Luis nodded. Before Carmen could finish crossing herself, Nina came into the room bawling and jumped into her mother's arms.

Reba went over to Luis and asked, "Luis, any more men upstairs?"

Luis shook his head. Reba said, "You saved some lives. I knew that Jack taught you to shoot, but I didn't know that he let you keep a gun. Thank God, he did."

Reba followed a trail of blood to the kitchen where B.A. lay in the corner gasping for breath with a large wound in his chest that was spewing out bubbles of blood with each breath. She knew that the knife had slashed the dog's lung. Reba knelt down by the dog. B.A. lifted his head and licked Reba's hand. His head then slumped to the floor and his labored breathing ceased. Reba's eyes filled with tears.

Carmen came back into the kitchen holding Nina with Luis trailing behind. She looked at B.A. and then Reba and mouthed the word 'dead?' Reba nodded.

Then Reba went to the phone and dialed a number. Victor was used to middle-of-the-night calls and answered almost immediately.

"Victor, Randy's men made a major assault on the restaurant a few minutes ago. Two men broke into the kitchen through the alley, and three men crashed a truck into the front door. As of now, the restaurant looks like a war zone with five dead bodies and lots of blood. I hate to say it, but poor B.A. got slashed in the chest and bled out after he ripped the throat out of one of the bastards. Carmen was afraid for her children and turned out to be very good with a gun, as was her son Luis.

"No, I think that we are safe now. It will take a while for word to get back to Randy that five of his professional killers are down for the count. No more time to talk now. I need you to drive me to the Medrano mansion, then come back and call the police and let them cart off all of the bodies from here. My sixth sense is ringing emergency bells. I'm afraid that all is not going well with Jack and the others' rescue mission.

"Dangerous? Hell, yes. But I still have several cat lives left. Carmen got shot in one of her shoulders, but I think it is only a flesh wound. I'm going to clean the wound up and put a gauze pad on it. Can you be here in 10 minutes?"

Reba put the phone down and went over to Carmen. "Victor is coming to drive me to the Medrano estate. I have a strong fear that Jack, Maria, and Becky may be in grave danger. You and the children should be safe here until Victor gets back to take you three to his house for the rest of the night. But you and Luis should definitely stay armed. Let's take a look at your shoulder now."

Carmen removed her blouse to let Reba see the wound. "You are really lucky," Reba said. "The bullet must have ended up in one of the walls. It just grazed your shoulder. I'll bandage it up. Tomorrow will be time enough to go to the ER and get a tetanus shot."

After the wound was dressed, Reba reloaded her pistol and grabbed some extra ammunition from a drawer in the kitchen. She walked over to Nina, who was still tearful in her mother's arms. "Nina, everything is going to be all right. Your mother and Luis will take good care of you until we get back with Linda Kay and Ryn. I bet your mother can find some milk and cookies for you and Luis. Then maybe you can go back to sleep."

The sound of a motor was heard in the alley. The bolt on the back door had been ripped off by the two men who had attacked first. The door was wide open but was still on its hinges. Reba paused to look back at Carmen and her children before stepping into the alley and closing the door behind her.

CHAPTER 71

UP A BROWN CREEK

Randy moved closer to the glass window. "I cannot tell you how excited I am to have the great pleasure of your company once again. We now have a world-class cinematographer along with an incredible sound technician on site and eager to get started with our amazing project. We are as of yet missing your charming wife, but rest assured that she will be joining you and your little whore shortly. I sent five of my best men out tonight to invite her to the party. And, of course, having the two new little whorelets, Linda Kay and Ryn, to play cameo roles in at least one of our films is an added bonus."

Randy's face darkened and hatred burned in his eyes beneath the scarred eyelids.

"See what you people did to me? I had extensive burns on my face and upper trunk. There is no way I should have survived the burns or the explosion of your uncle's compound. But I, like you, have lots of cat's lives. There was water in the bottom of the paternoster shaft that I fell into that put out the fire. Miraculously, I fell between the spikes. The explosion blasted a hole in the shaft that let me fall down into the underground aquifer. I was able to float several miles until I could crawl out at an artesian spring."

Jack interrupted Randy to say, "Obviously, your fantastic offer was not an offer at all. There was no way that you were going to trade Linda Kay and Ryn for my wife, me, and Maria."

Randy gave a short laugh. "Of course not. But you people are such fools that I thought that you might fall for it. I had already promised my men a fun time with the two new girls. Mig did me the favor of luring them out of the restaurant, so I rewarded him with some special play time first. Too bad Mig stupidly walked into a bullet in the courtyard tonight. However, there was no way we would ever have let him leave this place alive."

Randy continued, "Armando Cabral was kind enough to let the Chicago people know that you three had survived and were living under assumed names in San Lindo. I received immediate orders to bring some professionals with me here to settle some scores. The KGB remains willing to pay a large price for punishing Ava for becoming a dirty turncoat and working for the CIA. All they asked is to have access to the films of her slow and painful death. And, of course, our cartel friends in Mexico City are pleased that we have assumed the responsibility of removing an impediment to their taking over this fair town."

Jack said, "You seem to forget that we are armed and won't be easy to take."

Randy laughed. "As I have said before, you people are so stupid. You may wonder why Juan Medrano's son Isidro does not spend much time in his father's mansion that he inherited. Let me simply say that the son has discovered great opportunities in Chicago that enable him to live in a large penthouse overlooking Lake Michigan with a steady flow of spectacular women and generous income. Isidro's father was a Renaissance man in many ways. He incorporated some amazing features in this mansion. This large glass window with a sound system enabled him to become a voyeur when his friends used this room for romantic liaisons.

"As to the alleged problem of encouraging you armed people to cooperate with us—this is simply not a problem. Medrano's elegant sex boudoir is equipped with a ventilation system that enables us to flood the room with a special knockdown gas to send all of you off to dreamland while we collect your weapons and handcuff your wrists and ankles. As far as using your weapons to break out of this space, don't waste your time. The walls are solid concrete and this glass spy window will withstand a barrage of AK-47 bullets. Also, the so-called 'secret' door that you used to come in from the outside has now been protected with heavy iron bars that dropped down from the ceiling."

Randy laughed again. "So, Mr. All-American CIA stud, you and your friends have just run out of your cat lives. To put it bluntly, you people are now way up shit creek without a paddle. Please do excuse my indelicate language. I know that you are praying that your guardian angel Rebecca Reagor will soon come to your rescue. Don't hold your breath on that one. I just received word that my men trapped her on the grounds and killed her since we really don't need another bit actor for our film production. You would be surprised how much we know about the CIA from various leaks. Sources have told us that Officer Reagor was one of the best assassination experts in the entire agency and was active around the globe. Tonight was an inglorious ending for her."

Jack walked closer to the glass window. "My wife is pregnant. How about keeping me and letting the other people go?"

"Ah, my naïve friend, you overlook how important your pregnant wife is to us artistically as well as financially. Her spectacular demise, along with the baby, is worth hundreds of thousands of dollars to us from our Middle East customers, as well as the KGB. I have been told that the Russians will use the movie of your wife's painful and protracted death as a training film for KGB recruits to show them what happens to people who are traitors.

"You will need to excuse me now. I have to work with the producer regarding the planning of some of the most exciting scenes as well as how best to use our sound system to accentuate screams. Oh— and one other thing: Blowing up the guard and ramming him into this room was not at all smart. I note globs of flesh stuck on the walls and ceiling. They will soon begin to smell so bad that you will realize you are indeed up that famous brown creek. Have a pleasant rest of the night."

CHAPTER 72

CATOMETER READINGS

The sound of the hand grenade explosion drew immediate attention to Reagor, who was standing at the outer entrance to Medrano's private boudoir. A guard spotted her and began shooting wildly. Reagor returned fire. Her aim was deadly, and she dropped the man almost immediately. She tried to follow Jack and Maria into the love suite, but the outer door was already closed and locked. Reagor heard yelling voices in the distance and decided it was time to change her geography. She kept low and worked her way to the front of the house, finding enough hand and toe holds to scale the stone wall up to a second-floor balcony.

The room that fronted the balcony had thick curtains behind a large plate-glass window that was locked from the inside. Reagor tried to lift the window without success. She then took off her backpack and knelt down beside it as she reached inside and retrieved a small object. Reagor took the glass cutter and made a circle just below the lock. A slight tap caused the circle of glass to fall inside the window almost noiselessly. Reagor reached through the hole and opened the lock. The window was very heavy. It took almost all of Reagor's strength to open it. She parted the thick brocade curtains and stepped carefully into the pitch-black room, closing the window behind her.

Reagor shielded her small flashlight to look around the room. On one wall there was a shelf full of ghastly shrunken heads. As the light moved around the room, Reagor was startled to see the preserved body of a nude woman that Sofia had talked about. The body had been prepared by an expert taxidermist and was standing on a marble base. Reagor came closer to the woman and gently touched the bronze skin that had the feel of soft leather. The eyes were very realistic, but obviously were professionally done prostheses. Reagor cast a dim light on the marble base and saw a small gold plaque. She knelt down and could read the single cursive word—'Pandora.'

Reagor walked cautiously across the room to a large oak door. There was no handle, but there was a small brass keyhole located at the top of the door almost up to the high ceiling. Reagor tapped on the door and confirmed her suspicion that it was solid wood. The door did not budge at all when Reagor pushed on it. Reagor began to wonder if she would be forced to go out through the window and risk being seen by one of the guards. Then she became aware of a strange smell and started to feel queasy. She quickly realized that there was some type of toxic gas flowing into the room. Reagor quickly went back to the window and found that it had relocked and could not be re-opened. She began a frantic search for a key to the door, opening the drawers of an antique desk and feeling the tops of books in the rows of bookshelves. Her movements were beginning to slow down, and she had an overpowering urge to lie down and sleep. Suddenly a book on one of the shelves caught her eye when the cover twinkled as her light passed across it. She looked closer and read the title—*La Esperanza.*

Something clicked in Reagor's head when she translated the Spanish book title to English. She kept forcing herself to stay awake as she looked frantically about the room for a box—Pandora's box. Her thoughts were becoming scrambled, and she was feeling very dizzy. Then she remembered seeing a small ornate box way at the back of one of the bottom drawers of the desk she had searched while trying to find a key to the door. She forced herself to go back to the desk and retrieve the box. It was locked, but Reagor was able to break the lock using a letter opener that she found on the desk top. Inside was a brass key. It took all of Reagor's strength to move the desk chair to the door and stand on her tiptoes to put the key in the lock.

Reagor had become so weak that turning the lock was a huge effort. Sleep was all she could think about. Reagor began to totter on the chair, and the room started to spin. Her breathing became very shallow. She stood immobile on the chair for a moment, then fell forward into the door, which opened due to her weight. Reagor landed awkwardly in the dark hallway and passed out. Unbeknownst to her, the door slowly closed behind her. She did not hear the voice at the far end of the hall that said, "What the hell was that thumping sound? I'm going to turn the lights on and go check it out."

* * * * *

Reba was urging Victor to drive faster as his car left the town and headed up toward the high hills. Victor was clearly reluctant to be the chauffeur for Reba.

He looked at her and said, "Once again, Reba, what you are doing is foolish and beyond dangerous. You seem to have forgotten that you are carrying Jack's baby and are five months' pregnant. Randy sent professional killers to capture you, but you, miraculously, took out all of the killers with the help of Carmen, Luis, and the dog. You and Jack frequently brag about how many cat lives each of you has left. My estimation is that you have more than used up all of your lives."

Reba interrupted Victor to say, "I checked on my Catometer just before we left the house, and I have at least three lives left."

Victor shook his head and replied, "Reba, this is not a joking matter. Randy Williams is an animal. His sole purpose in life is to make you suffer as much as possible with horrendous acts of cruelty."

The road became worse the higher it rose toward the hills, punishing the passengers as the old car's shocks squealed in protest.

Victor broke the silence by saying, "I hope that all of this bouncing around doesn't put you into early labor. The hospital in town has no way to care for preemies."

Reba replied, "Going into early labor is way down on my list of worries. Helping Jack and the others stay alive is number one."

Victor shook his head and said, "What if you get captured?"

Reba hesitated, then replied grimly, "I still have my cyanide tablet handy."

CHAPTER 73

SUITE RULES

Once Randy closed the screen to the glass window, Jack began studying the walls of the suite, looking for anything that would suggest a hidden entrance that the men who kidnapped Linda Kay and Ryn might have used to deliver them into the room. The girls were certain that they did not enter the room by the outside door like Mig and the film crew. They both distinctly remembered being harshly commanded to bend over before being shoved inside by the kidnappers. The women were also positive that there was a sliding sound before the men left.

Maria asked Jack with great concern, "Do you think that horrible man was lying about Reagor being killed?"

Jack answered, "Reagor survived many undercover years in the field. And if she really was a CIA assassin, I'd put her up against Randy and his thugs any day. She may be our only hope to get out of here alive."

Ryn began to sob. "I've had such a crappy life. I'm not ready to die before I get a chance to live like a normal person."

Maria went over to Ryn and hugged her. "The fat lady has not yet begun to sing, Ryn. We all have some cat lives left to spend."

Suddenly the curtain behind the thick glass window parted. Randy's leering face appeared again. "I don't know if you have had time to read the Suite Rules that are in the drawer in the nightstand, but Rule 17 distinctly states that visitors are not permitted to have weapons. So, it's nighty-nighty time for all of you so we can assist Jack and Maria in complying with the rules. It will just be a short nap. Sweet dreams to one and all."

There was a subtle hiss as gas began to flow into the room from ceiling vents. Linda Kay and Ryn immediately clapped their hands over their mouth and noses and stopped breathing. Jack shook his head. "It's no use, girls. Randy has the trump card."

Very quickly, all four people began to wobble and collapsed on the huge bed. Two men wearing respirators entered the room from a panel below the large window. They confiscated Jack and Maria's revolvers and extra ammunition. Then the men used large handcuffs to secure the feet of the passed-out people. One of them looked at the glass window and asked, "How about their wrists, Boss?"

Randy smiled and replied, "Cuff them behind their backs. These people just ran out of cat lives and good luck. I just can't wait to start filming!"

* * * * *

The man down the hall from the shrunken heads room turned on the hall light and started walking briskly toward the sound that had gotten his attention. He had a pistol in one hand. Suddenly everything went dark.

"Shit! We lost power again." Then he thought to himself, "The boss is going to be pissed. I'm ready to get back to Chicago where the power never goes out, and a person can eat the food without having to camp on the shitter half a day."

A voice called out, "Bruno, we need to go check the breaker box. I've got a flashlight."

Bruno turned around and walked down the dark hall toward his partner's flashlight.

A few minutes after the men left, Reagor began to stir. She remembered standing on the chair before everything went black. Reagor had been out of the room with the knockdown gas long enough that its effects were wearing off. The door's spring hinges had closed the door automatically after Reagor fell forward, which kept the gas from flowing into the hall. She checked to make certain that her gun was still in her waist holder and that she still had her backpack. Reagor stood up carefully as her head continued to clear and began to move cautiously down the dark hall.

* * * * *

Victor pulled his car off the dirt road and killed the headlights. He turned to Reba and said reluctantly, "If you walk down the road about one hundred yards to the top of the hill, you will be able to spot the lights on the front gate of the Medrano Estate. But if you had any regard for the life of your child and yourself, you would let me turn this car around and head back to town. Reagor promised to have you extracted if things went wrong tonight. I fear that your bad choice to come here may be just as fatal as putting the strychnine capsule that you have been saving into your mouth and crushing it with your teeth. I beg you to reconsider, Reba."

Reba shook her head. "The die is cast. Wish us all luck." As Reba opened the door to get out, Victor reached into the back seat and retrieved a backpack. "Here's a little going away present for you that is cram full of goodies."

Reba took the backpack, then gripped Victor's hand. "Don't forget that I'm counting on you to deliver my baby." She exited the car and began to walk down the road using a small, shielded flashlight occasionally. When Reba crested the hill, she could look fifty yards down a side road that led to the estate. She moved into the heavy brush and started cautiously toward the lighted gate.

CHAPTER 74

NEAR MISS

As Reagor moved down the dark hallway, she reviewed the details of the Medrano house that Sofia had provided. The master bedroom was on the second floor at the back and opened up to a large balcony that had a view of the swimming pool and the higher hills to the west. Randy surely would know by now that he had lost a number of men and that, contrary to what he had told Jack and the women about Reagor's supposed death, she was still unaccounted for. Sofia had also described a large basement toward the rear of the house. That was the likely place where the torture and exotic filming would take place.

The power outage made it much safer for Reagor to move about the house. However, just as she reached the central staircase, a voice from the darkness called out, "Mike, is that you?" Reagor slipped behind an ornate column and began to groan. The beam of a flashlight started coming rapidly up the stairs. Just as the man holding the flashlight reached the landing, Reagor threw several pesos over his head. He abruptly whirled to shine his light in the direction of the sound.

A split second was all Reagor needed to place her garrote around the man's neck.

His death was quiet and quick.

Reagor collected the man's gun and flashlight. The guard was light enough for her to carry his body to a nearby powder room and deposit it there. Reagor continued toward the back of the mansion until she approached a corner room that she felt certain was the master bedroom. As she watched from a distance, Randy Williams emerged with a man carrying a rifle and a large flashlight ahead of him. They started walking away from where Reagor was flattened against the wall. Randy was angry and started venting.

"Nobody sleeps until we find that Reagor bitch. She could be real trouble. Have the men search the grounds and go room by room through the house. Once we have Reagor, we can meet the camera and sound men in the basement and go over the script and how our little stars will be sequenced. I want to be certain that Stressel is still conscious enough to witness when his baby is ripped out of his wife's belly and splattered on the floor. And I plan to think of something very special for that whore Leta who shot me in the neck and almost paralyzed me."

Reagor heard a "Got it, boss," before the voices faded away.

The hall lights suddenly flashed on. Reagor headed straight for the master bedroom door and tried to open it. Locked. There was an ornate brass keyhole that made it easy to use a lock pick to open the door. Inside there was a beautifully furnished sitting room that led to a huge bedroom with an antique four-poster bed. There was a half-empty bottle of tequila with a large worm in it by the bedside table, along with some shot glasses. Reagor set her backpack down on the floor and reached inside to find a small glass vial containing a clear liquid. She poured the entire contents into the tequila bottle.

Reagor searched the room methodically. She found a Smith and Wesson .38 Special revolver under one of the bed pillows. Searching again in her backpack she found several .38 caliber cartridges, which she exchanged for the ones already in the revolver. Reagor then took a small needle out of her backpack and pricked one of her forefingers. She pressed the finger and collected several drops of blood on the glass cover of the nightstand. Using a toothpick as a brush, Reagor wrote the number 312 on the pillow that lay on top of the revolver. She then used the remaining blood to add a small red cross before wiping the top of the nightstand clean.

Reagor locked the door from the inside and surveyed the room before stepping out onto the large balcony. A high-powered spotlight mounted on the outside wall illuminated the pool area very brightly. Reagor took a cloth and partially unscrewed the hot bulb. The pool area was now very dark. Reagor climbed over the balcony railing, dropped a few feet, caught a branch of a Baja Elephant tree, and swung for a minute before dropping to the ground. She quietly moved to the corner of the house that Sofia's drawing had shown to be above the basement.

Reagor almost stumbled into a fresh excavation in the ground. Using her partially covered flashlight, she judged the excavation to be approximately seven feet by five feet with a depth of ten feet. Reagor puzzled for a minute and then shuddered when she suddenly realized why the pit had been dug.

There was a metal grating extending out from the wall of the house. Reagor shined her light down and saw pool equipment. There was a small hinged door in the grating with a padlock. Reagor found a bolt cutter in her backpack and squeezed hard to cut through the lock shank. She opened the door, squeezed through the opening, and started climbing down the metal ladder. When she reached the bottom, she found a locked metal door in the concrete foundation. The lock was hard steel with a shank that the bolt cutter could not cut.

Reagor worked with a lock pick for several minutes before finally defeating the lock. She cautiously opened the thick door and found to her surprise that the inside of the door was heavily covered with soundproofing material. There was a small amount of space between the door and a heavy glass window that was totally blackened with thick paint. Reagor used a pocket knife and, after much effort, was able to scrape a small hole in the paint. She looked through the hole and had a hazy view of Randy and the man with the rifle in animated conversation.

There were several metal gurneys in the room with wrist and foot restraints.

Randy started walking over toward the window. Reagor ducked down and did not move for several minutes. She then looked and saw that the room was empty. She wondered if she had been seen and was about to have unwanted company.

Reagor heard the sound of feet coming down the metal ladder. She moved to the side and stood waiting with her garrote in hand. Once the person's feet touched the floor, Reagor tried to apply the garrote, but the person sensed her presence and whirled to strike Reagor in the face, driving her backward. Reagor grabbed her revolver and was stopped just in time when the person said "no!" in a distinctly female voice.

CHAPTER 75

ALMOST MOVIE TIME

Reagor knew the voice immediately. "Thank God, Reba," she gasped. "I would have garroted you had you not been so quick to slap me away. Then, I was a millisecond away from putting a bullet into your chest. You are the last person on earth I would have expected to see here. I told you that plans were in place to extract you if things went south with our rescue mission."

Reba responded, "Shortly after you three left the restaurant, two of Randy's thugs broke in through the back door just before three more knocked in the front door with a truck. With help from Carmen, Luis, and B.A., we sent all five of them to hell." She choked up, then said, "B.A. is dead. One of the men slashed his belly open before Carmen put a bullet in the man's chest. I had a strong sixth sense that things were not going well out here."

Suddenly there was a loud metallic clang as the hinged door above the two women was slammed shut. Bright lights blinded Reagor and Reba. Then they heard the taunting voice of Randy Williams. "'Come into my parlor,' said the spider to the fly. You two are just dumbass stupid to let yourselves get trapped in a blind cul-de-sac. It gives me great pleasure to say that all of the future cinema stars are now on site, and it's almost time to start rolling film.

"Just to avoid any more ill-advised moves on the part of you two espionage wannabes, please be aware that behind these bright lights are men with machine guns. The door above is once again locked shut. I know that you two women still have weapons, but fear not. We will soon confiscate them. Now, please excuse me. I need to supervise the transfer of our other esteemed guests to the movie set. We will come get you two in due time."

Reba turned to Reagor and said, "I was very careful sneaking onto the grounds but someone must have seen me. From Sofia's sketch, I figured that the basement had to be in this area. I was hoping that there might be a way to see if you, Jack, and Maria were in there. It's my fault that we got caught."

Reagor shook her head. "There's a blackened window behind the wall door over there. I scratched a small hole in the paint to try to look in. Randy and one of his men were in the basement, and I think they must have seen the hole and come running with some backup help. This mess is likely my fault."

* * * * *

The knockdown gas only lasted fifteen minutes. Jack and the three women returned slowly to consciousness to find that they had ankle cuffs, and their arms were fixed behind their backs with handcuffs. Maria looked down at her waist and said, "No handgun." Jack nodded in agreement. Ryn's lips were quivering, and she was trying hard not to burst into tears.

Maria moved closer to Ryn and said, "Reagor is still out there somewhere. Don't give up hope. I'm not planning to cash all of my cat lives in tonight."

The curtain behind the glass window opened to reveal the scarred face of Randy Williams. He gave a crooked smile with his deformed lips and said, "Rise and shine, my little ducklings. It's almost time for you four lucky people to realize your thespian aspirations. I cannot tell you what excitement is in store for all of you.

"The cinematography gods have smiled on us and delivered both Reagor and Jack's lovely bride into our hands. You all will be reunited with them soon." Jack and Maria exchanged worried looks.

"And now a word about our specific ground rules. The noise you just heard was the outer door opening and the metal bars being lifted. You will soon be able to say a friendly 'hello' to three very nice men with AK-47s. But I do need to warn you that they all have very itchy trigger fingers. Any step out of line by one of you will be immediately fatal. We owe it to our wealthy buyers to film any sudden violent deaths, so you will note a large man with an expensive camera entering the room behind the men with guns. I can promise you that he is hoping that one of you will try something stupid that he can immortalize in celluloid."

A well-built tall man with a stocking cap perched on top of a bald head came into the room carrying a fancy camera and tripod. He had a black tattoo on one cheek and large gold hoops in both ears. The cameraman looked disdainfully at the four hostages as if they were vermin, then began setting up his camera.

Randy continued, "Here's the deal for you future stars. I'm going to open the panel under the window that you people were not smart enough to find. Harold will come through the panel and escort you one at a time back through the opening. Since it is not possible to walk with ankle cuffs on, once on the other side, we will gently assist each of you into an upscale cage on wheels that will convey you in comfort to the beautiful movie set."

The panel opened, and a swarthy man with a bushy beard and one blind eye with a white cornea came into the room. "Who's first, boss?" the man asked.

"The woman named Ryn looks tearful and anxious. Let's let her have the honor of being first. And, Sweetie, I was just wondering if your folks named you after the famous movie star Rin-Tin-Tin." Randy gave a loud chuckle.

The bearded man grabbed Ryn's arm and pulled her toward the exit. "Stop blubbering, you bitch, before I pop you in the mouth." As Ryn bowed her head to pass through the exit, the one-eye man gave her a lecherous pinch on the buttock. Ryn began wailing.

The cameraman looked up at Randy and said, "I got that on film. Your customers are going to like having some human-interest footage before the big event. We can get better sound on the set when the acoustic engineer is set up. I'm sure that babe will be hollering from start to finish."

CHAPTER 76

COUNTDOWN

Jack, Reba, Reagor, Maria, and her two expats from the Barlow whorehouse had all been secured in heavy metal chairs. Their handcuffs had been tightly fixed to the back of each chair with heavy zip ties. There were four tough-looking men with AK-47s occupying each corner of the basement. Two metal gurneys with wrist restraints were in the center of the room beneath large overhead lights. The cameraman with the stocking cap was setting up his camera and taking readings with a light meter. A short, kyphotic man with bushy eyebrows and a wrinkled face was moving about the room, setting up microphones.

Randy made a grand entrance into the room with a jaunty beret perched on his head and a small megaphone. He was carrying the bottle of tequila from his bedroom and placed it on a small table by a folding movie director's chair.

Randy sat down and announced with a crooked smile, "Move over, Alfred Hitchcock. There's a new director in town!" He paused, then said, almost plaintively, "I have wanted to be a movie director ever since I was a child. And now I am one."

A worried look suddenly crossed Randy's face, and he pointed to one of the armed men and said, "Over here, Harold." The two had a brief conversation. Jack was the closest to the man and was able to strain and hear the number 312 spoken several times. When the talk was over, Harold nodded and left the room.

There was a binder on the side table by the whiskey. Randy opened the binder and flipped through several pages. He poured himself a full shot glass of the tequila and downed it in one swallow. "Delicious." Then Randy looked intently at the six captives.

"I have worked hard to make a captivating script for our affluent buyers in the Middle East. Several of them called to make special requests that I will endeavor to honor. As I am sure each of you is aware, none of you will survive the filming. However, it may be a consolation to know that this will be an expertly documented dramatic end of the road for you people. A slow and painful death is essential for the best artistic effect. Sad to say, you have all just exhausted your mythical cat lives.

"My second fondest dream after becoming a movie director has been to become a surgeon. If you will kindly look at the Mayo stand beside each gurney, you will note a variety of surgical instruments. Yours truly will be using the scalpels and knives to remove body parts as spelled out in the special script that I spent hours honing and polishing. Frankly, I cannot wait to get started."

Reagor looked directly at Randy and said harshly, "You are the lowest form of human garbage. It is a real pity that you didn't burn to death at the desert compound. I swear that within the next few hours you will die a horrible death. Never forget the number three twelve."

Randy's face turned red, and he stood up and screamed, "Shut up, you bitch! I was considering letting you survive, but you have just bought a ticket to die first. Men, hook this miserable slut up to the overhead hoist."

Two of the men with rifles laid them down on the floor and rushed over to Reagor while the third man stood back with his weapon sweeping across the other captives. The men freed Reagor from the chair and dragged her over to where a hoist chain descended from the ceiling. One of the men roughly placed a shoulder harness on her and used a control on the wall to lift her up until her feet were dangling. He looked at Randy and asked, "OK, boss?"

Randy nodded and said "perfect."

Randy referred to the script folder again, then closed it and began to speak. "To continue the show after Reagor is through screaming, we will move to the two little whorelets from Barlow. Whiny Ryn will achieve cinematographic greatness first as she is placed nude on one of the gurneys. I will selectively remove body parts, starting with her nose and lips and working down." He turned to the sound engineer. "Nick, be sure to have good microphones close to the gurney to capture all of her screams. I think three or four minutes will be long enough before I finish her off."

Randy looked at the photographer. "Oscar, be sure that you are using the best color film to show the blood well. Our clients really like gushing blood. I may just slice Ryn's carotid arteries at the end to let her have a wonderful ending."

Ryn was crying hysterically and struggling to free herself. The photographer pointed the camera at her and exclaimed, "More wonderful human-interest stuff!"

Randy continued. "Linda Kay will be next in a déjà vu episode, but I may decide to harvest some organs. Then, sweet Maria will move to center stage. My work on her will be classic improv. She is the little bitch who shot me in the neck with a lipstick gun and almost paralyzed me. Her death will be slow and extremely painful. Building toward the dramatic highlight will occur next, with the super stud Woody Stressel being neutered with dull scissors. We will prop him up on his gurney so he can watch what is in store for his beloved and pregnant wife lying on the other gurney. The KGB was explicit that comrade Ava should die an agonizing and slow death so they can use the film to show new recruits the penalty for being a traitor to the motherland. I have some special plans for her baby."

Randy paused and took another large swallow of tequila. His face darkened, and he looked nervously toward the door to the basement. "Make sure that door is double locked," he ordered. Then he walked over to Reagor with his Smith and Wesson Special revolver in his hand. He turned to the photographer and said, "Oscar, if I stand about five feet away, will you be able to get both of us in the picture?"

Oscar replied, "Randy, if you stand back ten or twelve feet the composition will be better. I would suggest that you shoot the bitch in one of her eyes. I will start out showing both of you just before you fire, then immediately zoom in on the face. Seeing the blood and vitreous jelly spurting out of the eye will make for a great sequence. For the finale, I plan to back off to show the dirty bitch screaming and dancing on the hoist chain. Then I will swing back to you for a big thumbs-up. But before we film, I need to move in to take some quick light readings off her face."

Oscar walked up very close to Reagor with his light meter. He stared straight at her as he moved the light meter around. "Whore," he warned, "if you try anything funny while I am in close, you will be dead on the spot." The photographer finished his readings, then pinched one of Reagor's breasts and laughed before he walked off. Reagor did not flinch.

Randy smiled and responded, "That bitch should have gotten a cheap boob job before going on camera." He walked closer to Reagor and said, "You know for a CIA super ace, you really are kind of stupid to get caught. I've thought for a long time that most of your agents are people too dumb to get into law school." Reagor looked straight at Randy, then spit in his face.

Randy bellowed, "Change of plans. I'm going to shoot her in several slow-death places before the *coup de grâce* shot to her head." He backed off and pointed his revolver at Reagor's upper abdomen.

Oscar shouted, "Do a countdown, Randy. Your clients will love it!"

Randy smiled and started to count—"Five, four, three, two, one…"

CHAPTER 77

LETHAL CAMERA

The loud crack of a pistol reverberated around the room as Reagor gave a horrendous cry of pain and pulled her legs up into her chest. Oscar shouted, "Straighten her up so I can film the blood coming out of her belly!"

Randy ran up to Reagor, jerked her hair, and screamed, "Straighten up you bitch! You're ruining the movie!"

Reagor suddenly thrust her feet very hard into Randy's chest, knocking him backward to the floor. His revolver skittered across the concrete and slid close to the photographer. Oscar picked up the weapon and fired a quick burst of shots at Reagor who was screaming and swinging around on the hoist chain. "Die, you bitch!" Oscar yelled as he pumped one more shot into Reagor. One of the men with an AK-47 rushed to help Randy to his feet. Just as he bent down over Randy, there was one more muted shot, and the guard's head exploded. There was pandemonium.

Randy bolted to his feet and screamed, "Three twelve is here!" He then raced out of the door. The two remaining men with rifles looked nervously around the room trying to find the person who shot their companion. They edged toward the door. There were two quick additional muted shots and two loud groans as the guards fell down. Nick, the hunchback sound man, had been watching all of this without moving. Just as he reached for a gun, Oscar pointed his camera at him. Another muted shot knocked Nick to the floor.

Reagor stopped screaming and gyrating on the hoist and looked at the photographer and said, "Hulga, I have never been so happy to see anyone in my life. You saved us all from a horrible death."

Hulga answered, "My pleasure. I told you before I left that you folks needed to grow some balls. Once you each grew a pair, I decided to come back to help you."

Maria interrupted to say urgently, "That bastard Randy is escaping. Hulga, can you get us out of these handcuffs and zip ties."

Hulga went to one of the Mayo tables and grabbed a large orthopedic bone saw and a pair of wire cutters. She went to Jack and snipped the zip tie, then quickly used the bone saw to cut through both of his cuffs. She said only, "Cheap cuffs with soft metal."

Once Jack was free, he grabbed tools from the second Mayo table to help release the other people. He went first to Reba while Hulga cut Reagor out of her harness. As soon as Maria was free, she grabbed one of the revolvers and ran from the room shouting over her shoulder, "Randy's mine!" Just as she left there was the faint sound of gunfire outside followed by a loud crash.

Hulga had a large photographer's bag. She reached inside and pulled out several pistols. Jack said, "Reba, I don't think Ryn and Linda Kay are in any condition to help us. You need to take a pistol and stay here until Hulga, Reagor, and I find Maria. You can lock yourself in. There is no way to know how many goons Randy has left to defend him. Maria may be rushing into a trap. If I were Randy, I would try to use a vehicle to escape from here. But that crash outside may have spoiled his getaway plans."

Reba looked at Jack and said, "I'm really wiped out." She put one palm on her abdomen and smiled, saying, "Woody Junior is still kicking." Then she added, "Please be careful. This kid is going to need a father."

Jack gave his wife a quick kiss. "I knew that we all still had some cat lives left."

He turned to Reagor and asked, "How come you aren't dead?"

Reagor answered, "That and a whole lot of other things deserve an explanation. But now is not the time. Let's all arm up, fan out, and search the house." Just as the three of them headed for the door, all the lights went out. Ryn began to sob.

CHAPTER 78

JUST SAY "PLEASE"

Maria hurried up the basement stairs, listening for any voices. She knew the general layout of the Medrano mansion from Sofia's sketch. Thinking that Randy might have decided to make a run for it, she headed for the door that opened into the garage. Maria stopped short when she turned a corner in the hall just as the lights flickered and came back on and saw Randy leaning on the banister of the stairs that led down into the garage. She could hear his heavy breathing. Suddenly there was a loud crash followed by several gunshots.

Harold came running up the stairs back into the house. "Some dickhead just rammed into our truck as soon as I opened the garage door! I jumped out and put a burst of fire into his windshield. Since he returned fire, I may not have killed him."

Randy shouted, "Those 312 bastards must have tracked us down here! We need to get to the trophy room and lock ourselves in. There's a hidden door in the room that leads to a tunnel that comes up into a shed at the edge of the property. There is a motorcycle in the shed."

Just as Maria was about to squeeze the trigger of her AK-47 to take out Harold, the lights went out again. There was a loud "Shit" from one of the two men. Then Randy said, "I'm feeling pretty bad, Harold. I need you to give me a hand. My legs are like rubber."

Maria tried to stay behind Randy and Harold as they headed for the central stairs. It was pitch black, but Randy seemed to be able to navigate by memory. The lights suddenly flashed back on and showed Randy and Harold near the top of the long flight of stairs, with Harold helping support his boss. Maria stayed out of sight near the bottom of the staircase. She had a good view of Harold once the pair reached the second-floor landing. Maria took careful aim. There was a single loud shot with an almost simultaneous scream from Harold. He lurched into the railing and cartwheeled to the main floor with a heavy thud.

The gunshot seemed to have energized Randy. He broke into a clumsy run and headed for the front of the house. Maria ascended the stairs like a gazelle and was only fifteen yards behind him when Randy reached the trophy room door.

The door was closed but had not been locked after Reagor had left the room earlier. Randy pushed the door open and tried to close it behind him. Maria forced her way into the room just as the lights went out again. The door closed behind her followed by an audible click. She stepped cautiously farther into the room with her finger on the revolver trigger. It was deathly quiet. Randy had been panting earlier, but Maria could hear no sound of breathing.

A taunting voice broke the silence, "Poor little whore girl. You will not get out of this very special room alive. Medrano was a very paranoid genius. This was his safe place with hidden controls. I have just locked the door. There are some other nice features that I may want to show you before you cash in your last chips."

Hidden behind a column in the room, Maria responded, "Talk is cheap, you asshole. You are only a tough guy when you are armed. Your revolver is still down in the basement." There was a sudden gunshot that clipped one of Maria's ears. She reached up and felt blood.

Randy's voice appeared from a different location in the room. It was slightly garbled. "Close call, Sweetie. Medrano had weapons hidden in several places in this room. And I know all of those places. The man had a number of enemies. It was very thoughtful of him to stash a pair of night vision goggles in his safe room. I can see every move you make. My next shot will be the last one since I have places to go and important things to do." Randy stopped talking and could not suppress a loud yawn.

Maria felt around the column, then jerked her hand back in surprise. The column had breasts and hips. She decided to send a burst of fire in the direction of Randy's voice if he spoke again. The lights suddenly flashed back on, and Randy got off a quick shot that struck the taxidermy woman in the chest. The bones and internal stuffing absorbed much of the impact, but the specimen pushed hard enough into Maria to knock her backwards. Randy fired a second time just as Maria dived to the floor. She fired back wildly as she rolled to one side. There was a loud groan and the sound of something metallic hitting the floor. Then there was pitch blackness as the lights cut off again.

Maria very cautiously stood up with the revolver in her hand. There was the sound of gasping breathing in front of her in the darkness. She moved slowly toward the sound. Suddenly, a strong hand grabbed her ankle and pulled her down, pinning her to the floor under the weight of a heavy body. Two hands were instantaneously around her neck. Maria struggled to free herself but the pressure on her neck intensified. Her arms were pinned to the floor by the weight of the man on top of her. Just before Maria started to lose consciousness, in a desperate last-second burst of adrenaline, she freed the arm with the revolver and jammed it into the abdomen of her assailant and fired. Randy gave a guttural scream, released the grip on Maria's neck, and curled up in a ball gasping.

Maria wiggled free and stood up with the gun in her hand. She was careful to move away from the man still on the floor. The lights flickered on and off, then stayed on. Maria's second shot had landed low in Randy's groin area. The first shot had struck him in the outer shoulder. There was very little blood staining his shirt or trousers. He sat up clutching his groin and said, "We can easily straighten out this little misunderstanding. Several hundred thousand dollars in U.S. bills are hidden in my bedroom. Let me go, and I swear to tell you how to find the money. You will be a rich woman. I know a secret way out of this room. You will never hear from me again. I swear on my sacred mother's grave. Just say yes, and I'll be gone forever."

Maria appeared to be weighing the offer. She hesitated, then said, "Say 'please' and it's a done deal."

Randy's eyes lit up. He said, "Leta, I've always known that you are a very smart woman. I never really meant you any harm."

Maria replied, "I need a 'please' to seal the deal."

Randy started to stand up and said a wheezy "please." Maria put two quick shots into his head with no hesitation. There was a fountain of blood welling up as Randy fell to the ground with a look of disbelief on his face.

CHAPTER 79

VAMPIRE MANAGEMENT

Maria looked down at Randy, who had already stopped twitching as the pool of blood around his head continued to expand. She stared at the body and her face contorted in rage. She screamed, "No more cat lives for you, you piece of human garbage! I hope that your fat ass burns forever in hell!"

There was a heavy knocking on the door. She could hear Jack's voice, partially muted by the thick door. "Maria, are you in there? Are you all right?"

Maria walked to the door and shouted, "I'm OK. Randy and I are just having a philosophical discussion about whether there is life after death. Not sure how to open the door. There's no handle or doorknob on the inside."

"There's a key way up high, Maria," Reagor yelled through the door. Maria looked up. "Got it," she shouted back. "I'll stand on a chair and try to open the door with the key. But first there's one quick thing I need to do."

Maria walked over to a large full knight of armor suit on a marble stand. She struggled to lift the heavy silver sword and walked back to Randy's corpse.

A minute later, Maria was up on the chair and turning the key. She pushed on the door and it slowly began to creak open. Jack and Reagor rushed into the room with weapons drawn while Hulga kept watch in the hall. Randy was sprawled on the floor in a puddle of blood.

"Oh, my God!" Reagor exclaimed as she stared at the silver sword that had been plunged through the heart of Randy Williams and into the floor. Both Reagor and Jack whirled to look at Maria who said matter-of-factly, "If it works to keep vampires from coming back to life, it should work to keep Randy in hell."

Jack gave Maria a hug. "Good work, Agent Maria. We all have a lot to tell, but we need to get back to my wife and the girls to be certain that they are safe. No sound of gunfire from the direction of the basement is a good sign, but with the door closed it's virtually soundproof."

* * * * *

Reba breathed a prayer of relief when she heard a knock on the locked basement door and a voice that said, "It's Jack. Everything is fine." She rushed to the door, then stopped just as she started to open the deadbolt. The voice had a slight New York accent. Silently, she motioned for Linda Kay and Ryn each to pick up one of the revolvers that Hulga had pulled out of her photographer's bag. "Hang on, honey, this lock is a little hard to work."

Reba pointed to either side of the door to position the girls. Ryn began to sniffle and shake. Reba gave her a cold stare and shook her fist. Then Reba suddenly pulled the door open. A man rushed in firing wildly. Linda Kay coolly put a bullet in the man's chest. Reba and Ryn shot simultaneously and dropped a second shooter who ran into the room firing.

Ryn began to cry hysterically. "I killed a man. I killed a man." Reba looked out of the door cautiously to make sure there were no more armed men. Then she slammed the door and locked it. Reba walked over to the sobbing Ryn and slapped her face very hard. "You didn't kill a man. In fact, your shot barely grazed his leg. The person on the floor is not a man—he is an animal. I know that all of this has been tough on you and Linda Kay, but it's time for you to grow up."

Ryn slowly stopped blubbering. She raised her head, looked Reba in the eye, and hissed "Bitch." Reba put a gentle hand on Ryn's shoulder and said, "Feel between your legs, Ryn. I think something is beginning to grow down there."

There was a furious knocking on the door and a voice yelling, "Reba! We heard gunshots. Are you people OK?" Reba teared up as she moved to the door. "That's Jack for sure." She opened the door but kept a gun in her hand. Jack came in cautiously, also armed and ready. He looked about the room quickly, then put his arms around his wife. "It's good," he shouted. Reagor and Maria entered the room with obvious relief on their faces. Hulga kept a watchful eye in the doorway.

Maria looked at the two dead men on the floor and said, "Looks like you three had fun while we were gone. I want to officially announce that Randy is absolutely dead now and forever. His head stopped two bullets in that weird room with the stuffed lady."

Reagor added, "Maria went all in for overkill and stabbed a silver sword through Randy's heart after she shot him—which I thought was a nice artistic touch."

Jack said firmly, "We have lots of things to discuss at a safer place. Our job now is to get out of this cursed house and figure how to get back to town. I'm sure that our garbage truck ride is long gone."

Reba responded, "Against his will, Victor drove me out here, but he headed back to take care of Carmen and her children and to get someone to start removing all of the bodies lying about the restaurant."

Maria joined in. "When I was following Randy and his guard, they went to the garage to get a vehicle to escape. There was a loud crash followed by gunfire. The guard rushed back out of the garage and reported to Randy, who was standing at the top of the garage stairs. His exact words were: 'Some dickhead just rammed into our truck as soon as I opened the garage door. I jumped out and put a burst of fire into his windshield. Since he returned fire, I may not have killed him.'

"Randy was in a panic mode and screamed that the 312 bastards, whoever they are, must have tracked them down. The two men headed for what Randy called the trophy room to access a secret tunnel that would lead them to the edge of the estate where a motorcycle was stashed."

Jack said, "Let's hope that there is another vehicle in the garage that I can hot wire to get us back to town. We need to pray that there are no more of Randy's heavies lurking around. I think that Reba, Maria, and my days in Camelot are over."

CHAPTER 80

DEEP FREEZE

The seven people left the basement with two bodies lying on the floor and headed up the stairs toward the garage. Jack walked point with his revolver in hand. Hulga and Maria followed Jack, with Reba in the rear of the procession along with Linda Kay and Ryn. The slap on the face seemed to have been effective in bringing Ryn back to reality since she was no longer crying. The trip to the garage was uneventful. Jack took the stairs down into the garage. One of the four garage doors was open with a black Land Cruiser station wagon turned partially sideways just outside in the motor court. There was a white Ford sedan with a crumpled bumper a few feet away from the Toyota workhorse. The Ford's windshield was shattered, and there were several bullet holes in the car.

Jack walked slowly over to the Land Cruiser—prepared to duck and fire if need be. The vehicle was empty, and the keys were still in the ignition. Jack moved to the Ford and looked in an open side window. The sedan was not empty. Victor was slumped over the steering wheel with shards of glass on his face. There were several bullet holes in Victor's head and torso. His lifeless eyes were open with corneas that were starting to cloud.

"Fuck," Jack said almost reverently. His eyes started to tear up. Reluctantly, he started back up the garage stairs into the house. Reba looked at his face and moved to his side with great concern. "What is it, Jack?"

Jack paused, then said softly, "Victor is dead." Reagor had a quick startled look on her face that she quickly erased.

Reba shook her head and said bitterly, "The killing and dying never stops. Victor left me to go back and take care of Carmen and her children. Why did he come back here?"

Jack replied, "After Victor drove home to move Carmen and the children to his house, he must have decided to come back to try to help us. There was a Walther pistol on the bloody car seat by him. Just as Victor drove up, he must have seen Randy's guard getting the Land Cruiser fired up so he and his boss could make a run for it. Victor rammed the Cruiser to keep Randy from escaping."

Maria asked, "Any chance that either the Land Cruiser or the Ford will still run?"

Jack answered, "Not sure. I'll go check. Be sure to stay armed and ready. There may still be some rats in the house."

Jack came sprinting back up the stairs. "The Land Cruiser has a bashed in side, but it still runs. Victor's Ford has a crumpled front end with a flat tire. I think we can back the Cruiser up and push the sedan out of the way. Since it is a station wagon, we should be able to cram everybody in it."

Reba asked, "What about Victor? We can't just leave his body here."

Jack answered, "Two options. There is a tarp in the garage. We can wrap him up and tie him on the top of the Land Cruiser. But the better option for now would be to put him in the large chest freezer that is in the garage for safe storage."

Reagor said, "With all of the bodies here and at the restaurant, there are bound to be Federales heading for town. My vote is to leave Victor in the freezer and get out of here as fast as we can. My plan to extract Reba, if necessary, is still available. There is no way any of us can stay in Mexico and be safe."

Reba gave a thumbs-up. "I'm starting to feel short on my cat lives. This baby is really draining all of my energy. All we have done so far is just buy a little time. No question that the KGB will keep coming after us. Eliminating ten members of the Chicago mob, including Randy Williams, is not likely to win us any new friends. I vote for going somewhere that we can sleep at night without wondering if we will wake up dead or not."

Reagor asked, "Hulga, do you have a better idea?"

She shook her head. "I'm all for getting the hell out of Dodge."

There was a brief silence. Then Jack said, "Victor must weigh an easy 300 pounds. Even though I am a modern-day Hercules, I could use some help getting Victor out of the car and over to the freezer. Hoisting him into that tall freezer will be a gut-buster." Hulga quickly said, "I'm all in."

Jack replied, "Great. Once we get poor Victor into cold storage, we can all squeeze into the Land Cruiser and blast out of here."

Victor was heavy, and Jack and Hulga were struggling to get him out of the car. Reagor called out, "You need another person. I'm coming down." She gave her revolver to Ryn and said, "Help Maria watch out for rats while I give Jack and Hulga a hand."

It took great effort, but with three people it was possible to drag Victor over to the freezer. Fitting the corpulent doctor into the cold space took considerable contortion of his body. Suddenly there was a loud scream, "Duck!" followed by two almost simultaneous pistol shots and a loud guttural cry.

Jack and Reagor rushed up the stairs. Reba was sitting on the floor with blood on one shoulder. Ryn was standing close by with a pistol in her hand and an angry look on her face. Down the hall, there was a man writhing on the floor and groaning. Ryn marched down the hall and ended his misery with a bullet to the head.

Jack knelt down anxiously by Reba. She smiled and reached up to take his hand. "Missed anything vital. Just a superficial wound. Looks like I had at least one cat life left. Reba looked at Ryn as she returned to the group. "Ryn, you saved my life. If I had not dropped down when you yelled, that bullet would be in my chest now and not in the wall."

Hulga had stayed by the freezer and had finally succeeded in getting Victor stuffed into it. She had to sit on the lid to get it to fully close and lock. Hulga yelled up the stairs, "Let's get the hell out of here while we still can."

Everyone piled into the Land Cruiser station wagon. Jack was able to back into the crippled Ford and slowly push it to the side. He turned to Reagor, who was sitting beside him, and said, "We have a lot of money stashed away at the restaurant. Even if it is dangerous, I need to stop by Ellie's and grab the funds. We can ease down the dark alley with the headlights off, and I can slip in through the back door."

Reagor nodded. "Go for it. We will keep you covered, but stay armed. Once you're back, we will be heading to the beach to look for seashells."

CHAPTER 81

MONEY STOP

The trip back to town was uneventful. There were two police cars in front of the restaurant with lights flashing. An old hearse sitting low on its rear springs was slowly pulling away. Jack carefully eased into the alley behind the restaurant with lights out and coasted the last thirty feet. The back door had been closed, but it would no longer lock after the two men had broken in earlier. Jack cracked the door slowly and looked in. There were no longer any bodies, but there was still blood on the floor.

Jack slipped into the kitchen and tripped the breaker box. Everything was suddenly pitch black. There were excited voices speaking Spanish from the front of the restaurant. Jack quickly entered the pantry and swung a shelf out. By feel, he located a safe built into the wall. It took him two tries in the dark to dial in the proper sequence of numbers. Jack reached inside the safe and located the handle of a heavy leather valise. Thirty seconds later he jumped into the back of the Land Rover.

As had been previously agreed, Reba was in the driver's seat. Her extensive experience in defensive driving during her KGB training would be available if needed. She slowly backed out of the alley. Reagor said, "Head south on the beach road. I'll tell you when to slow down."

Reba had driven only two blocks before a police car pulled out of a side street, turned on its siren, and began rapidly accelerating. She gunned the Land Cruiser station wagon and made a screeching donut at the next intersection, heading directly back toward the police car with her bright lights on. The driver of the police car chickened out at the last minute and swerved into a light pole with a loud crash.

Reagor shook her head in the front seat. "This little pregnant lady can drive like an ace. Our Cruiser could never have outrun the police car. Kudos to Reba." Reagor turned to her and said, "Once you hit the beach road, you'll be going south for about six miles. There is an abandoned beach hotel project that is our target for tonight."

Reba tromped the accelerator, and the 125 horsepower in-line six engine responded with a roar. The passengers were bounced up and down on the uneven asphalt beach road. After five minutes Reagor said, "Reba, way ahead and toward the ocean you can just see the outline of a steel framework. When you get closer, slow down and look for a gate. I'll need to get out and open it."

In another minute, Reba slowed down, pulled off the road, and stopped in front of a large gate. The headlights illuminated a faded sign over the gate that read, "Beach Heaven." Reagor got out, walked to the gate, opened a heavy padlock, and pushed the gate open with some effort. She motioned for Reba to pull into the dirt road behind the gate.

Once Reagor had relocked the gate and was back in the Cruiser station wagon, she instructed Reba to drive another thirty yards and stop in front of a metal building. Reagor left the vehicle again to unlock and slide open a large metal door, which she closed after the Land Cruiser drove in. The only light was from the Cruiser station wagon's headlights, which Reagor signaled Reba to turn off. Reagor used the flashlight to guide the group to a flight of metal stairs that led to yet another locked door, which she opened. Inside was a large room with a high ceiling and no windows. Reagor shined her flashlight on the wall to find a switch. Once she flipped it, the muffled sound of a generator was heard. Overhead lights came on dimly, then quickly brightened. Ceiling fans began to turn.

Reagor said, "There are several cots and a stack of bedding over in the corner. This place is not the Manhattan St. Moritz with Swiss chocolates on your pillow at bedtime, but at least all of us will be safe. In the pantry there are C rations, which we will have to eat cold. There are also a number of canteens full of water that is safe to drink. The door in the back leads to a squat toilet room with a piss tube. This place is meant for short stays only."

Maria asked, "How long will we be here?"

Reagor answered, "If all goes as planned, as soon as it is dark tomorrow night, a produce van will pick us up and take us to a private pier where we will board a fishing boat. Once we are in international waters, there will be a Coast Guard escort to a private dock in San Diego. What happens next is still undecided. The CIA director has been very concerned for your welfare. Catching some sleep would be well advised."

Maria announced, "I have dibs on the squat toilet first. Then, I plan on getting some shut eye. This will be the first night in forever that Jack, Reba, and I won't have to sleep with a gun under our pillow. I am planning on a very pleasant dream about the devil having Randy on a skewer and roasting him in the fires of hell as he screams."

Linda Kay piped up, "How about having a second skewer for Mig?"

Reagor interrupted with, "Lights out in fifteen minutes. You women can entertain yourselves tomorrow by playing Dante and assigning people to various punishments in hell. Now is the time to grab some C rations and to hit the bathroom. We need to be fresh for any unanticipated miscues between here and the fishing boat."

Maria could not resist saying, "And we all need to hope and pray that Jack can aim well in the dark."

CHAPTER 82

A PARTIAL REVEAL

The Army cots were not designed for comfort, but Linda Kay and Ryn slept until mid-morning. Reagor was awake early and made coffee using a hot plate. She waited for Jack, Reba, Maria, and Hulga to wake up and have a C ration breakfast before motioning them to follow her to a small room with a heavy padlocked door. The room contained a number of rifles, pistols, and hand grenades. There was also a short-wave radio. Reagor went to a small window and looked out.

"Perfectly quiet out there. This is the only window up here. The main room is totally blacked out so no lights can ever be seen from the highway that might give away this safe house. This property has been deserted for several years after the company building a beach resort hotel went bankrupt. The U.S. government bought the property for the CIA through a sham Mexican holding company. I am not at liberty to tell you all that I know about CIA operations in this area, but you are all due some clarifications.

"First, you need to know that Hulga has been a clandestine operator for the CIA for ten years. She lives in Detroit, but is not on the police force. Her uncle was the owner of the El Caballo Restaurant in San Lindo, who was burned to death when local thugs set fire to his business. I'll let Hulga fill in some details."

Hulga had a grim look on her face as she began to speak. "I took time off from work to come back to Mexico to settle the score with the men who killed my uncle."

Reagor interrupted to say, "Let's be clear that Hulga's plan for revenge was not a CIA-approved endeavor. She was totally on her own."

Hulga continued, "Once I arrived in San Lindo, I was quickly certain that Rodolfo Mendez was the man behind the cruel death of my uncle. The goal to repay him has been accomplished. And there is nothing more about that topic that I am going to share."

Maria asked, "Will you at least explain why you and Victor concocted the story that you were on the Detroit police force?"

Hulga looked at Reagor, then replied, "CIA business that I am not at liberty to discuss."

Reagor said, "I think it only fair to let you know that Victor has been a CIA local asset for several years. The U.S. government has had an interest in this part of Mexico for some time in terms of the drug trade."

Jack nodded and said, "That explains why Victor had a never-ending supply of armaments and other unusual things. I really hate it that he felt a sense of duty to come back to the Medrano estate to help us."

There was a moment of silence, then Reba asked Reagor, "Becky, did you have any idea that we had survived the explosion at the desert compound until you recognized Jack in the restaurant?"

Reagor replied, "I must admit after the explosion I kept thinking that as smart as Jack's uncle was, he must have had some sort of amazing escape plan if his enemies closed in on him. My next thought was if you three survived, where would be a logical place to hide? Mexico seemed to be a likely candidate. When my cousin returned from her vacation in San Lindo and mentioned eating in a restaurant named 'Ellie's,' I immediately thought of your friend Ellie Edwards, who was killed at the compound. The girls had been wanting some beach time, so I booked a vacation in San Lindo."

Jack turned to Hulga and asked, "How in the world did you ever end up as a photographer for Randy's horror movies?"

Hulga replied, "I can't tell you everything, but when the original movie equipment as well as the photographer in the truck were blown up, that made an opening for a replacement. My camera was very special and had a concealed pistol that proved to be very useful."

Maria asked, "How did you know that the gun Randy had was loaded with blanks and would not kill Reagor?"

"When I moved close to Reagor to take light meter readings, she mouthed the word 'blanks.'"

Reba asked, "How did the blanks get in the gun in the first place?"

Reagor replied, "The noise from the explosion of the hand grenade at the door of Medrano's secret bedroom brought men running toward the sound. I had to relocate in a hurry and climbed the wall at the front of the house. After almost getting gassed to death in the trophy room, I found the master bedroom as well as Randy's pistol under his pillow. Victor had supplied me with a backpack full of useful items, including several blanks, which I used to replace the real bullets. I also laced Randy's bottle of tequila at the bedside with chloral hydrate powder."

Maria said, "That explains why Randy was having so much trouble navigating when he and Harold ran out of the basement. But why was Randy panicked about three twelve—whatever that is?"

Reagor replied, "Three twelve is the area code for Chicago and is the name of a powerful rival Chicago gang that is in a turf war with the group Randy was in. A number of murders have been instigated by both sides. When I was in Randy's bedroom, I pricked my finger and wrote '312' in blood on his pillow just to give him something to think about."

Suddenly there was a crackle from a small shortwave radio on a desk in the room.

Reagor sat down at the desk and listened to a string of Morse code. She immediately replied by rapidly tapping on a telegraph key. Then she looked up and said, "Change in plans. Things are heating up. The produce van will be here in thirty minutes. Let's get organized and be ready on time."

CHAPTER 83

DÉJÀ VU ALL OVER AGAIN

Ava was propped up in a hospital bed with a unit of packed cells flowing into an arm vein. Woody was pacing nervously in the room. Ava said, "I'll be fine once I get some new red blood cells into circulation. You are going to wear a hole in the floor. Why don't you sit down and relax?"

There was a knock on the door, and a middle-aged physician in blue scrubs came into the room. His name tag read, "William Shuster, MD, OB/GYN." He was prematurely gray, with strands of hair peeping out from beneath his surgery cap.

He walked over to Ava and felt her pulse.

The doctor smiled and said, "Your heart rate is much lower. I checked your hematocrit after the first unit of packed cells, and it has risen to thirty-four. You lost a fair amount of blood, but the vaginal bleeding seems to have stopped.

"This second infusion should get your crit up to a good level. An ultrasound confirmed the diagnosis of marginal placenta previa. That means the placenta is only blocking part of the cervical opening."

Ava asked, "Doctor Shuster, what can we expect with this pregnancy going forward? Will I bleed again?"

The doctor replied, "Marginal locations like yours usually don't bleed this much in the sixth month. But it is entirely possible that the placenta will migrate superiorly as the pregnancy progresses with no further bleeding. If it does move up away from the cervix, you may still be able to have a vaginal delivery. If the placenta stays the same or moves farther downward, you will need a C-section for sure. We will need to keep you in the hospital for three or four days to make certain you don't bleed again. Then you can go home with a lot of bed rest and no strenuous activities."

Woody asked, "Does home mean back to Camp Peary?"

The doctor replied, "I know that Camp Peary has a medical facility with blood available. Your wife is AB positive, a so-called universal recipient, so she can receive any blood type in an emergency without cross-matching. Peary is only thirty miles away, so with the medical help at the camp, I think staying there is safe as long as you watch carefully for spotting and have a hematocrit done every week."

Woody said, "One more quick question, Doc. Could you tell the sex of our child by the ultrasound?"

"Absolutely. You folks have a healthy-looking male."

Woody gave a little smile and said, "Just to be certain about paternity, did the child have an unusually large penis?"

The doctor laughed and replied, "The size was normal for a six-month-old fetus."

Ava shook her head and looked at the physician. "You'll have to forgive my husband. In some ways he never matured psychologically beyond junior high."

Dr. Shuster smiled and replied, "Believe it or not, I've had a number of prospective fathers ask the same question." He walked toward the door, but stopped to say, "Unless you have problems, I'll be back in the morning to see you. I don't know who you folks are, but I've never seen an armed guard outside a hospital room before except for prisoners."

Woody sat down by the bed and took Ava's hand. "Becky had me tracked down in the hospital this morning, and we had a nice little catch up. She had a lot of news to share. Hulga was sent to Europe on some sort of secret CIA mission. Linda Kay and Ryn are back in school at a small, private place with a locked campus. Strangely enough, neither one of them seems to be exhibiting great stress. Even though Becky is still officially retired, she is acting as a consultant to the director."

Ava asked, "Any news about Carmen and her children or about Sofia?"

Woody replied, "Becky seems to have access to CIA sources in San Lindo. I learned from her that Victor was cremated and had a small Catholic mass. Sofia seemed bereft at first, but cheered up considerably when Victor's will was read. She will have plenty of money for a long time. Carmen has decided to try to keep Ellie's Restaurant open. She has recruited a number of friends to help. The really surprising thing is that Sofia approached Carmen and offered to help support the restaurant financially if Carmen would agree to change the name to 'Victor's.'"

Ava responded, "Wow! That is unbelievable!"

Woody added, "One other bit of news is that Sofia is now seeing a wealthy older man from Mexico City. It obviously didn't take her long to get over Victor."

Ava looked toward the window and said sadly, "It's déjà vu all over again being warehoused at Camp Peary under CIA protection. The director has been really nice to us, but I don't want to spend the rest of my life like a rat in a cage."

Woody replied, "My sentiments exactly. But we really have no choice until the baby is born. The director remains willing to relocate us."

Ava said, "You didn't mention how Leta is doing."

"You know how shocked we both were when she agreed to go with Becky and the girls. Leta is so bright that she is taking freshman courses at Georgetown. She understands the risk, but was adamantly opposed to being essentially incarcerated with us. Becky will obviously keep a close eye on her."

There was a pause in the conversation. Woody looked at Ava. "Honey, how many cat lives do you think we have left?"

Ava laughed and replied, "We obviously started out with more than nine. But I would just as soon not have to find out."

Woody thought for a minute, then said, "One thing I didn't share with you is that the doctor told me earlier in the hall that intercourse is a definite no-no until the baby is born."

Ava smiled and replied, "You forget what a creative woman I am."

Dwain Gordon Fuller is a retired Dallas retinal surgeon who finally has found time to try his hand at writing. A demanding premedical curriculum in college has a way of damping down literary interests. However, Dr. Fuller found time to write stories and poems for the college creative writing journal. The mantra in medical school was survive—not write fiction. But during residency, Dr. Fuller was able to rekindle his interest in writing and pen and publish several nonscientific articles. Once in practice, Dr. Fuller coauthored a medical book about evaluating eyes with opaque media and also published a number of articles in scientific journals. Being retired has given Dr. Fuller the time to unleash whatever creative spark remains.